Hawaii
State Facts

Nickname:	The Aloha State
Date Entered Union:	August 21, 1959 (the 50th state)
Motto:	*Ua mau ke ea o ka aina I ka pono* (The life of the land is perpetuated in righteousness)
Hawaiian Men:	King Kamehameha the Great, *king* Father Joseph Damien, *leper colony worker* Hiram L. Fong, *first Chinese American senator* George Parsons Lathrop, *journalist, poet* Ellison Onizuka, *astronaut*
Flower:	Pua Aloalo (hibiscus brackenridgei)
Tree:	Kukui (candlenut)
Bird:	Nene (Hawaiian goose)
Song:	"Hawaii Ponoi" (Hawaii's Own)
State Name's Origin:	Thought to be based on the native Hawaiian word for homeland, *Owhyhee*.

Ashley forgot she shouldn't be doing this....

Parker held her against him, and his hands felt so strong and good, his desire blatant. Her tongue danced with his, her breasts pressed to his chest. She pushed back a little, self-conscious that he could feel how wildly her heart pounded.

Parker broke the kiss and pulled back too, gazing at her with such intensity, she wanted to look away. Using his thumb, he brushed a soft caress across her lips before tracing her jaw. "Isn't this better than fighting, Ashley?" His whisper was hoarse and close, his breath mingling with hers.

She groaned. "Rule number—"

"I think I just showed you what I think of your rules." Parker nudged her chin up. "Shall we go over it again?"

Ashley willed herself not to react. Slowly, calmly, she slid her hands up his chest. She slanted her mouth over his, leaving only a breath between them and whispered, "Enjoy the couch."

American
HEROES
AGAINST ALL ODDS

DEBBI
RAWLINS
Marriage Incorporated

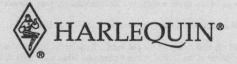

HARLEQUIN®

TORONTO • NEW YORK • LONDON
AMSTERDAM • PARIS • SYDNEY • HAMBURG
STOCKHOLM • ATHENS • TOKYO • MILAN • MADRID
PRAGUE • WARSAW • BUDAPEST • AUCKLAND

To my critique group:
Brenda, Crystal, Karen, Kathy and Maureen,
who were always there to nudge and encourage me.

And to my husband, Peter,
who always believed I could do it.

HARLEQUIN BOOKS
225 Duncan Mill Road, Don Mills,
Ontario, Canada M3B 3K9

ISBN 0-373-82209-X

MARRIAGE INCORPORATED

Copyright © 1995 by Debbie Quattrone

About the Author

A native of Hawaii, **Debbi Rawlins** married on Maui and has since lived in Cincinnati, Chicago, Tulsa, Houston, Detroit and Durham. One of her favorite things about living on the mainland is snow—she can't get enough of it! When Debbi isn't busy at the computer, she is usually lost in the pages of a book, or headed for the airport and parts unknown.

Books by Debbi Rawlins

Harlequin American Romance

Marriage Incorporated #580
The Cowboy and the Centerfold #618
The Outlaw and the City Slicker #622
Love, Marriage and other Calamities #675
Marry Me, Baby #691
The Bride To Be...or Not To Be? #730
If Wishes Were...Husbands #741
Stud for Hire? #780
His, Hers and Theirs #808

Love & Laughter

I Saw Daddy Kissing Santa Claus #34

Dear Reader,

Over the years, Hawaii has meant many things to me. It's the place where I was born and raised, where I walked to school barefoot along Kailua Beach, then quickly pulled on my Oxfords and adjusted my uniform before the nuns saw me.

During my rebellious teen years, Hawaii was the place I couldn't wait to leave. I wanted to see fall leaves, and snow and to be able to drive a hundred miles without ending up in the ocean.

At twenty-seven I finally did "escape" after marrying my New Yorker husband, and for many years (I won't say how many) I've missed Hawaii. Sure, I go back every year to visit my family, but it's not the same. Being able to tell Ashley and Parker's story and seeing Hawaii through their eyes has been such a delight. If any of you plan on visiting Oahu, don't stick to Waikiki. Head for the windward side, where I grew up and where Ashley and Parker call home. You won't be sorry.

Debbi Rawlins

Please address questions and book requests to:
Harlequin Reader Service
U.S.: 3010 Walden Ave., P.O. Box 1325, Buffalo, NY 14269
Canadian: P.O. Box 609, Fort Erie, Ont. L2A 5X3

Chapter One

Parker James watched the gloved waiter balance each champagne glass strategically on the rim of the next until the pyramid was complete. It cleared the chandelier by only a foot. Parker smiled. The whole thing would probably come crashing down any moment.

With pompous flourish, the waiter stood over his creation and poured the bubbling wine into the top glass. The elegant ballroom quieted but for a few appreciative whispers. The champagne artfully cascaded down the crystal pyramid, filling each goblet with its effervescent promise. A round of refined highbrow applause followed.

Damn. For a moment there, Parker had thought the evening might have possibilities, after all. He cradled his own slim-stemmed glass, wishing it were a beer instead, and surveyed the well-heeled crowd. Where the devil was his attorney? The collar of his tuxedo seemed to be shrinking by the minute, and he still had no idea why he'd let Harvey Winton talk him into coming to this benefit dinner.

"I see you made it." Harvey's voice came from behind him.

Parker turned to face the older man. "Me? I've been here for twenty minutes."

Harvey adjusted the monogrammed cuffs of his custom shirt. "Well, I knew you'd be deliberately late—if you showed up at all—so I hedged my bet."

"Fine. Now, can we leave before I have another attack of visual indigestion?"

"Leave? If your curiosity weren't piqued, you wouldn't be here in the first place."

"Curiosity, hell. You said you may have an answer to…" Parker glanced around, uneasiness tickling the back of his neck. Two of his investors were over by the caviar. He lowered his voice. "We both know why I'm here."

"That we do." The sympathy in the attorney's voice did not equate with the amusement in his cagey brown eyes. For an instant it disturbed Parker. But he was probably just being paranoid. So much was at stake.

"I don't understand why we had to meet here." Parker pushed a frustrated hand through his tawny hair. "Why not at my office?" He looked out the plate-glass windows and trained his eyes on the fading Hawaiian sunset framing Diamond Head—anything to avoid the other man's scrutiny. Harvey was more than his attorney, more than a friend. He was the father that Parker James II had never been. And right now Parker couldn't let Harvey see his self-doubt.

"I have my reasons. Can I get you a fresh drink?" Parker shook his head. The attorney started to turn away, then hesitated, slanting him a wry look. "Have a beer, Parker, you don't have to drink champagne just because you're a James."

Parker swallowed a resigned chuckle. It wasn't even safe to *think* around Harvey. He turned his attention back to the elegantly decorated room, scanning faces and recognizing many of those in attendance as people with whom he did business. But, in general, most of the people here nauseated him. They were more his parents' crowd. Not his.

Parker's gaze swept the room again, stopping to rest on the entrance.

"He's not coming," Harvey said, returning with his drink. "I talked with your mother this afternoon. They had a scheduling conflict."

"Who said I was wondering?"

"Weren't you?"

"No." Damn but Harvey knew him too well. "You're sure we need to be here."

"Quite." The attorney looked around at the prominent guests. "Besides, it's good for your image."

Parker didn't need the reminder. There was a lot of money riding on his project. A lot of ego, too. And as much as Parker would like to disagree with his friend, Harvey was right. His family name and his newly earned reputation as Honolulu's most promising up-and-coming real-estate tycoon would only take him so far. Rebellion had gotten him into a lot of trouble a decade ago. And now, in some ways, he was still paying.

"I've got enough to worry about." Parker dusted imaginary lint from his tuxedo jacket. "Now, when are you going to explain how being here will solve anything?"

"As a matter of fact," Harvey said, nudging his chin toward the door. "I think the solution to your problem just walked in."

Parker followed Harvey's gaze to the young woman coming through the door. She wore a simple black strapless dress. A single strand of pearls fell upon flawless tanned skin. Her glossy black hair might have hung to her waist, but it was wildly out of place as if she had just climbed off a motorcycle. She went from one person to another, smiling and shaking hands, never once apologizing for her appearance.

Parker liked that. A smile formed on his lips. "Who is she?"

"Ashley King."

"My savior, huh? Does she have a small fortune looking for a home?"

"Quite the contrary. Besides, you need a miracle, not money."

"Spit it out, Harvey. What's the angle?" He craned his neck to get a better look at Ashley King. Annoyed as he was, Parker's impatience faded.

The woman was petite. Only about five foot two, if he had to guess. Small and curvy, her hips swayed to a gentle, silent rhythm as she worked her way around the room. He couldn't get a good look at her face though, and he had already resigned himself to the fact that being that small, she'd most likely have a high, squeaky voice.

She finger combed her hair away from her face and tilted her head back, laughing at something a young man had said. Her neck was long and graceful and beckoning. Parker fastened his gaze on that silken expanse of vibrant skin and something flared inside him. He swallowed hard. Quickly he raised his eyes to her face, but it was too late.

Like a black satin veil, her hair fell forward, obscuring her profile. Frustrated, Parker maneuvered himself to within a few feet of her. Then he heard her laugh. Deep, throaty— a Kathleen Turner kind of laugh. Staring in surprise, he watched her turn wide hazel eyes on him.

"Hi. I'm Ashley King," she said and offered him her hand. "Isn't this a lovely party?"

He was still recovering from her voice when she favored him with a wide, enticing smile. Beads of perspiration formed at his hairline. "I'm Parker James."

"I know the name well." A small disapproving frown appeared at her brow but just as quickly fell away. "You must be the third."

"The third what?" There it was again. That seductive laugh.

"Parker James III. You're far too young to be the second."

"Oh, yeah." Parker cringed inwardly. He'd always hated being addressed as "the third" and had subconsciously put it out of his mind. Catching sight of an amused Harvey out of the corner of his eye, he gestured the man forward. "This is Harvey Winton." He paused. "Or do you two know each other?"

"I don't think so." Ashley turned her attention to Harvey. "But you do look familiar."

While Ashley and his friend exchanged greetings, Parker used the time to study her. She wasn't pretty in a classical sense, but she possessed a certain magnetic charm. He'd already sensed that, as she had made her way around the room, people were drawn to her. His gaze lingered on her small oval face, her eyes, warm and golden like maple syrup. How could she possibly help him?

Unless it was to seduce some high-ranking government types. But that wasn't Harvey's style. Besides, the thought repulsed Parker. He was no Boy Scout, and there certainly wasn't much he wouldn't do to get out of this jam, but he felt oddly indignant that she could be involved in anything so sordid.

"And what type of law do you practice, Mr. James?" Ashley's low, soft voice floated through his reverie.

"Me?" Parker tried to keep the stiffness out of his tone, but when her natural assumption finally sunk in, he felt his answer tangle in his mouth. His bow tie seemed to tighten a notch. "I'm not a lawyer."

"Oh…" A spark of interest brought out green flecks in her guileless eyes. "I thought the James name was synonymous with law and politics."

"I'm not like the rest of my family." Amazing, there was someone on this island who didn't already know that.

Ashley flashed a puzzled look at Harvey, who was busy studying the olive in his drink. "Well, I'm certainly glad you could attend our benefit. Obviously you think it's a worthy cause," she said, her smile still brilliantly intact. "Wasn't it wonderful of the board to lend us the museum for the evening?" She placed her hand on Parker's arm. Just as quickly she withdrew it.

Startled, Parker had felt the electric current between them. He looked deep into her astonished eyes and found some consolation there. She'd felt the connection, too. He could see it in the small heave of her chest, hear it in the slight quiver of her voice.

"It looks wonderful, doesn't it?" She gestured around

the grand room where each flower was fastidiously in place, each glass crafted from the finest crystal and each dress more glamorous than the next.

And although Ashley looked as elegant as any woman there, Parker instinctively knew this wasn't her scene. So what did she have to do with all this? And how was she going to help him?

She had averted her gaze and laughed again at something Harvey said. Even though Parker had no idea what they were talking about, he felt his own lips curve in response. A tiny dimple had formed at the corner of her rose-tinted mouth and a twinkle of gold and green sparkled in her flashing eyes. The sensuality of her throaty laughter vibrated throughout his body.

He wanted her to tilt her head back again. He wanted to feast on all that silken skin dipping into soft cleavage. He wanted to...

Parker shook himself. There was something dangerously infectious about Ashley King. And if they were going to do any kind of business together, he'd better remember to keep it just that—business.

"May I get you a drink?" Parker asked all of a sudden. The air was closing in on him. He needed space.

"No, thanks. I'm fine," Ashley said. "But if you'll excuse me..."

Parker had already begun backing away, a lump blossoming in his throat. Just before he turned toward the bar, he saw the curiosity in Ashley's face, the amusement in Harvey's.

Where was all the Ivy-League confidence his parents had paid for? At the moment, gone. He had downed half his champagne refill when Harvey caught up with him.

"Slow down, man. You're going to be needing a clear head."

"A clear head for what, Harvey? I'm tired of the riddles. I'm tired of this evening. I'm just plain tired. Tell me what the hell is going on. And who the hell is Ashley King to me?'' He gulped down the rest of his drink.

"Your fiancée, hopefully.''

Parker almost lost his mouthful. Instead, it made a painful jerking descent down his tightened throat. "Are you crazy?" he finally spat out.

"Sometimes more than others, but in this particular instance I'm quite lucid." All traces of indulgence vanished from Harvey's face. "And dead serious."

Parker grabbed the other man's arm and hauled him over to a private corner. Voice lowered, he asked, "What's going on?" He made a cursory sweep of the room, pinpointing the proximity of each of his financial backers.

"I've tried every loophole, called in every favor. That Hawaiian homestead land is like sacred ground." The attorney shook his gray head. "There's a long list of hopeful and eligible applicants. Distributing it is a hot political issue. Not only does that put it out of reach, but if it were common knowledge that you want it to protect your resort, all hell would break loose. We need a backdoor approach."

"Even for one lousy strip of it?" Parker asked in frustration, not really needing an answer. He wasn't keen on ripping off the Hawaiian people, not even for "one lousy strip." But this was a complication he hadn't anticipated, and right now he felt plastered up against a brick wall. If just one investor got wind of this and pulled out, no telling how many others would follow suit. He exhaled deeply. He couldn't begin to fathom the predicament that would put him in. "What does this have to do with Ms. King?"

"It seems…" Harvey sighed and pulled out a cigarette. "The only way you'd be able to gain control is to marry into it. And Ms. King is a very eligible candidate."

"You *are* crazy." Parker stepped back, fumbling with his tie. For a hundred and twenty bucks, it should be able to unknot itself.

"Of course, getting her to agree is another matter. But that shouldn't be too much of a problem."

"Why not?" Parker threw up his hands, shaking his head. "More importantly, why am I even asking? This is absurd."

"Because she needs the money."

"And where is this money supposed to come from? If things don't get ironed out soon, I'll be bankrupt."

"Exactly. So to put it in your own vernacular, this may be the only way to save your butt."

Parker jammed his fisted hands into his pockets. The evening had gone from bad to worse. And as if he didn't have enough of his own problems, now all he could think about was why Ashley King would need money badly enough to marry for it. But he wouldn't give Harvey the satisfaction of asking. Anyway, it was irrelevant. Marriages of convenience, business marriages or whatever the hell they called them, were a thing of the past. Archaic. Out of the question.

"You could do much worse." Harvey took a long, seemingly bored drag off his cigarette, then blew a stream of smoke in Ashley's direction.

"Nasty habit, Harvey. Give it up." Parker pretended not to follow his friend's gaze, but darted a quick glance in time to see her flick that magnificent black mane over her bare, silky shoulder. "Besides, I prefer blondes."

"I don't think your investors much care what you prefer. Do you?"

Parker winced at the reminder. There was more at stake than his reputation and money. "This is just plain crazy." He paced a little, knowing how wild animals felt in a cage. "There's got to be..." He stared at his attorney. "You know, Harv, I don't see what the hell you find so funny about this whole situation. Every time I look at you, you've got a damn smirk on your face."

"Amusing," the other man corrected. "Not funny."

"Amusing?"

"It's too bad Ms. King wasn't as susceptible to your charms as the other ladies about town."

Parker glanced over his shoulder at whatever was capturing Harvey's attention. Two women, one blonde and one redhead, were looking his way. He knew them both socially but had never been impressed enough to pursue anything. He gave them the expected wave. They smiled their reply.

"Honolulu's finest," Harvey murmured and raised his glass in salute to the two women.

"Spare me," Parker said. He turned back to face his friend and rolled his eyes.

"You might have been a bit more charming to Ms. King. It wouldn't have hurt to bat those popular baby blues of yours at her."

Parker slammed down his glass and reached for a bottle of beer off the tray of a passing waiter. "Give it a rest, Winton," he ground out through clenched teeth, then headed for the door and away from Harvey's irritating snicker.

Across the room, Ashley kept Parker James in her peripheral vision. It was easy to do, since his tawny head was visible above most others. Something about him interested her. It wasn't physical, she assured herself, ignoring the quickening of her pulse as she recalled the sleepy blue of his eyes, the fullness of his lips.

He wasn't anywhere near her type, not that her social life was hopping these days, especially with her tight volunteer schedule and her daily visits to the hospital. But there was something intriguing about him....

Ashley turned her attention to the impeccably manicured woman who'd cornered her and tried to concentrate on what the wealthy matron was saying. After all, the woman had just donated a king's ransom to Ashley's beloved Hawaiian Immersion Program. With the contributions Ashley and her committee had secured, the program was about to get its start.

She breathed a happy inward sigh, then caught sight of Parker heading for the door. He carried himself with purpose and confidence...the best money could buy. If only some of that James fortune would make its way to one of her pet charities. But that was unlikely—and surely what accounted for the pang of disappointment she felt at watching his broad shoulders disappear through the smoked-glass doors.

Besides, Ashley had a far graver problem to worry about. Her heart heavy, she forced a smile for her chatty companion, ignoring the irony that she and her father were one step away from being a charity case themselves.

IT WAS A PERFECT MAY afternoon and Parker decided to do something he never did…skip out of his office two hours early.

He pulled up beside his sprawling beach house, then stepped out of his cherry red Porsche and walked to the mailbox. God, it was a great day. He squinted up at the bright sun and cloudless sky. Today, nothing would stop him from that swim and game of tennis he'd promised himself. Two of life's little pleasures that he never seemed to have time for anymore.

While sorting through the mail, he meandered back to the house. Bills. A pizzeria advertisement. More bills. Then a small linen envelope caught his eye. He tore the seal.

"A wedding invitation? Oh, Christ." He jammed the contents back into the envelope. His life had been a spinning top ever since Harvey had presented his harebrained idea, and now reminders of it were popping up when least expected.

At least he had made it clear to Harvey. Absolutely, positively no way would he marry Ashley King, or anyone else, to secure that strip of homestead land.

He thought about the posh resort he'd broken his back to have built during the past three years, and about the overlooked tract of poverty-afflicted homestead land that would threaten wealthy consciences if visible from the resort windows. And only one lousy strip of unclaimed land separated it all.

It was also the only thing separating him from redemption.

Not only were a lot of investors with big money riding on him, there was his father—and his father's long, unforgiving memory.

Maybe Harvey's attempt at creativity hadn't been such a bad thing after all. It certainly had gotten Parker moving. Since Saturday, he had had architects and landscapers working around the clock to camouflage the stretch of unsightly homestead structures. He'd also promised large bonuses to keep it quiet.

The relocation of trees alone was going to cost him a small fortune, but he already had his accountants liquidating some of his assets. Although his latest effort was no guarantee, he would overcome this problem. He'd make a hefty profit, reestablish his name, and he'd do it by himself. Not that the money was particularly important. Parker'd known wealth most of his life. Then he'd had next to nothing during his more rebellious years. And although having money was better, it wasn't essential—no matter what his family seemed to think. For him, money had merely become a by-product of his personal success. And not having it handed to him made it a whole lot sweeter.

Parker shifted the mail to one hand and fumbled with his key ring until he found his house key. He let himself in the entrance of his suite rather than in the front door, hoping he could sneak off to his room without fending twenty questions from his housekeeper.

He slipped out of his jacket and hung it on the valet. He tossed his tie on the chest of drawers.

"Parker?" A tentative voice called out.

"Yes, Mrs. Lee, it's me," he assured the housekeeper and dropped his shirt near the hamper. The woman had always had sharp ears. In his teen years, it had been his cross to bear.

"You're home early. Anything wrong?" She called from the kitchen where she spent most of her time.

"Nothing at all." His socks landed somewhere near his shirt.

"And Parker?"

"Yes, Mrs. Lee."

"Pick up your clothes."

Parker grinned. Only Mrs. Lee and Harvey would think of speaking to him like that. When he had returned from the mainland for good, he'd noticed how much older she looked. She had worked for his parents for as long as he could remember. But the large plantation-style house had become too much for her, and he was pleased it hadn't taken much convincing to get her to work for him. She was a proud woman and would never accept anything resembling charity, but at least this way Parker could make sure she didn't overdo it.

He kicked the clothes into a pile, promising himself he'd get to them before Mrs. Lee. All he could think of right now was diving into that pool and soaking up some sun. He pulled on a pair of battered old trunks and headed outside.

After only five laps, Parker was winded. When had he gotten so out of shape? Harvey had tried to tell him how all-consuming this project had become, and he'd probably been right. As well as his friend knew him though, Parker suspected the attorney didn't fully fathom the importance of making this resort a success.

He hauled himself out of the pool and was about to settle onto a chaise longue when he heard a car pull up along the side drive to the house. The distinct purr of the engine alerted his senses. Only one person he knew had a car that finely tuned. Sweat mingled with the chlorinated water. He toweled off both and waited.

"Good afternoon, Parker. Beautiful day."

He draped the towel around his neck and turned to study his father. Even in his late sixties he was virile and commanding. His shock of white hair was perfectly styled. It wouldn't dare not be.

"Afternoon, Father. What brings you by?"

"I wanted to have a word with you. I stopped by your office but they said you'd already left, so I just took a chance you'd be home."

Why didn't his father just come out and ask him, Parker wondered. Ask him why he saw fit to leave work for a senseless afternoon in the sun.

Parker could feel residual defiance begin to fester. He squelched it fast. He wasn't perfect, no matter how much his father wanted him to be. He'd reconciled himself to that fact long ago, but deep-rooted hurt had a way of sneaking up and stealing pieces of maturity and rationale. "Well, you've found me. Can I get you something to drink? Some iced tea?"

"I won't be that long. But I would like to retire to some shade, if you don't mind. My skin can't take the sun like it used to."

"Of course." Parker gestured to the patio. He watched his father walk ahead of him, shoulders slightly stooped. When had he allowed that small imperfection? Parker wondered. "Playing much golf lately?"

"No. Not much at all. I've been leaving that to the younger men. And you, playing much tennis?"

"I've been too busy." Parker shook his head. For the first time he could remember, his father looked old. "But I'm playing a couple of rounds with Tom Booker today."

"How is Tom?"

"Good. What is it you wanted, Father?"

Parker James II issued a short elegant snort. "A little pleasant conversation, perhaps?" He smiled wryly at his son's cynical expression. "All right, how about some news on the Makena project?"

"You heard everything there is at the last board meeting."

"No problems?"

"Everything is on schedule."

"Well, son, I thought you should know...." His father

paused, rare uncertainty shadowing his bright blue eyes that were so much like Parker's. "There are some rumors flying around."

"What sort of rumors?" Parker was glad for the towel around his neck. He didn't want his father to see him sweat.

"Nothing specific that I've been privy to. Just that there might be some problems."

Parker shook his head but was saved from responding by the phone's ringing. He twisted around, stalling, hoping Mrs. Lee would call him. His rescuer appeared.

"Parker, it's Harvey Winton." Mrs. Lee shrugged plump shoulders. "I tried to take a message, but he said it was urgent."

"Excuse me a moment." Parker swallowed a relieved sigh as he stepped past the sliding-glass doors and slid them closed behind him. He picked up the cordless phone and greeted Harvey.

"We've got trouble," the attorney said, his voice unusually tense.

"Go on."

"Rumors. None accurate, but they always cause questions."

"Do you know who's behind it?" Parker automatically glanced out at his father, who was watching him intently through the closed glass door.

"That's hard to tell. Not that it matters. I wanted to advise you right away, because there is one question you will have to answer and I'm not quite sure what to tell them."

"What's that, Harvey?" Parker pulled the towel from around his neck and mopped his sweaty forehead. At that moment Parker James II slid open the door and his gaze fell on the small but elaborate spider tattooed on his son's shoulder. The visible reminder of the day Parker'd had too much booze and too little sense. It was the day he had quit law school. The day he had disgraced his family. A day he would never forget.

"Parker, some of the board members want to know why

you're suddenly liquidating assets,'' Harvey stated after a significant pause.

''Tell them...'' Parker's gaze took in the piercing censure of his father, his disapproval almost searing Parker's skin. ''Tell them I'll be paying for a wedding.''

Chapter Two

"How much longer until she gets here?" Parker asked for the third time.

"She is still due to arrive at eleven-thirty." The ever-patient Harvey looked as if he were ready to bind and gag Parker.

"Are you sure she understands the terms of the contract?" Parker adjusted his tie and glanced at the office clock. Ten more minutes.

"Yes, she understands. Yes, she has enough Hawaiian blood to qualify. And no, I'm not certain she will agree. Now, how many more times would you like this repeated?"

"Until I hear Twilight Zone music, damn it. I hate this, Harvey, I hate this whole stinking thing."

"So you've said."

Parker leaned back in his leather chair, brought steepled fingers to his lips and narrowed his eyes. "If I didn't know better, I'd think you were deriving far too much pleasure from all this."

"I'll let that slide since you're under so much pressure." Even that was said with a slight—and annoying—smirk.

Parker stretched out his legs and the chair settled with a clunk. "It just seems so cold-blooded."

"Your getting married at the tender age of thirty-five or the business about her father?"

"For God's sake, the man's seriously ill. I wouldn't think joking about it would be your style."

"This isn't a joke. Mr. King's medical upkeep is very important to Ashley. That's the only reason you have a prayer at all."

Parker winced. "That's my point."

"That's business."

Parker tried not to think about the means, only the results. He looked at the wall clock again. This had to be the longest morning of his life. The only good thing about it would be seeing Ashley again. The thought of her sweet, serene smile calmed him.

"I think she's here." Harvey pushed back in his chair, straining his ears toward the reception area outside Parker's closed door.

Parker swept half a stale doughnut off his desk and into the wastebasket. He started to brush the leftover crumbs into his hand, but his palms felt gritty enough. He hastily arranged a stack of papers over them instead, then stood while Harvey opened the door.

Ashley King looked smaller, more fragile than she had the previous Friday night. Her wan smile, directed at Parker's secretary, faded as she came through his door.

Parker cleared his throat. "Nice to see you again, Ms. King." For a moment, Parker didn't think she was going to accept his proffered hand. Her eyes didn't sparkle as they had the other night. They were shadowed and dull.

"Let's not pretend this is anything other than what it is, shall we?" She withdrew her hand from his almost as quickly as she'd extended it, then accepted the chair Harvey pulled out for her. "I have a list of questions my attorney has advised me to cover. I'm sorry she couldn't be here. She's in court."

Parker didn't like the idea of anyone else—even an attorney—knowing of the proposal. Harvey had taken care of the confidentiality issue with a separate contract, yet it still made Parker uneasy. But Ashley was right. This was a business deal, no matter how you looked at it, and of course she should have legal counsel. This whole idea really stunk, but did he have a choice? Obviously Ms. King didn't either.

He watched her remove a typed sheet from the briefcase on her lap, then the contract Harvey had drawn up. Her hand trembled. Parker's gut clenched.

"First of all," Ashley began. "There is no indication as to how long this agreement would be in effect." She directed her statement to Harvey, and Parker got the distinct impression she was avoiding his gaze. Several times she flicked at her shoulder as if, by habit, adjusting her hair, only she had pulled it back into a tight knot at her nape. Right now, she looked like the schoolteacher she was.

"We purposely left that open for discussion, Ms. King," the attorney replied. "Obviously we would prefer an extended period of time, to protect our position. However, we understand that since you are only twenty-nine..."

Ashley's chin lifted a few cool degrees. "What else do you know about me?" Her eyes, flashing green with temper, found Parker's, then switched back to Harvey. "I imagine you've done a complete check, haven't you?"

"Well, naturally we needed to—"

"I expect the same consideration, Mr. Winton. At your expense, of course. I choose the investigator, you issue the check. Next point." She bent her head, perusing her list.

Parker felt a streak of indignation straighten his spine, and then he relaxed and smiled. Wouldn't he have done the same thing? He liked her spunk. He liked her. Maybe this wouldn't be such a bad deal after all.

"Mr. James?" He looked back just in time to see her blow absently at a softly curling tendril that had strayed. His gaze fastened on her full pursed lips. Then again, maybe he should run like hell while he still had the chance.

"Mr. James," she repeated.

"Parker," he said automatically. "Call me Parker." If they were going to be married, she should at least call him

Parker. The absurdity of the situation sobered him once again. He leaned forward, elbows resting on his desk. "Look, Ms.—uh—Ashley, this original contract," he said, tapping his copy, "is not etched in stone. It's a guide to meet both our needs."

"Fine. And I'm just trying to voice mine."

"Go on."

"With regard to my father," Ashley said hesitantly, and Parker could see the bittersweet emotions play across her face. The light that had entered her eyes only moments earlier vanished. "I want the type of medical expenses you'll cover clearly defined."

"Whatever he needs."

Harvey coughed. "He means whatever is reasonable and customary."

"You sound like an insurance agent, Harv." Parker looked at Ashley. "If it's within my ability, your father will have it." He waited for her eyes to respond, watched for some small reprieve, but she shuttered them from him.

"What is it exactly that you want, Ms. King?" Harvey asked.

"I want my father to be comfortable." Her words were soft. Tension lines appeared where her dimple should have been. And Parker felt like a bigger heel than ever. He tried to concentrate on the paperwork before him and ignore her wounded look. Forget heel. He felt like a snake.

"What else concerns you?" he asked gruffly before he said something utterly stupid.

Ashley raised her eyes level with his, resolve replacing sentiment. "I want a community center."

"A what?" Parker's voice echoed Harvey's by a second.

"I don't have to remind either of you how valuable and important that homestead land is to native Hawaiians. If it weren't available, many of them would be homeless. If only to salve your own conscience, I'd think you'd agree to that."

"Wait a minute." Now she was pushing it. No one was

going to beat up on his conscience but him. "This project is also going to create one hell of a lot of jobs. Don't tell me we don't need more of those."

"And are these great jobs going to pay enough to afford housing in this already inflated market?"

"Are you going to lay inflation on me, too?"

"That's the deal, Mr. James." Ashley looked directly at him, her expression impassive.

"You've drawn the mistaken conclusion that I have unlimited resources. Medical treatment is not cheap. Are you willing to compromise that for this community center?"

"Don't you have the James stamp of approval? That should count for quite a bit," she said, disdain in her tone.

"Leave my father out of this." Parker had lowered his voice to a monotone. "No one, absolutely no one, can get wind of this arrangement, or everything is off. And I'll leave both you and your father so high and dry you won't know what happened."

"We're not getting off to a very good start," Harvey interjected. "Maybe you should have your attorney call me, Ms. King."

Silence crackled like heat lightning. Parker leaned back in his chair, staring at the battle preparation on Ashley's face. Slowly he let out his pent-up breath. "You'll get your damn community center. But only after..."

"After what, Mr. James? After my father is dead?"

Parker had been gut-punched plenty in his younger days, but at this moment, nothing he recalled had felt worse than Ashley's accusing stare. "After the resort begins to turn a profit. That's what I was going to say."

Ashley turned her bright eyes away from him. "I'm sorry," she whispered. "That was uncalled for."

Briskly, he shuffled some papers on his desk. "Think about my offer. That's the best I can do. But I will add this, there's no question about the resort's eventual profitability. Take that for what it's worth."

"I don't need to think about it. That seems reasonable

enough." She paused. "As long as I have control of the land in the meantime." She blinked, then looked away for a moment, and Parker had the uneasy feeling he was missing something. "And I'd like that in writing," she added.

"Don't trust me?" Parker's eyebrows rose slightly.

Ashley merely smiled. "Do we have a deal?"

"As long as you agree not to build anything in the interim." Parker tipped farther back in his chair. "And I'll have that in writing, thank you. Anything else?"

He glanced at Harvey, who stared at him intently, an odd smile lurking at the corners of his mouth. The attorney wasn't getting any younger, and it was past time for him to retire. He hadn't been acting like himself lately. After this was over, Parker vowed he'd let up on him. It wouldn't be easy. Harvey had always been his most trusted friend.

"Well, there's the courtship..." Ashley finally said.

"Courtship?" Parker's eyes skidded back to her.

"I know it sounds old-fashioned." A faint pink tinged her cheeks. "And I agree, but my father will expect it. You see, Mr. James, it's just as important to me that this union seems real. I don't want my father to know I've compromised myself."

Her words stung. It made him sound like some kind of pervert. "For starters, I think you'd better get used to calling me Parker. Now, how long is this, uh, courtship supposed to last?"

"It depends on how well I can convince him there's been someone in my life."

"Is there?" The thought hadn't occurred to him before. Surely Harvey would have warned him.

"No. That's going to make it more difficult."

"Would he believe in love at first sight?"

"Not..." Ashley uncrossed her legs, then recrossed them in the opposite direction, darting an uncomfortable look at Harvey. "Please don't take this wrong. But not with someone like you."

"Meaning?"

"You're not my type."

"And what is your type, Ms. King?"

"You'd better get used to calling me Ashley."

"Ashley." Parker had never claimed to be a patient man. Now she was definitely pushing it. "What will it take to convince him?"

"Let's see. Have you ever done anything worthwhile…uh…charitable, that is?" Ashley demanded without a trace of apology.

A brief chuckle escaped Harvey before he turned it into a cough and cast an amused gaze at the ceiling. Parker could only hope Harvey had caught the warning look he gave him, even though Harvey already knew Parker's contributions and past involvements were either anonymous or a taboo subject.

"Nothing you'd be interested in. Have any suggestions?" Parker asked in a clipped tone.

"Well, I'm quite involved in the truancy tutoring program. If you were also involved…" she continued, doubt clouding her eyes, "he might believe we'd met there and that we'd hit it off."

"That's fine. Tell him that."

"Great. It might work. What day would you like to begin?"

"What?"

"Tutoring."

"I didn't mean I'd *really* get involved. I meant that you should tell him that."

Ashley shook her head. "That won't work. He'll have questions."

"And you'll have the answers."

"But he'll ask you when you go to the hospital."

"Why would I do that?"

She stared back at him. "As my fiancé, surely you'd want to visit him, ask his blessing."

This was getting far too complicated. Parker looked helplessly at Harvey.

"She's right, you know," his friend said.

"All right," Parker said through clenched teeth and reached for a notepad. "Where and when do I show up?"

Ashley gave him directions. After they'd come to an agreement and settled several other issues, she tapped her papers into a neat pile and put them in her briefcase.

Parker's stomach told him it was well past lunchtime, and he was considering an offer of lunch when Ashley, poised for flight, dropped the final question.

"I realize this doesn't need to be contractual, but what will the sleeping arrangements be?"

All of a sudden, food was the last thing on his mind. "I'm not sure I follow you," Parker said slowly. He really had to change cleaners. They were shrinking his collars.

"What percentage of the time will I be expected at your place? Do you entertain much?"

"I expect you to move in." He put both palms up. "This has to look like a real marriage. Don't you understand that? Harvey?" he pleaded for his friend's assistance.

The older man laid down his pen and abandoned the notes he'd been taking. "Ashley—may I call you that?" She nodded and he continued. "It is imperative that we don't leave ourselves open for speculation. You will have your own room and one that only appears, and I stress *appears*, to be shared with Parker."

"But that's—"

Harvey held up his hand. "Parker has a live-in housekeeper who must also be convinced. I'm sure you two can get around that, however, but not without a joint room."

"Can't you let her go?" Ashley flashed an agonized look at Parker. "I'll do the housework."

"She's been with me a long time," he said, shaking his head. Mrs. Lee had been a major concern. Although she had a heart of gold and would never do anything to intentionally hurt him, she also had a big mouth. One that had been a problem in the past, but something Parker had long ago accepted. He would never turn her out.

"She really should be retired, but Parker has a soft—" the attorney began.

"That's enough, Harvey," Parker warned, then faced Ashley. "Mrs. Lee stays. But don't worry, I'm sure it won't be difficult to stage a quarrel soon after the blessed day. Enough to justify separate rooms for a while." He hoped he didn't sound put off over Ashley's attitude toward him. After all, the only thing he cared about was her signing on the dotted line.

"We're adults." She sniffed. "I'm sure we'll be able to handle it. I'll keep my apartment, though. No one has to know about that."

"I have a big house, Ashley. There's plenty of room."

"I'm keeping it, anyway," she said, a stubborn green glint in her eyes.

"We'll leave that open for discussion." Not that Parker meant it. She could not maintain her own apartment and that was that.

"Sure," Ashley said with raised eyebrows and no conviction. It was obvious that issue was closed for her, too. She stood and smoothed out her slacks. "I'll go over what we discussed with my attorney and get back to you within the week."

"Tomorrow. I need to hear tomorrow."

"That's not enough time."

"Yeah? Well, I hadn't planned on a courtship. We don't have any more time." Parker stood, too. He towered over her by a foot. They couldn't agree on one blasted thing. And he still preferred blondes. What had he gotten himself into?

"I'll be talking to you in the next couple of days." She stuck out her hand. He engulfed it with his. Her palm felt damp. Or maybe it was his.

"I'd like to know before I show up for this tutoring thing," he said, not wanting her to have the final word.

"Of course," she replied with deceptive sweetness. "You wouldn't want to waste your time."

Without saying anything more, Parker watched her shake Harvey's hand, exchange a few words, then leave his office. Lunch forgotten, he lowered himself to his chair and gave a frustrated push away from his desk. "Couldn't you have found someone a little more contrary?"

"Do you blame her?" Harvey asked.

"This isn't exactly what I had planned for the next few years either."

"Nothing is signed. You can still pull out."

"And do what? Sign bankruptcy papers instead?"

"If I were you, I'd just be thankful we found someone eligible and in a tight enough bind to be useful."

The reminder of Ashley's problem humbled Parker. But just a little. "She doesn't look very Hawaiian." Parker looked up from the paper clip he was unbending when Harvey sighed. "I wasn't going to ask again. If you tell me she is, I believe you. I was wondering if there's any sort of relationship to *the* King family, as in mega land holdings."

"One and the same. She's one of the granddaughters."

"Then what the hell would she need money for?" He dropped the paper clip altogether.

"Her father fell out of grace years ago, before Ashley was born. Most of the family lives on Maui. I'll bet she doesn't see them much, if at all."

"But the man's ill, for God's sake."

Harvey shrugged. "Some things can't be forgotten."

Parker knew the truth of that all too well. "What did he do that was so unforgivable?" he asked, toying with a pencil, not sure if he really wanted to know. Tentacles of sympathy wrapped themselves around him. Her wounded look flashed in his mind. He snapped the pencil in half. This was a business deal, he reminded himself.

"He married a mainlander."

"Great." Parker rested his head on the back of his chair and stared at a faint watermark on the ceiling. For many Hawaiians it was almost sacrilegious to mix blood, especially with a Caucasian. "So if Ashley marries me, she'll put the final nail in her coffin."

"You're not a mainlander. Your family's been here for generations."

"We both know it goes beyond that."

"Sometimes," Harvey agreed. "But in this case the woman was a gold digger. She did a good job of spending King's money before she hightailed it back to the mainland."

"And she's Ashley's mother?" Unbidden sympathy once again skittered through him before he shoved it away.

"Yes, but she didn't stick around too long. I'm not sure what Ashley considers her."

"You certainly know a lot about the family," Parker said.

"I've been around a long time, and I'm nosy."

"Think this scheme has a snowball's chance?"

"Without a doubt."

"We're nothing alike, you know."

"Oh, I'm not so sure about that."

"She's a damn bleeding-heart liberal," Parker continued, shaking his head. "I can tell."

"Probably."

"She'll drive me crazy."

"I think you'll do your fair share."

"There's too much friction between us. People won't buy it."

"Friction. Interesting choice of words."

"Spare me the raised eyebrows. We don't see eye-to-eye and you know it."

"Then use it to your advantage."

"How?"

"The passion is already there, change the angle."

"That will *never* happen." Parker rolled his eyes and flicked the pencil halves away. "Think she'll do it, Harv?"

"She loves her father more than anything in the world. I don't see how she can pass it up."

This conversation didn't make Parker feel any better. In fact, it made him feel predatory. He had to keep in mind that she had just as much to gain as he did.

That wasn't quite true. For Parker, this was a tightrope he couldn't share. He had both everything to gain and everything to lose. Right now, he wasn't sure his soul could withstand the loss.

He messed with some papers on his desk before looking up into Harvey's inquiring gaze. "How about some lunch?"

"You go ahead. I have some calls to make."

"Can I bring you something back?"

"Sesame chicken salad or anything light. I've got a full calendar this afternoon."

Parker felt a little guilty. He had a full calendar, too. But he had to get out for a while. Harvey was looking tired these days, but Parker couldn't bring himself to push the idea of retirement too hard. His friend's ego had also suffered the ravages of age. Besides, Harvey had always been there and Parker couldn't imagine not having his reliable counsel.

"I won't be long. Just need to clear the cobwebs from my brain," Parker called over his shoulder as he headed through the reception area.

Harvey returned to his own office, and watching through the glass inset bordering his closed door, he waited until Parker stepped onto the elevator before picking up his phone. He waited a moment for the connection to be made. Hearing the anxious greeting on the other end, he smiled.

"Not to worry," he said, leaning leisurely back into his chair. "We have him right where we want him."

Chapter Three

"I wish you could have been there, Crystal." Ashley slid a hatbox under her bed. "The guy is unbelievable."

"So why are you even considering his proposal?"

"This, coming from you?" Ashley slanted her friend and attorney a wry look. Beneath the slicked-back hair, she knew there was a spiked punk rocker waiting to emerge as soon as the power suit came off. "The queen of adventure herself?"

"That's all right for me, not you. Besides..." Crystal tugged at her lapels. "I am trying to clean up my act."

"Right." Ashley suppressed a smile, then frowned as sobering thoughts flooded her overtaxed brain. "There's something you need to take into consideration when you review the contract."

"Such as?"

"Parker James is a shark."

"Oh yeah?" Her friend chuckled and waggled her eyebrows. "I don't recall quite that description after the benefit."

"That was before I knew what a low-down scheme he'd concocted." Ashley stopped, unable to keep from wincing at her self-righteousness. Especially after what she was about to admit to Crystal.

"So, tell him to take a hike."

"I wish I could." Ashley sighed, sat on the edge of her bed and kicked off her sandals. "But that's not an option."

"You could call your grandparents." Crystal said hesitantly, then made a show of touching up her lipstick.

"And start a war? My father would never forgive me, and I can't take the chance of exciting him." No one had to know they had already refused her calls. "That leaves me with the shark."

"But such a good-looking one. Half the women I know—"

"Don't even think it. This will be purely business, and that's why you need to make sure that contract is ironclad."

"No problem." Fingering out spiky bangs, Crystal asked, "Think I should wear my hair up or down?"

Ashley started to say something, then clamped her mouth shut. Crystal was not taking this seriously enough. Ashley stared at her friend's young Amerasian face and thought about the lines of experience and wisdom in Harvey Winton's.

In spite of being nothing alike, she and Crystal had been best friends since grade school. And although they had always championed each other, Crystal was new on the legal track and Harvey Winton had a hard-nosed reputation. So much was riding on this "blissful" agreement, it made Ashley nervous. Right now, she felt as if she were being sucked under by a tidal wave. Guiltily, she wondered if she should retain a more experienced lawyer. She could handle being shark bait, but not at her father's expense.

Ashley's thoughtful silence seemed to go unnoticed by Crystal, who was busy adding two more earrings to each ear.

Without further deliberation, Ashley made her decision. Whatever Crystal lacked in experience, she more than made up for in loyalty. No matter what else happened, Ashley wanted her father taken care of, and she knew she could count on Crystal for that. That left Ashley free to pursue the second part of her plan.

"There's something else," Ashley said nonchalantly, then took a deep breath while Crystal finished fiddling with a silver ear cuff. "I want that land, too."

Crystal's eyes briefly met Ashley's in the mirror before she swung around to face her. "Why?"

Ashley leaned back on the bed, bracing her elbows behind her head. "It's perfect for a shuttle service to Magic Island." A smile spread across her face. "I can see it now, the revolutionary new gambling mecca of the Pacific."

After a brief silence, Crystal laughed. "You had me going there for a minute." She turned back to spiking her hair.

"Think about it." Ashley sat up and spread her hands. "It would be only a fifteen-minute plane ride, forty-minute ferry ride, tops. That wedge of land is ideal for a short private airstrip and it butts up to enough ocean footage for a dock. It's perfect."

Crystal gave her a long, incredulous look. "Aren't you forgetting something rather major? Like Hawaii hasn't legalized gambling yet, much less allotted an island for it."

"It's only a matter of time. We both know that. And when it happens, I want a piece of it."

Crystal put down her hair pick altogether and turned slowly back toward her friend. "This doesn't even sound like you, Ash."

Ashley pulled her bare legs up on the bed and crossed them. Resting her chin in her palms, she sighed. "Do you know how much I have in my savings account? Zero. My teaching pension? Not worth mentioning. I wrote a check to the hospital last week that just about put me in there along with my dad." She shook her head. "It's scary, Crystal. I'm wiped out, and if anything else happens to either my dad or me…"

She threw up her hands. "Besides, I'm tired of living like this. Someone stands to make a bundle and it might as well be me."

"Look." Crystal nudged Ashley aside and sat down next

to her. "I know if gambling is legalized you'd like to see it confined to one island."

"Not just one island," Ashley corrected. "Kahoolawe, also known among my more enlightened peers as Magic Island. The navy doesn't need it for target practice anymore. It's useless as is. But with an amusement park, casinos and enough resort development, so much of the tourist traffic will be eliminated from the residential islands."

"You don't have to convince me," Crystal said, holding up a hand. "It's the resort owners here and on the other islands you have to worry about. They don't want to share the market, not with existing hotels and restaurants to fill. That's why they're pushing for the floating casino idea rather than a self-contained island. That way, they'll still have plenty of hungry and tired tourists coming back every evening. And there's a heck of a lot of money behind them to make sure things go their way."

"Don't be such a pessimist." Ashley lifted her chin, but her spirits didn't quite make the same ascent. There was too much truth in what Crystal said. "This is still a democracy and a lot of others believe as I do."

Her friend stared up at the ceiling for several minutes before commenting. "Okay, let's say that this Magic Island theory of yours has a chance. How would you fit in?"

"A service center." Ashley's eyes lit up. "With money exchange, translation assistance, concierge service—and the air and sea shuttles would, of course, be the most profitable. And best of all, it could be manned primarily by the kids I tutor. Most of them need jobs—"

"Hold it. And where, in heaven's name, would the money come from?"

"Parker."

"I knew it. You've gone totally bananas." Crystal started to leave, but Ashley grasped her arm.

"Not just from him. As long as I have the land, the state will have to take my bid for the shuttle service seriously, and once I've accomplished that, investors will start coming out of the woodwork.''

''Not Parker's woodwork. His money, his investors' money, his family's money is all heavily tied up in hotels here and on Maui and Kauai. And they sure as hell don't want to see any tourist moola going to other resorts.'' Crystal widened sympathetic eyes that suggested her friend had gone over the edge. ''Parker will flip.''

''Parker is not going to know.'' Ashley swept her hair back with a shaky hand.

''I'm going to be sorry I asked....''

''I sort of skirted around it. I told him I wanted a community center.''

''And?''

''And nothing. He didn't ask and I didn't volunteer. If he thinks it's for the kids I work with, then that's his problem.''

''You know damn well, Ashley King, that's exactly what he thinks.'' Crystal's lips curved up in conspiratorial joy.

''Oh, well...'' Ashley smiled back. That's exactly what she'd counted on. And having been named volunteer of the year twice in a row hadn't hurt. ''It's half true, anyway. Those kids need the jobs and I plan on giving them all a considerable amount of interest in it.''

''Don't try and rationalize your conniving little heart now, my formerly altruistic friend.'' Crystal rubbed her palms together in delight, ignoring Ashley's grimace over the well-placed jab. ''It's just getting interesting. But why didn't you apply for the land yourself?''

''Homestead land isn't supposed to be zoned commercially, but apparently Parker and Harvey Winton have friends in high places.'' Ashley rolled her eyes toward the ceiling. ''And truthfully, I'm not at all happy about how they're going about this, but since it's going to be done with or without me, I want in.''

''Oh, yeah, for the community.'' Grinning, Crystal picked up her purse and slung it over her shoulder.

"Believe what you want, but I won't be the only one benefiting from this deal," Ashley sniffed.

"If you pull it off."

"If I pull it off," Ashley agreed, trying not to think about the alternative.

"You know Parker won't give you a cent if he finds out."

"What he'd probably give me is a one-way ticket to the loony farm." He'd give her a heck of a lot more than that, she suspected.

"And you'll be giving him a run for his money. Sounds fair to me." Crystal chuckled, then hesitated at the door. "I was wondering…" she began, her forehead puckered in thought. "Do sharks mate for life?"

LONG AFTER HER FRIEND had left, Ashley sprawled out on her bed, wide-awake, an attack of cold feet well underway. Two glasses of milk hadn't eased the burning in her stomach. And Crystal's teasing words still stung, even though Ashley truly didn't consider herself in the same category as Parker. His reasons were purely self-serving, while her first concern was for her father.

And until now, wanting to turn Kahoolawe into the Disney island of the Pacific had been nothing more than a pipe dream. But with the land, Parker's money and the James name…Ashley could almost smell success.

She rolled over and stared at the ceiling. Dollar signs replaced the zeros in her teacher's pension fund, even as the foreboding thoughts of Parker's reaction fought for her more practical nature. Wanting a secure future didn't make her a bad person, she assured herself. And she wasn't so naive as to think Hawaii didn't need the tourist industry. But that didn't mean there wasn't a better way. And Parker, of course, was certainly getting what he wanted.

But when it came right down to it, even with all the rationalizing she'd done in the past two days, Ashley dreaded the time when she would finally have to face-off with Parker. Because no matter how she twisted the equation, Parker and his investors could stand to lose sizable profits with the development of a Magic Island. And he'd be far from pleased with her part in Project Teacher's Pension.

Ashley smiled at the impromptu name. It had a nice ring to it. She concentrated on that and tried not to think about the more dreary "what-ifs" that lay ahead. The many hours she'd spent at the hospital were beginning to take their toll. She hadn't cut back on volunteering, and she had another two weeks of teaching Hawaiian social studies before summer vacation.

Besides, time was no longer a viable commodity. She couldn't afford to use it for negative thoughts. That's why she wouldn't stall by investigating Parker. It wasn't necessary. The James family was well-known, but she had been miffed at her meeting with Parker and had felt like being difficult.

She shifted positions and prayed for sleep—sweet, numbing sleep. She had classes to teach today and Magic Island supporters to contact.

She thought about the enormous project she was about to undertake and about the father who'd always been there for her. Keeping perspective on his welfare would ultimately be her biggest asset. If her attention remained centered on that, she'd have her best chance of pulling this off. Life had to go on as usual. It would keep Parker from being suspicious.

Parker. Why did her thoughts keep returning to him? *Marriage.* That thought wasn't any better. Ashley punched her pillow and shook off the warm shiver that coursed up her spine. Maybe she'd squeeze in a Dale Carnegie seminar. What she needed was some basic positive thinking.

She let her mind drift back to Crystal, and the thought of her unconventional friend meeting Parker and Harvey for the first time made her smile. It turned into a yawn, and then she stared at the ceiling for the next two hours.

IF HARVEY TOLD PARKER not to be nervous one more time, he'd forget what a good friend the man was and pop him right in the mouth. Parker wiped invisible smudges from the marble pen holder and adjusted his leather blotter. "Hey, Louise," he yelled out to his secretary. "Turn down the thermostat, will you? It's hotter than hell in here."

The woman in a mustard cotton sweater rolled her eyes at Harvey as she passed Parker's open office door.

"I heard the elevator bell." The attorney straightened exaggeratedly in his chair. "Maybe you'd like to greet her with a lei in the hall?"

"Cut the sarcasm. I'm not in the mood." Parker snuck a glance pass the reception desk. "This is only a formality, right?"

"That's my best guess. We've already agreed to—"

"It's her." Parker cut him off in a lowered voice and rose from his chair. Harvey followed suit.

Her waist-length hair hung free this time, and he caught glimpses of it as it swayed gently like a mantle of black satin. Her hips moved in the same mesmerizing motion, and her dancer's legs were bare and brown.

"I'm sorry I'm dressed so casually." Ashley tugged at the skirt of her yellow floral dress, a soft pink heightening her cheekbones. "I have a tutoring session after this, and I didn't have time to run home and change."

Parker realized he was staring. Except he still couldn't stop himself, as he watched the fabric flutter from her graceful hands. Hula, he thought. She had told many stories with those hands. He wondered about what other kind of pleasure they could bring.

"Oh, no. You look great…I mean fine…you look fine." He yanked unnecessarily at a chair. "Here. Sit."

He looked from one pair of raised eyebrows to the other. "Please have a seat. You, too, Harvey." He swung the door closed, stopping it from slamming at the last moment.

"I understand we're in agreement," Parker said from his own chair, rubbing the familiar, reassuring leather arms.

"I made some minor changes. I believe my attorney had the contract delivered by courier?" Ashley looked to Harvey for confirmation. She didn't smile. Her mouth quivered a bit, and her beautiful hands had balled into small, tight fists.

"Yes, we have it," Parker said before his friend could speak. "Harvey, would you excuse us?"

"But I don't think—" Harvey turned his doubtful expression on Parker.

"Good. Then could you not think outside?" He exhaled a harsh breath, not liking his own curt tone. "The damned thing is already signed. Just give us a few minutes alone."

Shaking his head, Harvey rose to leave, but so did Ashley. "I really need to be going myself. I—I just thought I should stop by in person to confirm everything."

"Wait." She looked as if she were going to bolt for the open door through which Harvey was exiting, so Parker grabbed her wrist. "Don't go yet." He could feel her muscles tense beneath his fingers. Her eyes widened and she swallowed hard. He should have let her go, but he didn't.

"I don't need to be shackled, Mr. James. I'll stay for a few minutes." Slowly she curved back her hand, palm out, to escape his grasp.

He released her then, but let his fingers trail away. "Parker," he reminded her, remaining close.

Ashley took a step back, her progress halted by a wicker chair brushing her hip. Shooting swift glances toward the outer office, she extended her hands as if warding him off.

"I'm sure my entire staff is curious about you," he said in a low tone, not attempting to back off. "But of course no one knows of this arrangement but Harvey."

"What's your point?"

"Don't look so nervous. We're about to be engaged. Let's try to look like it."

"Now? Here?" She tried to back up the stubborn chair.

"Nothing dramatic. I merely don't want you to act so frightened when I get near you."

"Frightened? Of you? That'll be the day."

"Prove it." He edged closer. "For their sake, of course." His eyes held hers, as he nudged his head toward the open door and the gathering lunch crowd trying not to look interested.

"What do you want?"

"A smile would be nice, for starters."

Slowly, a small dimple appeared at the corner of her mouth. He put his hand at her waist and the dimple vanished.

"You're not trying very hard." He felt his own lips curve, unforced. He brought his lips to her ear, intoxicated by the blend of gardenias and sunshine that surrounded her. He felt his eyes drift closed.

"Parker?"

He pulled back. This woman was lethal. "That should do it for now." He glanced out at the few office stragglers oddly eyeing him and forced a smile. "Let's get out of here." He started to reach for her elbow, thought better of it and snatched his jacket instead.

"What are you talking about? I have a tutoring appointment."

"I'm supposed to be getting involved with that, remember?"

"Now?"

"Now." This time he did grab her elbow and headed full speed for the elevator. What the hell was he doing? He should be getting away from her. Not going with her. But they had unfinished business.

After a tense elevator ride and a short argument over who would drive, they left in Ashley's battered Toyota station wagon. Sprawled out as much as the small car would allow, Parker lounged back and said, "First thing we have to do is get you a new car."

"Forget it." The side mirror was missing. Parker watched Ashley roll down her window and stick her head out to clear a left turn.

"I don't think I heard you correctly."

"I said, forget it. This one suits me fine."

"Right."

She darted him a warning look. "There's something we need to talk about. As stipulated in the contract, I'll be where I need to be and I'll say what I need to say, but don't expect to change my life."

"I'm glad you brought up the contract. I can understand your attorney's involvement up until now. But no more. This can't look like a business deal."

"She's my friend."

"Then she is welcome in our home as your friend. No more of this communication-by-courier crap." *Our home.* The words sounded strange. He tugged his tie loose and glanced over at Ashley. He'd expected a scowl or at least a grimace; what he hadn't expected was a smile.

"Actually," she said, turning up the wattage directly at him. "I can't wait for you to meet her—and Harvey, too."

"I'd like that." Parker felt his shoulders relax. "Maybe we can have some sort of get-together with a few of our friends. Let them start getting used to the idea of us as a couple before we spring the news."

"Perfect." Ashley looked inordinately happy, still smiling, humming to herself. Parker felt somewhat uneasy but wasn't about to second-guess her sudden high spirits.

"When do you think we can legitimately pull this off without raising suspicion?" he asked with deceptive indifference.

"I've signed the contract." Her smile receded and her shoulders straightened. "Harvey is taking care of the paperwork to have the land transferred to my name. Using his political connections," she added with sarcastic disapproval. "I don't see what the rush is."

"I don't like loose ends."

"Sorry you consider me a loose end."

"That's not what I meant."

"Look." She slowed the car, veered off to the side of

the road and parked. "There had better not be something you two aren't telling me. I don't know how Harvey managed to get this in the works so fast. Or how he was able to get land for multi-family use assigned to me alone. And I don't think I want to know." She was jabbing her finger in the air now. "But you'd better be straight with me."

"Calm down, damn it. I'll just feel more comfortable when everything falls into place. That's all. There's no hidden agenda."

She stared at him for a long time, just on the verge of speaking. She was jumpy, he could tell, and he wondered how much of it had to do with him personally.

"You have my word," Parker added, not at all mollified when misgivings darkened her eyes. It made him want to take her reassuringly into his arms, and he had to blink away the absurd notion.

"Now," he said, looking around for the first time. They weren't in the best of neighborhoods. "Can we get going?"

Ashley issued a short, humorless laugh. "We're already here." She got out of the car and pulled a large canvas bag along with her. "Welcome to the rest of paradise," she said, shutting the door and leaving him dumbfounded in his seat.

It took a few seconds for realization to set in before he got out and caught up to her. She was nearing a run-down garage when he finally managed to regain her attention.

"Is this where you do that tutoring project?" he asked, his peripheral vision taking in boarded-up windows and rusted-out abandoned cars.

"Did you expect a country club?" She turned away from him and headed in the direction of a small weathered church.

"It was only a question," he replied softly, easily matching her angry stride.

"These kids need tutoring because most of them have to work and help the family. When they start missing too much school and fall behind, they drop out altogether."

She sighed and slowed her pace. "We have to break the cycle or they'll end up at dead ends just like their parents did."

"I don't doubt that, and I think what you're doing is admirable."

"But…?" She glanced warily at him only to find him smiling at a little girl who had stepped off a porch. Her face was dirty, her clothes torn and her thumb stuck in her mouth.

"Is it safe here?"

"No. She's about to mug us at any minute." Ashley threw up a hand. She cooled her harsh tone and spoke a couple of Hawaiian words to the toddler, making her grin from ear to ear. She patted the tangled mass of black curls, then picked up her pace. "These people are poor, Parker, not criminals. Or maybe you think it is criminal to be poor."

"Now, wait a minute." Firmly, but gently, he grabbed Ashley's arm, forcing her to stop. Her bare arm was warm from the sun. It felt fragile yet vibrant under the pressure of his fingers. Her eyes shot shards of firey green and her mouth parted in indignation. She had more passion bottled up in her than any woman he'd ever come across. He didn't know if he should shake her or kiss her.

"It doesn't look like I have a choice."

"What?" he asked, blinking.

"About waiting." She looked significantly at his hand locked around her arm.

He dropped it. "I'm sorry."

"It's ironic that after all these years of coming here, this is the most violence I've encountered."

"I said I was sorry," he said, wincing. "But did it occur to you that I might care what happens to you?" And amazingly, at this moment, he did.

She turned her incredible eyes on him, and her mouth softened into a wry tilt. "I believe Rhett Butler said it best. Frankly, my dear, I don't give a damn."

Chapter Four

Ashley didn't know what it was about Parker that irked her. Part of it was that everything seemed to come easy for him, but there was something else, too...something she couldn't quite put her finger on.

Anyway, she'd be smart to be a little nicer to him, to not rock the boat. She certainly wasn't in any position to be provoking him. And although all this wonderful rationalization was fine when she was alone, being in such proximity to him sent all her good intentions right out the window.

The fact that the past two hours had been no picnic didn't help. The kids were unusually restless and far too inquisitive about her "new friend." Playing twenty questions and fending off adolescent hostility over the unexpected intrusion had exhausted her. By the time they had packed up, she was itching to be rid of her companion. Her nerves had had enough of Parker James.

"I've got to get to a phone, Ashley," Parker said as they left the church. "Let Louise know how long I'm going to be. She'll have to cancel some of my appointments."

"There's no need for that." She waved to the kids and headed for her car at a fast clip. "I can have you back in twenty minutes."

"That anxious to be rid of me?" he teased, and she felt

the blood rush to her face. "And here I've been on my best behavior."

"By following me around?"

"I thought I'd been courting you."

Ashley caught his spreading grin out of the corner of her eye. "Are you trying to make me crazy on purpose?" She waved a hand around. "Or is this some natural talent?"

"I have many natural talents," Parker drawled in a low, sexy voice, and Ashley had to stop herself from glancing back over at him. "But patience with hostile kids is not one of them."

She slowed down near the car and sighed. One of her older pupils had verged on insolence. She was hoping Parker hadn't noticed. "Kimo can be a little trying and I really do appreciate that you didn't take the bait."

"A little trying? The kid looked like he wanted to carve me up for sushi. He obviously doesn't like *haoles*."

"Especially ones wearing three-hundred-dollar shoes." She slid her gaze from his feet, up his body, to his eyes. "And five-hundred-dollar suits." His silky gaze awaited hers. She stared back a moment too long before looking away. "If you're still interested in helping out, I think you'd be more effective if you dressed for the neighborhood."

"I'm still interested."

Her eyes flew back to his. Something in his tone sent her imagination off like a rocket, and his gaze roaming her face, sent a warm shiver through places that shouldn't be shivering.

Ashley took a quick, deep breath. "Well, I won't snub any help, as long as you're sincere." She walked around to the driver's side and tossed in her bag. "Those kids already have the deck stacked against them."

Parker climbed into the passenger seat as Ashley slid behind the wheel and laid his hand on her arm when she started the ignition. "I won't lie to you. I'm getting involved in this to make our relationship look legit. But I also genuinely admire your dedication, and as long as I'm involved those kids will have my full attention." His eyes were startlingly blue, earnest. And too close.

She shifted her arm a bit, telling him he could let go. He didn't.

"I believe you, Parker, but...even Kimo?" She arched a brow, ignoring the unsettling feeling caused by his warm palm on her flesh.

"Especially Kimo, probably," Parker groaned.

"He'll come around. He's real protective of me, and it didn't help that his girlfriend played up to you."

"So, the little sucker's got the hots for Leilani."

Ashley shot him an amused look and smiled. "I think you may just fit in after all."

He smiled back, allowing a few silent moments to pass, his thumb absently stroking her skin. And then he dropped his hand from her arm as if it were a hot potato. "Where to next, so I know what to tell Louise?" he asked, his tone all business again.

"The hospital," Ashley said, exhaling an uneven breath. "Are you still in?"

Parker hesitated for just an instant, pinching the crease in his pants. "I am."

"We're not far. You can call her from there." Ashley glanced over at his guarded face. "And you can wait in the lobby if you want."

"I'd like to meet your father, unless you think it's too soon."

"I'm not sure." She sucked in her lower lip. "I mentioned you last night so you wouldn't come as a complete surprise. But he's not expecting me today and I don't want anything to look amiss. I just want him to get used to you."

"This is your show," he said with a tight smile.

Something had spooked Parker, so Ashley respected his silence the rest of the way. She had enough of her own problems to worry about, anyway. She had no idea how her father would react, but the sooner he got used to the idea of her and Parker as a couple... Ashley drew in a large gulp of salt-scented air. Heck. The sooner *she* got used to them being a couple, the sooner she would have money for his medical bills and the land she needed to submit her bid to the state.

They arrived at the hospital in record time and were halfway down the long hospital corridor when Ashley broke away from her mental tailspin long enough to look at Parker. "You look horrible," she said. "You're as white as a sheet."

"Don't tell me. He's in the last room." Parker's lips thinned considerably. A light film of moisture shone at his temples and Ashley's eyes widened on him.

"You don't like hospitals, do you?" She pressed a comforting hand to his wrist.

"I hate them." He grabbed her hand in a death grip and pulled her along.

She had to slow him down when they reached her father's room. She knew others who had hospital phobias and felt a moment's pity for him. "We're here." She yanked her hand from his vise. "Maybe by the *next* visit he'll expect us to be holding hands," she said jokingly. Mentioning next time was an error. Deeper lines formed between his brows. "We won't stay long," she assured him and led the way in to the semiprivate room.

Keoki King sat up in his bed, his black eyes wide and alert, his flowered orange-and-yellow shirt a jarring contrast to the stark white sheets. A lunch tray was pushed to the side, a deck of cards and two haphazard stacks of quarters crowded the empty plates. The thinly disguised odor of tobacco lingered in the air.

"Leialoha, I was not expecting you." He opened his arms wide to his daughter.

"Oh, Dad, you haven't been taking money from the nurses again," Ashley scolded softly as she hugged him and kissed his cheek.

"Better than money." He grinned. "I have two more

weeks of not having to wear that.'' He pointed to a wadded-up hospital-issue nightshirt on a chair near the drawn privacy curtain around the other bed, then put his finger to his lips and said in a hushed tone. ''I have a new roommate.''

Ashley nodded and lowered her voice. ''This is the friend I was telling you about.'' She turned to Parker and grasping his forearm, pulled him closer. ''Meet Parker James.'' The special smile she turned on Parker was for her father's benefit, but the fact that it seemed to have a tension-easing effect on Parker pleased her.

''And Parker, this is my dad, Keoki King.''

''Mr. King, it's good to meet you.'' Parker stepped forward when the older man stuck out a weathered brown hand.

''Everyone calls me Keoki.'' His dark eyes were frank and measuring. ''So, you are the one making my Leialoha so happy these days.''

''Dad.'' Surprise and mortification seeped through Ashley's tone. Why would her father say such a thing? True, her spirits had been up because of the money raised at the benefit. And she had been terribly excited over the possible resurrection of Magic Island. But still, it was an odd conclusion for him to draw.

''I am an old man and time is short,'' her father said. ''I have to say what I think.'' Winking, a faint smile lighting his face, he added in a stage whisper, ''Is it serious? I may still see grandchildren?''

''Oh, Dad. Quit teasing.'' She chanced a peek at Parker, who had relaxed and was smiling. Was he enjoying this? *The jerk.*

''I'm glad I have you on my side, sir. Ashley's a tough one to catch. I'm flattered she's said so much about me,'' Parker said so earnestly Ashley could barely keep from gaping. He'd obviously missed his calling.

''I haven't,'' Ashley assured him.

''She did not have to,'' Keoki said, nodding his head with untold wisdom. ''I could tell. But she spends too much time with her charities. Make sure she pays attention to you."

"I have a feeling that'll be unavoidable," Parker said in a dry enough tone that it took all of Ashley's willpower not to give him a dirty look.

"Tell me about yourself, Parker James," her father continued, blithely unaware of Ashley's agitation.

Parker gave him a skeleton story—the truth sometimes embellished, sometimes distorted, but always in evidence. Ashley waited patiently, trying to gauge her father's reaction, until a nurse motioned that it was time to leave.

Trailing Parker out of the hospital, Ashley acknowledged that today's visit had been better than most. Her father was in unusually high spirits, which made hers soar. It also allowed her to consider her plans for Magic Island with minimal guilt. Everything seemed to be coming together, except Parker's earlier comment came to mind. No more loose ends, he had said. And now Ashley agreed. This marriage had to take place as soon as possible.

"THE COAST IS CLEAR, my friend." Keoki reached down under his mattress and produced a fat, half-smoked cigar. "Where are my matches?"

Pulling back the privacy curtain, a disgruntled Harvey Winton hopped off the adjacent hospital bed and meticulously smoothed his slacks with a nervous hand. "I don't know how you get away with all this," Harvey said, giving up his lighter. "One of these days those nurses are going to quit running interference for you."

Keoki grinned and patted the deck of cards. "They owe me far too much money. Trade is cheaper."

"Don't get too cocky. If they figure out you cheat, they just might let Ashley catch us together."

"Cheat?" Keoki pursed his lips around the unlit cigar, then removed it. "Huh. You are just a poor loser. I am right about this plan. You will see."

Harvey drove a reckless hand through his neatly arranged

hair. "Right. I should never have let you talk me into this." He shook his head. "If Parker finds out that there's no homestead land…"

"Parker? What about Ashley? You have not seen my Leialoha's temper. If she finds out it is we who own the land… It is best that we get them married right away." He tapped the side of his head with his index finger. "Before they have too much time to think."

"And before you're released from the hospital," Harvey reminded him. "You know she's doing this for you."

"Yes." Keoki stared out the window. "And I do not think I can keep her from finding out my treatment is nearly complete. We must move quickly."

"I'd say it's out of our hands. And none too soon, I might add."

"Oh, but you are wrong, my friend. We have much to do if I want to see little *keikis* soon."

"Really, Keoki. Grandchildren?" Harvey cocked his head, remembering the earlier conversation he'd overheard. "Wasn't that a bit overdone?"

"So, she can think I am a little senile." He clasped his hands behind his head and lounged back into the pillows.

"Senile? You old coot, you haven't changed in forty years."

"Has it been that long, my friend?" Keoki smiled at his boyhood pal.

"Longer, but who's counting? Like one long poker tournament, we've won some and lost some." A brief silence followed, each friend reflecting on their wins and losses.

"And this is our biggest gamble of all," Keoki said, suddenly very serious. "But I know *here*," he thumped his chest, "we are doing the right thing. Those two, they were made for each other."

"I truly hope so."

"Parker should have been your son," Keoki said lightly, wishing he could reassure him. Already Keoki saw the uncertainty of their impulsiveness in his friend's eyes...something he knew in his heart of hearts need not exist.

A wistful sadness crossed Harvey's face before he frowned. "Why? So he can disown me when he finds out about this stunt we've pulled?"

"You are doing a fine thing for him. You said yourself he works too hard, he is too driven. And my Leialoha is much too busy with her volunteer work. She will never have her own children if she keeps taking in strays."

"Well..." Harvey looked out the window to the green cloud-shrouded mountaintops. "I certainly hope she keeps this stray."

"She will, my friend, she will." Keoki clapped him on the back. "We will see to it." Then his brown face puckered in a frown and he picked up the battered playing cards. "The next shift starts at midnight," he whispered. "Think we'll need a new deck?"

"I'M TAKING YOU BACK to your office now," Ashley said as she coaxed her sputtering Toyota onto the freeway.

"Then what are you going to do?" Parker asked.

"Go home and grade papers."

"When do you tutor again?"

"Day after tomorrow."

Parker let out a soft whistle. "How often do you go?"

"At least twice a week, three times when I can get enough of the kids together."

"Pretty aggressive schedule."

"Time isn't on their side."

"It's not on ours either," he reminded her. "How about dinner tonight?"

"We've already spent most of the day together." Her tone made it clear she thought that was enough.

Parker sighed. "It's a good thing I have a secure ego. We need to be seen in public. It also wouldn't hurt to get to know each other better."

"I have a feeling that's going to be inevitable."

"Then don't fight it. Have dinner with me."

"But my papers..." He had a point about being seen.

"I'll help you after dinner."

"You?" Ashley looked over at him. He looked so sincere and charmingly boyish. He was still tieless, sleeves rolled up, tawny hair falling across his forehead. She wondered if he realized he'd gone to the hospital looking like that.

"I'll pick you up at seven. Okay?"

"Seven-fifteen," she countered, unwilling to give him the final say, and caught the smirk he was trying to hold back.

"Seven-fifteen it is." This time he out-and-out grinned, pinning her with an amused stare as they pulled up in front of his office building. "I think it's time we got something out of the way."

Ashley gritted her teeth. If he was about to deliver an "I'm the boss" speech, she'd throw up. "Yes?" She turned to him with thinned lips.

Parker twisted in her direction and curved his hand around the nape of her neck. He pulled her toward him. In astonishment, her lips softened and parted slightly. At that exact moment, he brought his warm, moist mouth to hers. A groan of surprise rumbled from her throat. Right away, she knew that to be a mistake. He held her chin in place and increased the pressure of his lips.

She felt the tip of his tongue tease the seam of her lips, felt his breath, warm and beguiling. She didn't pull away. She didn't kiss him back. Totally floored, she did nothing.

It was Parker who finally, in a lingering fashion, broke away. "I'll see you tonight." He grabbed his jacket from the back seat, unfolded his tall body from the confines of his seat, then strode away from the car.

Ashley sat motionless, watching his broad shoulders disappear through the revolving door. She swore she could still feel the heated pressure of his hand at her neck, smell the faint scent of after-shave clinging to her warm cheeks.

A horn blasted from a car behind her, waiting for her to exit the loading zone. "Damn him." She dropped the hand that had somehow made its way to her awestruck mouth and threw the car into gear.

"I'VE RESERVED YOUR favorite table," the waiter said as he ushered Ashley and Parker through the main dining room to an open candlelit balcony overlooking the ocean.

"I appreciate it, Larry, especially on such short notice." Parker tried to slip the man what looked like a twenty-dollar bill, but the waiter pushed it away.

"Please, Mr. James, you've already done so much," the older man said in a hushed tone and hurried away.

Ashley busied herself with settling into her seat and pretended not to notice the interchange, but she couldn't help but be curious about what the other man meant.

"Nice view," she said as she removed the artfully arranged linen napkin from the wineglass with a little too much snap. She had to shake this mood. She hadn't wanted to let Parker get away with that unwelcome kiss and had almost stood him up for dinner. But then she'd decided that would give the kiss too much weight.

She had, however, considered getting even by borrowing one of Crystal's outfits, but then she scratched that. Too obvious. In the end, she picked out her nice white sleeveless silk dress and decided to be an adult about everything...which basically meant she would pretend that brief scintillating kiss had never happened.

"Nice menu," she commented, her eyes glued, unseeing, to the elegantly scripted writing.

"Nice conversation."

"I'm tired." Ashley wasn't in the mood for his teasing.

"Try to look somewhat cheerful, will you? I purposely came to this restaurant because I wanted some quick exposure for us. And I know a lot of people here."

Ashley struggled to turn up the corners of her mouth. The attempt was only half successful.

"Look." Parker waved at an older couple, then leaned across the table and reached for her hand. "If it's about the kiss this afternoon, I'm sorry. It was bound to happen, and I thought we should get it out of the way."

Get it out of the way. Everything was calculated and arranged for him. "I haven't thought twice about it."

"Liar."

She looked over the top of her menu and realized he had his fingers on the speeding pulse at her wrist. She snatched her hand to her side. "We can end this dinner right now."

"Good." He waved at someone else being seated. "Let's get something to go and take it to your place. We can tackle those papers."

"I've already done them," she lied. No way was he going to her apartment.

"All of them?" He eased back in his chair and narrowed his gaze on her. "Your father's right. You work too hard."

"I'll determine that. Shall we go?"

"To your place?"

"No."

"Mine?"

"No." She flicked at her hair, then remembered she'd put it up in a twist.

He laughed. "Might as well stay here then. The lobster is exceptional. I strongly recommend it."

She watched Parker peruse the menu and started to relax. Lobster did sound awfully good. It had been a long time since she'd been able to afford a small luxury such as that. And after the day she'd just had with Mr. Self-assured she deserved it. She closed her menu and Larry promptly appeared.

"Two lobsters," Parker said, handing the waiter his menu. "Extra butter."

Ashley darted Parker an incredulous look and held her tongue for as long as she could...a whole two seconds. "And I'll have the *ahi*." She flashed the confused Larry a brilliant smile. "Broiled, please."

Parker grinned and nodded to Larry, who frowned and took the menu Ashley extended to him.

"And we'll also have a bottle of your finest champagne," Parker added.

"Very good, sir," Larry said with a nod before heading for the kitchen.

"You must be hungry," Ashley commented sweetly when the waiter was out of earshot.

"I am." Parker agreed, leaning back and patting his flat stomach. "Especially for this particular lobster dish. Did I tell you it's their specialty? They coat two perfect tails with garlic and herbs, and it comes out on a sizzling platter with lots of drawn butter and warm french bread."

Ashley swallowed, then sipped from her water glass.

"It's a shame you don't want any." Parker's lips curved up slowly. "But if you're real good, I may give you a taste."

Ashley was about to give him a taste of something, but a couple of his friends stopped by their table. Parker was quick to draw her into the conversation and Ashley had to hand it to him, he sure could play the attentive date.

Once they were alone again, Ashley swept a glance around the dining room and asked, "Pleased with your audience?"

"Pardon me?"

"For my...coming out."

"Oh, yeah." Either he had missed her sarcasm or was ignoring it. "Lots of key people, lots of big mouths, too."

Surprised by his disdainful tone, she studied his sullen profile while he surveyed the crowded restaurant. For an odd moment, Ashley felt like Parker was playing a role. He didn't seem to belong to this social circle.

In fact, she'd sensed that at the benefit the first evening she'd met him. His mere presence had meant a large contribution to the Hawaiian immersion program, and for that she was grateful. But unlike many of the others, she'd gotten the feeling he wasn't there for the sake of being seen.

He'd even seemed downright uncomfortable. Just like he looked now.

Ashley turned away from him and looked out over the darkened ocean. A scattering of city lights reflected like sea stars. She squinted into the blackness beyond, wondering if bright lights from Magic Island would some day be visible from Waikiki. Closing her eyes briefly, she sniffed the salty air and listened to the waves crash to swells before they rippled and licked the shore. God, how she loved these islands. How could her mother have left?

"A nickel for your thoughts?" Parker asked. He was his old smiling self, his personal demons momentarily gone. Even though she didn't want to, she wondered about him.

"Inflation," he said, misinterpreting her puzzled look. "A penny doesn't work these days."

She laughed. "Tell me about it." And then the reminder of why she was sitting here in the first place wiped all humor from her face. Even worse than inflation these days was her empty bank account.

Watching her, Parker, too, turned somber. Absently he rubbed his chin.

"Let's get married right away," he finally said out of the blue. "This week. That way the contract can go into effect and we don't have to worry about..."

"Me backing out," Ashley finished for him, leveling him with a steady gaze.

"It's not that." He looked long and hard at her. "I think it'll take off some of the pressure."

"I don't feel pressured."

"Sure. Then why do you look like you're going to bolt for the door at any minute?" Ashley barely got her mouth open to refute him when he leaned forward and tilted up her chin with his long, tanned fingers. "We don't have to be adversaries, Ashley."

"Then what are we?" Ashley sucked in her lower lip, cursing herself for the stupid remark and even more for its throaty delivery. She angled her head out of reach, but he caught her hand and stilled it from its fidgeting.

"We could be friends," he said lightly, while he stroked her inner wrist with his thumb.

Ashley turned her hand over into his, ignoring the hint of surprise in his face. She merely didn't want him anywhere near her pulse.

"Would that be so bad?" he asked, his voice raspy.

"Just friends," she cautioned, hoping the wind and surf disguised the breathless quality in hers. It would be far easier, she acknowledged, if he weren't so attractive.

He squeezed her hand tighter and she gave him a shy smile. The champagne he'd ordered arrived, but Parker didn't let go. And Ashley didn't let go either. Only when the pop of the cork startled them both, did Ashley slip away from his touch. She looked into his smiling blue eyes, caressed by moonlight and the soft glow of candles, and all but sighed.

Parker sent Larry away and assumed the task of pouring the sparkling wine. "Before we make a toast, I have something for you." He topped off both glasses, then reached into his breast pocket and produced a small velvet box.

"I guessed on the fit, but we can have it sized." He looked like a kid at Christmas. Ashley knew the feeling. She'd always been happier giving her father gifts rather than getting them herself. She smiled at his endearing enthusiasm, then peered into the box he'd flipped open.

"What the hell is that?" Her eyes were almost as big as the three-carat monstrosity that stared back at her.

Parker blinked several times. "What do you mean? What does it look like?"

"You can't expect me to wear that."

"No. I thought you'd dangle it from your car mirror."

"Do you know how many people that could feed?"

"Only one and his dental bill would be outrageous." His blue bedroom eyes were narrowed into impatient slits.

"Why, that thing could buy groceries for a family of ten

for a year." Or part of an airstrip, Ashley's incensed mind suddenly realized.

"Probably three years. Tough." Heads turned and he had to lower his voice. "You *will* wear it." He glanced around the room, shaking his head. "I told Harvey you were a damn bleeding-heart liberal," he muttered under his breath.

"Mr. James," she hissed back in an even lower tone. Remember Magic Island, the rational side of her brain valiantly tried to whisper. "Would you like me to tell you what you can do with that ring?"

Parker slumped back and sighed. "I can hardly wait."

Chapter Five

Their meals arrived and Parker quickly shoved the ring box back into his pocket to avoid a scene. His appetite was gone and so was his good humor.

He watched Ashley through arms and plates and fresh pepper being ground, and even with all the activity he could see the angry sparks of green brightening her eyes.

Well, he was angry, too. The ring had little to do with status. She'd been so unselfish in this arrangement that he'd been anxious for her to have something personal. But she'd thrown it back at him.

In silence he watched her eat, doing more poking than eating, before he picked up his own fork. Pushing his champagne aside, and sloshing most of it onto his hand, he signaled for Larry and ordered a beer. Ashley still made no attempt at conversation.

In no mood to be civil or socially correct, Parker waved off the chilled glass the waiter brought with his beer and tipped the bottle up to his lips. He chugged a long, hard swallow and put it down with a small thud.

Without skipping a beat, he stabbed a chunk of lobster, dipped it in the melted butter and nearly bit the fork tip off as well. Her silence suited him just fine. He chanced a look at her.

Although he'd never have classified her as pretty in the traditional sense, he'd always considered her attractive. But he had to admit that on her, bullheadedness looked pretty damn good. Thick black lashes cast long shadows on flushed satin skin and her lips formed an unconscious, sensuous pout. A new kind of tension eased into his consciousness.

Parker took another pull of his beer. He resumed his routine of spearing his lobster and splashing butter all over, when he heard a muffled sound and looked up.

She had been watching him but glanced away. The dimple at the corner of her mouth begged to appear. Ashley took a small bite of the fish she'd ordered, taking a long time to chew, then the grin emerged.

"What's so funny?" he growled.

Ashley shook her head and looked down at her plate, pressing her lips together. Parker felt his own mood lighten in response to her ill-fated attempt at composure. But in the space of a heartbeat, her good mood seemed to evaporate.

"Not our wedding, that's for sure." Ashley raised her eyes, resignation clouding them. "Like it or not, I think we need to talk about it."

Parker didn't particularly like it, but the fact that Ashley appeared to like it even less annoyed the hell out of him. When had he become so thin-skinned? This wasn't personal. "Not to mention the ring," he tossed in. Then, pushing aside any unaccountable irritation, he asked, "When do I see your father again?"

"Not for a couple of days," Ashley replied, stubbornly ignoring further discussion of the ring. "I don't want him to think we're rushing things."

"He seemed rather receptive to me."

"Yes," she replied with a trace of sadness. "I don't quite understand that. Of course with all the medication and everything else, he's not exactly himself these days."

Parker's defenses once again shot up, even as reason tried to step in. He was taking it personally again. Ashley's confusion over her father's response was valid, he knew.

But emotionally it stung. He swallowed some beer, and along with it any tempting sarcasm.

Parker allowed the conversation to lull, giving them both some reflection time before decisions had to be made. He watched Ashley watch his plate and an undeniable nasty streak snaked its way to his tongue.

"Want some of this lobster before it gets cold?" he asked, forking a healthy piece and dipping it in hot butter. He poised the mouthful in front of her and let it drip temptingly back into the small chafing dish. A satisfied grin threatened him at the longing look she gave it.

"Oh...I've got plenty here."

"C'mon. It's good. Best on the island." He drowned the lobster in the butter once more, then put it to her lips.

She hesitated a moment, then plucked the morsel off his fork with that full, luscious mouth. He reveled in the look of ecstasy that crossed her face, her eyes shut, tongue licking remnant traces of butter from her lips.

"Have another bite." His fork was ready for delivery, even as she shook her head.

He wanted to recapture that exquisite expression. She'd look that way in bed, her hair spilling out over the sheets. The sudden thought startled him. He pushed it from his mind. So much for paybacks.

"I've been meaning to ask you something." He took a cool, calming sip of beer and changed the subject, knowing full well that it was the subject of their marriage they should be discussing. "Doesn't Leialoha mean 'welcoming flower'?"

"Yes. It's my middle name."

"I'm surprised it's not your first." Steeped in tradition as Ashley was, like the rest of the King family from what he knew of them, he'd been curious about that.

"My mother wouldn't have it." She shrugged indifference that wasn't quite believable. "She said her family wouldn't understand a foreign name. Not that I ever met any of them."

"Where is she now?"

"Somewhere on the mainland. Idaho or Iowa, someplace like that."

Parker struggled with his conscience for a moment. He was prying and he could tell she was uncomfortable, but he wanted to know about Ashley. "Do you miss her?" he asked quietly.

Ashley looked out over the darkened ocean, the sea breeze blowing escaped tendrils about her face. She rested her arm on the balcony railing and wrapped her graceful fingers around the decorative bamboo. "How can you miss something you never had?" she asked softly.

Good question. Parker followed her gaze out to the water. He should be able to answer that himself. He looked back at her, wanting to tell her he understood. He couldn't, though—not without baring his soul. "When did she leave?"

"When the money ran out. I was five." That shrug again, but this time smaller, less confident. "But that's ancient history." She straightened, leveling her eyes with his. "What about your family? Do they know about me?"

Another pleasant topic, Parker thought wryly. His succulent dinner suddenly looked bland and he pushed his plate aside. He was about to tell her that what his family thought didn't matter, when someone with a mass of white hair caught his attention at the entrance of the restaurant.

"Speak of the devil," Parker murmured, peering over Ashley's head. When she turned to see what he was staring at, he captured her hand and her attention. "My parents just walked in. Do me a favor and follow my lead. Okay?"

"But—"

"I don't have time to argue, Ashley." He hated the edginess in his voice, hated Ashley hearing it. "Would you trust me on this?"

Ashley hesitated for a brief second and he could feel the unspoken questions in her fingers as they flexed in his palm.

Her eyes darkened with uncertainty but she slowly nodded her head.

He looked back up to greet his father's surprised expression, quickly forced a smile and stood.

"Oh, Parker." His mother was the first to approach and stood on tiptoes as he kissed both her unlined cheeks. "I was just commenting to your father that you haven't been by in ages. And here you are." She stood back, holding both his hands, looking at him as if he were ten years old again.

"You look great, Mother." Parker freed his hands and slipped an arm around her. It really was good to see her. She looked as young as always, and Parker was pleased that his father's overbearing personality had never daunted her spirit. "You look good, too, Father," Parker added, just as he was expected to, and nodded to his father.

"You're looking quite well yourself." His father's intense gaze descended to Ashley, who sat quietly with wide, curious eyes.

Parker cleared his throat. "Mother, Father, this is Ashley King. Ashley, these are my parents...." Her eyes widened a fraction more on him and he knew he sounded too formal. It abruptly struck him how well she could already read him, how well he thought he could read her. And how much more comfortable than his own family she made him feel. "Parker and Barbara James."

Smiling, Ashley promptly stood and shook each of their hands and before Parker knew it, she had invited his parents to join them.

"We don't want to intrude," Barbara responded and looked longingly at her son, who quickly altered his expression and ceased the warning looks he'd been sending his meddling companion. "Besides, Karen and her husband will be joining us, and your table is only meant for four." She stopped and glanced at Ashley. "Have you met Parker's sister?"

"No. But I'm sure I will." Ashley smiled sweetly at Parker.

"Don got a new car, that's her husband, and he simply won't allow the parking attendants to touch it yet. So he let us off, but they'll be along any minute," his mother rattled on while Parker shifted positions.

His father's tolerance for standing in the middle of a crowded restaurant looked just about spent, and Parker couldn't be more relieved. This wasn't exactly the way he'd planned on having them all meet, especially since he hadn't told either party anything about the other. Ashley wasn't exactly shy about saying what she thought and a little prep time might be in order. He reached up to loosen his tie and felt a protusion at his breast pocket. He patted the unfamiliar object and was suddenly reminded of Ashley's ring. In that instant, an unexpected idea took hold.

His sister and her husband had come through the door and he waved them over. With damp palms, he pulled two borrowed chairs to their table, ignoring his parents' look of surprise. He made short work of the introductions, ordered another bottle of champagne along with four more glasses and got them all seated before anyone knew what had happened.

"Well," Parker said, taking a deep breath and drumming his fingers on the edge of the table. He looked from one expectant face to the next. "What's new with all of you?"

His sister's eyes narrowed on him for several seconds before she glanced at Ashley. A slow, mischievous smile Parker knew all too well, spread across her face. The fact that maybe this wasn't such a hot idea crossed his mind.

"I think your answer to that question might be more interesting," Karen said and took a long, deliberate sip of the champagne she'd just been poured.

She'd handed him his opening. Parker fenced with a moment of well-warranted doubt and rested his gaze on Ashley's amused face. The hint of smugness that slightly curved her full rose-tinted lips, along with the tiny mocking dimple that flexed at the corner of her mouth, was his undoing.

Slowly he dipped his hand into the inside breast pocket of his jacket. The small velvet box was firm and real under his unsteady fingers. He took a quick breath.

"For one of the few times in your life, Karen, you may be right." Parker gave her a teasing grin that belied the tension knotting his gut. Nonchalantly he withdrew the small box, concealing it from view, his hand wrapped tightly around it. No one seemed to notice. No one except Ashley.

She reached for her glass and dropped her napkin to the floor. He felt a hard pinch at his calf before her head bobbed back up. His eyes begged her panicked ones for understanding. Before he could change his mind, he transferred his gaze to his family.

"Actually, I'm glad you're all here." He fumbled with the box under the tablecloth, silently cursing his clumsiness, as he slipped the size four ring on to the end of his index finger. "Now, maybe Ashley won't say no when I pop the question."

He turned to her and stared into the angry sparks of green cutting him to shreds. Her reaction was far beyond the notice of his family, who all stared slack-jawed at him. He pried the diamond off his fingertip and picked up Ashley's limp hand.

"Well, I'll be damned," Karen murmured into the brief silence.

"Ashley, will you marry me?" Parker asked, slipping the ring on Ashley's finger.

A long, dry swallow traveled Ashley's throat and her mouth quivered into a scant smile. "I'm speechless," she finally croaked out. And Parker pressed his lips to hers to keep her just that way.

"WOULD YOU TRUST ME on this?" Ashley mimicked an hour later as she briskly led the way to the car. "Great beginning, Mr. James.''

"Don't call me Mr. James." Parker handed the valet attendant a book of the restaurant matches by mistake. He muttered a single succinct curse that netted him several sidelong glances, then fumbled in his pocket and replaced the matches with a five-dollar bill.

"Maybe I should call you sir, or maybe master would be better." Ashley jerked her seat belt in place. "Except slavery has been outlawed. They actually pay people to work in the pineapple and sugar plantations now, or didn't you know?"

Parker slammed his door. "Look, isn't it better that we got it over with?"

"Better for whom?" Ashley waved her hand around, caught sight of the flashing diamond and made a disgusted sound. "Give me the ring box," she ordered, crossing her arms and tucking her hand out of sight.

Parker simmered while he abruptly fished in his pocket and produced the object of her request. He felt her fingers tremble as she snatched it from his hand.

"We have to tell my father immediately." Ashley sighed and rested her head back against the leather seat. "Before he hears it from anyone else."

For the first time, Parker experienced a flicker of remorse. Being surprised by his family's sudden appearance had done strange things to him and he hadn't stopped to consider Ashley's position. He had taken advantage of the situation for his own benefit and now her defeated look really got to him.

Parker drove the car away from the restaurant's entrance and pulled into a parking stall near the street. He let the car idle and took her cold, reluctant hand in his.

"We can go to the hospital right now. I'll even ask him on bended knee, if you want." Just the thought of going to the hospital again invited a cold sweat, but he couldn't help grinning at the way she suddenly straightened, even though it was too dark to get a good look at her face.

"On *both* knees. That's what I ought to make you do." She tapped a finger against his palm as if seriously considering it, and before Parker realized what he was doing, he brought her hand to his lips and stilled her fidgeting.

He pressed one kiss to the tip of the restless finger, then another to the back of her silky hand. When she didn't resist, he turned it over and buried his mouth in her soft palm. He felt the cool metal of the ring against his cheek and felt a sense of deep satisfaction that she hadn't yet removed it.

"What do you think you're doing?" Ashley asked in a tight, breathless voice.

"Practicing." He kissed his way to her wildly beating pulse and felt his own speed up.

"What for?"

"To convince your father." He trailed up farther with a light touch of his tongue.

Ashley yanked her arm back and landed a hard whack on his lips in the process.

"Ouch." Parker jerked his head up and put a reflexive hand up to his bruised mouth.

"You let me worry about that," Ashley said in a clipped tone. "All you need to practice is writing checks." She pulled the ring off her finger. "Because, Buster, I'm going to cost you plenty."

PRACTICE. Ashley couldn't shake the word from her brain even after a night of fitful sleep. Parker was smooth, charming, a real snake. And Ashley was a damn fool.

Chemistry. Now here was a word. She'd been poor in that particular subject in high school and she was proving to be even poorer at it now. She never could understand it then, and now, when Parker touched her...well, all she understood was that he simply couldn't touch her anymore.

She had barely gotten off the phone with her father when

Parker pulled up to her apartment in his showy red Porsche. Out of a perverse sense of revenge, she insisted on driving, well aware of his aversion to her beat-up Toyota.

"Did you talk to him?" Parker asked after they were on their way to the hospital.

"Yes." Ashley sighed. She knew who he was talking about. Her father had been on her mind most of the night. "I dropped more than enough hints. It shouldn't be too much of a surprise when we do tell him."

"How did he take it?"

"Too well."

"Ashley? About last night." Parker adjusted the air-conditioning vents directly at his face. Ashley fidgeted with her hair.

"Forget it, Parker."

He didn't say anything for a long time, and Ashley did all she could to keep her eyes on the road and off him. "I think I have a happy medium with the ring deal," Parker finally said, glancing at her bare fingers.

Ashley remained quiet with her eyes straight ahead. She had already come to a decision about that herself, but she was curious about his peace offering.

"Wear the ring for the duration of our marr..." The word seemed to stick in Parker's throat. "Wear the damn thing and when our arrangement is over, you can sell it and do whatever you like with it. Feed five families if you want." Ashley had the feeling that hadn't come out as he had planned, and she had to hide a smile when he tried to roll down the window but it stuck halfway. "And get this piece of junk fixed."

Lifting her chin, she took a corner a little too fast. She owed him one for that last crack. If she had felt a tad guilty knowing the ring would pay for part of the airstrip, she didn't now. When he acted like a horse's rear end by ordering her around, it took away some of the sting.

Ashley pulled into the hospital lot and parked the car. The sight of the dismal gray building reminded her that there was more at stake than quibbling over a diamond. Ignoring Parker's curious look, she withdrew the burgundy velvet box from her purse and slipped the ring onto her finger. "It's a deal," she said and got out of the car.

Parker had to move fast to keep up with her. He was having enough trouble keeping up with her fleeting moods, he didn't want to have to physically chase her down. He reached out and grabbed her upper arm to slow her. "Hold it."

She stopped and he saw her body settle on a deep sigh. He'd accomplished his purpose, but he didn't want to let her go. Her hair, black and glossy in the bright sun, was lifted off her shoulder by a tropical breeze. It floated away and then back, long and heavy to her waist.

"Are you ready to tell your father now?" He loosened his fingers, lingering on her sun-heated flesh.

"I think so." She nodded, turning to him, and he immediately sensed that for whatever reason some of her earlier fire had fizzled out. "Oh, Parker, something is very wrong with him." Rare vulnerability clouded her eyes and his heart thudded. "He's seeing things that aren't there."

"Hallucinations?"

"No." She shook her head, her hair billowing like a satin sail. "About us I mean."

"That's good. It'll be easier on him." And us.

"But it isn't like him to be so gullible. It's simply not credible that you'd pop into my life like this. Besides, he knows how stubborn I am."

Parker laughed softly. "If he's having trouble remembering that, I'll vouch for it."

Ashley laughed a little, too. "If he forgot that, I'd really be worried." The humor fell from her face and large, sad eyes met his. "I *am* worried."

It seemed natural for Parker to hug her to him. He wrapped his arms around her, her head nestled under his chin. Closing his eyes, he placed a light, undetectable kiss on top of her head and inhaled the now familiar scent of sunshine and gardenia that spoke her name.

He blinked at the sunlight and stared ahead of them at the gray hospital outlined by green mountains and blue sky. His phobia forgotten, he rested his slightly roughened chin in her soft hair.

"Maybe it's wishful thinking," he said after a while. "Maybe he's so anxious to have you happy and settled, he's convinced himself."

"You think so?" Ashley angled away from him, looking so trusting, wanting to believe.

"People do it all the time. It's a form of survival." She was doing it now, Parker thought, and he brought her in close again. He had done it many times himself.

"You could be right." She moved back, and he had little choice but to let her go.

"The doctors have always been straight with me," she said, a shy smile of gratitude on her lips. "I don't see why they'd hide the truth at this point, although it's strange. I could swear they seem to be avoiding me. Probably just my imagination." She smoothed her hair and the diamond caught the sunlight. It sparkled like a million stars in a black, cloudless sky and bespoke promises of romance and commitment.

And for just an instant, Parker wondered what it would be like to be gifted with the love of someone like Ashley Leialoha King.

"SO, YOU WANT TO marry my daughter." Keoki King expertly shuffled two stacks of quarters with one hand. Not once did he look at what he was doing but kept his eyes directly on Parker as if he could see right through him.

"Yes, sir, I do." Parker shifted from one foot to the other.

Ashley fluffed her father's pillow for the fourth time.

"Don't call me sir, Parker. I have told you before, my friends call me Keoki. And in my experience, people have been either friend or foe.'' The older man pierced him with an unwavering stare and managed to look quite formidable despite the ludicrously bright blue-and-green aloha shirt he wore.

"Keoki," Parker promptly corrected. He was being tested. Perhaps all fathers were demanding and manipulative. Not just his. But Parker would play the game. For Ashley's sake.

"Do you love her?" Keoki asked bluntly.

Parker heard Ashley's small gasp and he slipped his arm around her waist, pulling her up against him. He gave her a reassuring squeeze, his gaze fastened on Keoki.

"I do," Parker said clearly, without stammering, without hesitation.

A slow, wide smile lit up Keoki's face. "Then you have my blessing." He clasped Parker's hand and held out an arm to Ashley, who immediately fell into his embrace. To anyone watching, it looked like a Norman Rockwell scene, only Parker knew the quiver in Ashley's shoulders was not from joy. And that undeniable fact dealt a strange blow to his gut.

"When is the happy day?" Keoki asked after a fair amount of hugs and sniffles had been exchanged.

"We haven't gotten that far." Ashley swiped back her hair and glanced at Parker.

"I'm free tomorrow," Keoki commented.

Ashley laughed.

Parker laughed.

Keoki didn't. Frowning, he looked from his daughter back to Parker. "You're right. We need time to prepare."

"Prepare?" Parker and Ashley said together and looked apprehensively at each other.

"We weren't planning a big wedding," Parker stated slowly. "Something private, maybe a civil ceremony."

Keoki's frown deepened. "But everyone will want to share your happiness. Your friends, family…"

Just what he needed, Parker thought, a big production

made out of this outrageous farce. What they *did* need was for it to be quick, quiet and legal. It would make the ultimate break easier. He darted a solicitous look at Ashley. "Well, actually..." he spouted. "Tomorrow sounds like a great idea."

"I agree." Ashley immediately jumped in. "I don't want a big fuss."

"But, Leialoha..." Keoki shook his head. "I must insist."

Parker watched Ashley's shoulders sag a fraction. Then her eyes turned that warm honey brown that made Parker's insides feel soft and gooey like melted caramel. Her mouth was soft and yielding...and she clearly was unable to say no to her father. And if push came to shove, Parker, without a doubt, would be putty in her hands.

"The truth is, sir, uh, Keoki," Parker said before he surrendered his last shred of control. "I can't wait any longer." He pulled Ashley into his arms and, feigning an intimacy between them, kissed her long and hard.

Reflexively, Ashley put her hands flat on his chest. He braced himself for the inevitable shove. But her warm palms rounded up to his shoulders and her surprised mouth softened against his.

He felt her moist invitation and his heart did a double somersault. He pressed her to him by the small of her back before sliding his hands to the curve of her buttocks. Somewhere in the distant fog, an intrusive sound penetrated his muddled consciousness. It sounded suspicously like a cough. Parker cocked open one eye.

Keoki grinned.

Parker reluctantly but quickly disengaged himself from the man's daughter. He took a large gulp of air and looked at Ashley's flushed face. Her formerly honey brown eyes were shooting a dangerous assortment of green. She was embarrassed. And angry.

And Parker didn't say a damn word.

"I see your point," Keoki said, still grinning. "Shall we say, day after tomorrow?"

KEOKI PULLED OUT THE half-smoked cigar from its hiding place, almost before he saw the last flash of his daughter's pink sundress disappear around the corner. He was so excited he nearly forgot to bring out the can of air freshener along with it. He was on his last warning from the nurses, but he just could not help it. He had a lot of celebrating to do.

He puffed on what was likely to be his last cigar for a long time and thought about his next plan of action. Things were moving along better than expected, but he wasn't out of the woods yet. It would not do at all for Ashley and Parker to have a private wedding. That would make a divorce far too easy.

And Harvey wouldn't be much help, Keoki figured, since he was getting entirely too squeamish about the whole matter. Keoki pondered the problem for another few minutes while he enjoyed his final puffs, then smiled and reached for the phone. He had another trump card, and if he played his hand right he would not have to incriminate himself at all. He coughed into his hand until his voice was suitably raspy and hoarse, then leaned back into his newly fluffed pillows and waited for the connection to be made.

"Crystal?" he queried in his most pathetic voice. "I need your help."

Chapter Six

"We have some fast moving to do," Parker said when they'd reached the hospital lobby. "We need a marriage license, a minister. What else?"

Ashley hurried on, ignoring him. He reached out and grabbed her arm. "I'd like some cooperation in this."

"Oh? Now you want my opinion." She glared at him and tried to shake loose of his hold.

"You weren't exactly helpful back there."

"And you were? You had a lot of nerve acting that way in front of my father."

"We're supposed to be getting married, for Pete's sake." Parker realized he'd raised his voice and sighed. He knew what she meant, and he hadn't intended on getting carried away as he had, but she hadn't had any business looking at him like she had, either. Her eyes all warm and dewy... geez, just thinking about it made him nuts.

Several people stopped to stare, so Parker pulled her toward the more private parking lot. He knew she'd noticed the gawkers, too, so she let him get away with it. When they reached her car he blocked her from opening the door, tilted her face to his, then trapped her with his other hand.

"Look, lady—" Parker began.

"Can't get your way by manipulating a harmless old man, so now you'll try bullying me?" She was so small that even with her chin lifted in indignation, he had to really lower his head to look into her unblinking eyes.

Different as night and day, he thought with a mental shake, in so many ways. In looks, ideology, temperament…well, maybe not temperament. The idea made him smile.

Her tongue darted out to moisten her lips—her pouty, coral-tinted lips. He felt her warm breath, smelled the butterscotch candy her father had given her. And try as he might, he couldn't remember what he'd been about to say. Nor could he drag his gaze away from her mouth.

"Not at all," he whispered before his lips descended upon hers.

She remained rigid at first, but her lips softened a little, and her hands made their way up to rest tentatively against his collarbone. It was weak encouragement, but Parker ran with it. He tangled his hands in her hair, gathering it away from her neck and throat, and wondered how all that black silk would feel against his naked chest.

With eager lips, he traced the delicate skin along her jaw. Her floral scent teased and drew him to the soft flesh of her ear. He lingered—nipping, tasting, feeling the increasing pressure of her fingertips, hearing her soft, unguarded sighs.

Somewhere a car door slammed, followed by another. It could just as well have been a faint echo to him, but apparently it was like a cold shower to Ashley. The sensual clawing of her graceful fingers turned into a hard shove.

"We need to get to my apartment," she said on a deep breath. "Get in."

"Sounds like a helluva good idea to me." His breathing wasn't any better as he struggled to get all his masculine accessories back to a socially acceptable state.

"So you can get your car and go home," Ashley hissed, making him hurry around to the passenger side. If her tone was any indication, she'd probably take off without him.

"I only meant we should probably start preparing for

your move,'' he replied with exaggerated innocence. Too much sexual energy flowed between them. It would only be a matter of time before they both responded. He knew it. And whether she liked it or not, he could tell Ashley knew it.

''I'll take what I need to your house when it's necessary.'' She threw the car into gear and jerked out of the parking stall.

Parker didn't like the way she said that. It lacked a sense of gravity. ''It might be a good idea to do that now,'' he said warily. ''Besides, you need to meet Mrs. Lee.''

Ashley glanced over at him and slowed the car. ''Your housekeeper.''

He nodded. ''I've casually mentioned your name to prepare her, but she's certainly not expecting me to bring home a *bride* the day after tomorrow.''

Ashley gave him a dirty look that had him regretting his choice of words, but she nodded in tight-lipped agreement and steered the car in the direction of his house.

An hour later Parker peered out the wide glass window that overlooked his pool and the ocean and idly watched his dog chase the outgoing tide. Mrs. Lee had cornered Ashley the moment they had arrived, and now Ashley was the victim of his housekeeper's requisite tour. He loved the older woman, but she was a real busybody. She'd also be a good test for their pretense, he reminded himself as he waited impatiently.

Parker tried to cast an objective eye on the natural wood interior of the split-level living area. Most women he brought to his house were impressed. For that matter, anyone who'd ever seen it had been.

But not Ashley.

Parker took great pride in having designed most of it himself, had even participated in the manual work. It had been a labor of satisfaction for him. A gratifying reminder of all those years he'd spent bumming around the mainland, learning one odd job after another, relying on his wits and two hands and not his grandmother's trust fund or a high-powered attorney's salary.

Ashley, however, saw it differently. He had felt it in her disapproving appraisal, heard it in her censoring silence. And for that, he couldn't really blame her. Most people only saw the silver spoon, they couldn't know that he'd never liked the taste. That's why the arguments with his father had started, culminating with his withdrawal from law school. The first James in generations not to carry on the tradition. What a disgrace. What a crock.

Parker's patience had been all but spent when he heard voices approaching.

"You should have told me sooner, Parker. This is very sudden." Mrs. Lee wagged her customary finger at him. Her eyebrows drew together in suspicion and she cast a pointed look at Ashley's stomach. "You not *hapai*, are you?"

"Mrs. Lee," Parker warned.

"I have a right to know." She sniffed. "If there is going to be a *keiki* around to take care of and diapers to wash, maybe I have to charge you more money."

"Don't worry." Ashley laughed. "No *keikis*."

"Soon." Smiling, Mrs. Lee patted her ever-present bun.

Ashley and Parker both opened their mouths to deny it, but the ringing of the telephone curtailed the need to vent their indignation. The older woman moved her bulk in the direction of the den and had barely barked out a greeting when they heard the door close.

Parker shrugged. "Well, I guess it's not for me."

"She's quite a character," Ashley commented.

"That she is. Did she give you the third degree?"

Ashley rolled her eyes. "Did she ever."

"Do you think she bought it?"

"It helped that you've been talking about me for the last week and a half." She cocked him a wry look.

Had it only been that long? The realization stopped Parker. Impossible. "Yeah, well…exaggerating is another one of her faults." He rubbed the back of his neck. "She may have overheard me talking to Harvey but I know she doesn't suspect anything or I'd have gotten a lecture."

"I think she may be in shock," Ashley said, smiling.

Parker shook his head. "She probably thinks you're someone I've brought here..." He cut himself short, surprised at his own callousness.

"It's okay, Parker." Ashley's smile faltered. "This isn't love, honor and cherish for real." She stepped up to the window. "That's a great pool."

"What do you think of the house?" he asked, watching her perfunctory assessment of his creation. A small part of him still wanted to dazzle her with the unlikely talent he'd discovered in his own two hands.

"It's fine." She moved away and reached for her purse, which dangled from a dining-room chair. Her gaze snagged on the marriage license he'd left on the table, and the same anxious look crossed her face as when they'd picked it up not more than an hour ago.

"Will you be ready to do this?" He narrowed his gaze on her. If her feet were getting cold, he wanted to know now.

"As much as I'll ever be." She sighed.

"You don't have to like it. But you do need to be enthusiastic." His voice lowered as he slanted a look toward the den.

"For an audience, I will."

"Is it going to be that bad, Ashley?" His ego asked the question, but something else inside him wanted the answer.

"I don't know," she admitted.

"Well, it's not going to be any picnic for me, either." He jammed his hands in his pockets. Three or four years of her stubborn self-righteousness were going to make him certifiable. "Just keep in mind what you have to gain."

Ashley looked straight into his eyes, not really seeing him, and then her solemn gaze drifted toward the ocean. She stared out at the solitary horizon for several seconds and then a slow, confident smile blossomed across her face. And once again Parker had the uneasy feeling he was missing a big piece of the puzzle.

ANYONE WOULD HAVE THOUGHT it was Crystal getting married today and not Ashley. She was as jumpy as a tourist walking barefoot on hot Waikiki sand at noon. She'd started off by being late and now, every time Ashley turned her back, it seemed Crystal was on the phone. Ashley supposed she should be glad that her friend was being so cavalier about the exchange of vows. After all, it really was no big deal.

"Higher heels," Crystal said, casting a critical eye at Ashley's reflection in the full-length mirror. "And nail polish." She paused, a thoughtful look on her dramatically made-up face. "Although you don't want to compete with the ring." She shoved bracelet after bracelet up her arm. "But definitely higher heels."

"Not with a *holoku*," Ashley said, gathering her hair in one hand and draping it over her shoulder in front of her. She picked up her hairbrush and glided it through.

"Does Parker know you're wearing that?" Crystal eyed the traditional Hawaiian wedding dress with misgiving. The collar was high, the sleeves long and fitted, the satin skirt floor-length and full.

"It was never a topic of conversation."

"Will he be freaked?"

"I don't know." Ashley hadn't given it a thought. She'd never had wedding-day dreams like many of her friends, but she'd always known that if the time came she'd wear her grandmother's dress. The one her mother had chosen not to.

Crystal took the brush out of Ashley's hand. "Let me do that." The two friends exchanged a familiar smile, filled with shared childhood memories. "Remember when we were eleven and I rolled your hair in bubble gum?"

"How could I forget?" Ashley laughed. "Your mother

made you pay for my haircut with your allowance, and you never let me hear the end of it.''

"That was brutal," Crystal said, grinning. "But your father paid me back. He let me win at poker."

Ashley gasped. "You never told me that."

"He made me promise." Crystal worried her lower lip. "You know I'd do anything for him, don't you? I mean, I never could refuse your dad a thing."

"I know." Ashley frowned at her friend's sudden fidgeting and took the brush from her hand. "Is anything wrong?"

"No." Crystal widened her eyes under lifted brows. "I just wanted to be sure you understood that. Well..." She twisted each of the four rings on her fingers. "What do you think of Parker's house? Is the pool perfect for skinny-dipping orgies, or what?"

"Oh, please." Ashley chuckled, then narrowed her gaze on Crystal. "How do you know he has a pool?"

"A guess. He probably has everything else, too." Crystal released the bracelets she was twirling up her arm with a clang. "So, any skinny-dips in the near future?"

"Can you see Parker James skinny-dipping?" Ashley laughed. But a tempting picture came to mind, which put an abrupt end to her amusement. She didn't want to imagine the new Parker who was beginning to emerge. The one who smiled at little girls and took the time to reassure an old man he didn't know. The Parker who made her heart beat much too fast.

"Actually, I'd love to." Crystal looked at her and sighed. "Lucky you."

"That isn't part of the deal." Ashley sank onto her bed and tried on a pair of shoes, refusing to engage in destructive fantasies. Any type of personal relationship with Parker would be just that...a fantasy, or maybe fallacy was more appropriate. "How about this pair?"

"Perfect." Crystal nudged her aside and sat next to her.

"According to the grapevine, interest in Magic Island is alive and well. I even got roped into some legal work."

Ashley nodded, familiar excitement skipping down her spine. "My phone's been ringing off the hook."

"Better not let Parker get wind of it."

"No kidding." Ashley flipped her hair out of the way. Most of the time he looked as if he needed little excuse to wring her neck, as it was.

"If he dumps you over it, I get first dibs on him." Crystal tried to hide a grin.

"You can have him."

"The hell you say. I know you too well, Ashley King," Crystal said, leaving the bed and wagging her finger. "You are hot to trot with that man, whether you'll admit it or not." She strode past Ashley, ignoring her look of astonishment.

"Do you actually think I want anything to do with that pushy, self-centered, egotistical, social snob?"

"You might've convinced me with three less adjectives. But you gave it away by almost hyperventilating." Her friend, perilously close to being ex, gathered the makings for her newest hair color and threw them into a sack. "Are you sure you're not doing anything special after the ceremony?" she asked breezily.

"For the third time, no." Ashley made a face. "This is business, Crystal, that's all." Only business. Ashley hoarded a deep breath and smoothed out the skirt of her *holoku*. "Why do you keep asking me that?"

Crystal shrugged and turned to give her a long, serious look. "No reason." She took Ashley's hand and squeezed it, her eyes misty. "You just look so...so gorgeous."

On impulse Ashley hugged her friend, pretending for a moment that her life was not about to be turned upside down. "And you're the best." She fought the catch in her throat. "Ready?"

An uncharacteristic blush climbed Crystal's face. "I'll remind you of that in a couple of hours," she muttered as she headed out of the room. "I need to make one last call before I lead us both to the slaughter."

ANYONE WOULD HAVE THOUGHT it was Mrs. Lee getting married today and not Parker. He hadn't gotten a moment's sleep the previous night with all her bustling around, making room for Ashley's things and rearranging the house until he almost didn't recognize it anymore. They had argued over that, and then they'd argued over what he should wear for the exchange of vows. By the time the vanload of flowers had arrived that morning, he'd had it. So he'd picked up his things and bolted for the nearest hotel. Though not before threatening his housekeeper with every bit of blackmail he could, if she told a single living soul before he gave her the go-ahead.

And now, even after a brief nap and a five-mile run, tension still cramped Parker's shoulders. Karen was going to kill him when she found out she'd been excluded. So would his mother. He could have called them—should have, actually. But the thought of his father's unwanted judgment had kept the phone out of his reach. After all, this wasn't his family's business.

He was disappointed, though, that Harvey couldn't be here today. The attorney had declined Parker's request to be his witness, having made a prior commitment. The ceremony was a farce, merely a means to an end, but Parker had wanted Harvey there. Tom Booker, another friend, had accepted. He'd been off the island lately, so he hadn't found the situation odd or asked a lot of questions.

But now, both Tom and Ashley were late. Parker waited outside the hospital, cursing under his breath. He hadn't wanted to have the ceremony at the hospital, even if it was in the open courtyard, but when it came right down to it, he couldn't refuse Ashley. She wouldn't disappoint her father and Parker couldn't disappoint her.

He shifted the long florist box from one arm to the other and shook out his clammy free hand. It was unseasonably cool for mid-May, but he was about to shed his sport coat and roll up his sleeves. His body heat was up at least ten degrees. Even quitting law school hadn't seemed this taxing.

He looked longingly at his fast red Porsche and thought about heading for the airport. San Francisco had to be nice this time of year.

And then he saw her.

The long ivory *holoku* she wore barely cleared the ground as she walked toward him, giving her an ethereal air. A large gardenia, startlingly white against her black flowing hair, was tucked behind her ear. A small and fragile package of pure and earthy beauty, housing determination and a will of steel. An unexpected serenity chased the edginess from his body. A smile came unbidden to his lips.

"You look lovely, Leialoha." Her startled hazel eyes searched his. He'd even surprised himself. Silently, he praised her father's sixth sense for so aptly naming her "welcoming flower" twenty-nine years ago. A self-fulfilled prophecy in Parker's opinion, and without conscious thought the name had fallen from his lips.

"Thank you, Parker," she said in a soft voice, the dimple at the corner of her mouth appearing slowly. "This is my friend and attorney Crystal."

He blinked, not having had the slightest clue of anyone else's presence. He cleared his throat, looked over at the taller woman and tried not to gape. Somehow the label of "attorney" didn't quite compute. "Nice to meet you, Crystal." He transferred his package, then shook her multi-ringed hand.

"Same here." Crystal ran fuchsia-tipped fingers through her spiked hair. They were unsteady and he could tell her smile was forced. Great. Even she was nervous.

"Is the minister here?" Ashley asked, her voice low.

"He's with your father. I don't know what's keeping my friend Tom." Parker gestured to the air and noticed the florist box. "Here, this is for you." He lifted the top and with great care removed the *maile* lei.

The wariness in Ashley's face stopped him for a moment. "I'm doing this right, aren't I?" He looked from one woman to the other. "Isn't *maile* supposed to be for weddings?"

Ashley nodded, unspeaking, her eyes uncommonly bright.

What the hell was wrong with her? He'd thought she'd be pleased. Did she want a bouquet instead? "Look, you don't have to wear it. I just thought—"

"I want to," she broke in, putting a hand on his when he tried to stuff the lei back into the box. "This is very sweet, Parker." She stroked the *maile* leaves with a feather-light touch, her lashes lowered. "I'm afraid I don't have one for you." Eyes widening, she searched his face. "It's traditional for the groom, too, but I didn't think—"

"That's okay, Ash." He took her hand and brought it to his lips, a smile forming there. "It's okay."

Crystal cleared her throat. "Why don't you two go inside? I'll wait for your friend Tom. I have a feeling I'll be able to spot him."

Ashley glanced heavenward, and Parker flashed a grin. "I wouldn't bet on that." He grinned further at Crystal's inquisitive look, then took the lei from Ashley's fidgety fingers and placed it around her neck. He pressed a firm, warm kiss on her unsuspecting lips before steering her toward the hospital.

"I think I like Crystal," he said after they'd entered the lobby. He stuck close to Ashley, his hand at her back. Inhaling her sweet scent, he was able to ignore the odor of drugs and ether, which for reasons he had yet to comprehend had always managed to permeate the air clear to the lobby.

"You do?" Ashley's eyes grew round and her dimple peeked out at him.

"Yeah, but maybe I'd better reserve judgment." He slid

his hand to the curve of her neck and grinned down at her obvious surprise. She didn't shy away from his touch and the steady pulse he found there reassured him. "She may be a bad influence."

Ashley laughed. "I promise I'll never color my hair ravishing raspberry, and blue shadow will not touch these eyelids." She cocked her head to the side and gave him a teasing grin. "But the quadruple ear piercing I'll have to think about."

"Heaven help me." He cast his gaze up briefly before looking back at her. "Actually, what I want to ask her about is some harebrained project called Magic Island. Rumor has it that she's somehow linked to it, and I want to know what those fanatics are up to." He felt the pulse at her neck leap at his fingertips just before she stepped out of reach. "It has to do with the new gambling law up for vote. Nothing you need be concerned with," he assured her. "I doubt your friend's even involved. Those idiots are to the left of left field."

Parker tried to take Ashley's hand but her fingers tightly intertwined with each other and she averted her sweet face, her chin making a defiant ascent. He cursed his stupidity. Magic Island had nothing to do with Ashley, and even if Crystal was somehow involved, she was Ashley's friend. And, of course, Ashley would be defensive.

He pulled his tie a fraction looser and eyed the ugly green walls closing in on him. If the powers that be didn't keep this death trap so hot he wouldn't have been such an insensitive cad, Parker thought with absolute certainty as he glanced down at the trembling hands of his soon-to-be bride.

CRYSTAL AND TOM, in his gray suit and worn sneakers, caught up with them just as they reached the open courtyard. Quick introductions were made at the entrance, where torches has been stationed on either side and twin flames shot up to meet the waning sun. A small gathering of nurses, patients and other strangers huddled around a trio softly singing Hawaiian love songs.

Ashley watched Parker's jaw slacken. His incredulous gaze swept the transformed courtyard. Ashley herself was only mildly surprised. She'd heard the whispers and caught the secret smiles this morning when she'd snuck in for a brief visit with her father.

Now that she stood at the entrance, she realized that in true Hawaiian style the nurses had invited themselves and had staged quite a backdrop for the ceremony.

Flowers were everywhere. Sprays of white and lavender orchids weeped from the arched entryway and fanned the air just above Parker's head. Petals from snowy-white gardenias and pink plumerias carpeted the ground before the minister, their potent and heady fragrance dancing with the breeze.

And under a large corner palm, her father waited, a flower in his hand. He hadn't seen her yet, as he continued teasing a pair of orderlies. He looked good, better than he had in months. And Ashley felt a layer of anxiety vanish.

Parker touched her arm and she turned to look at him. "I thought we agreed on privacy." He shook his head in bewilderment, his gaze skimming the crowd.

"My dad's nurses." She shrugged helplessly. "I think they're responsible." Her attention rested on Parker and the fine lines of tension bracketing his mouth. He looked handsome and tanned in his white dress shirt and taupe blazer, his jaw so strong, his eyes bluer than the sky. His slacks fit his long legs to perfection.

Ashley swallowed around the lump in her throat and let her eyes close briefly. Magic Island notwithstanding, she was out of her ever-loving mind for going through with this arrangement.

Looking back at Parker, she slipped her hand into his and was pleased to see some of the tension immediately disappear from his face. She gently urged him the rest of the way through the entrance.

As soon as they entered the actual courtyard, the crowd quieted and Ashley felt the pressure of Parker's hand increase. Certain all eyes would be on them, she cast a reluctant gaze around at the unwanted fanfare. But her dread proved groundless. All attention was on her father, who strode, straight and proud, toward her and Parker.

A nurse stopped him to drape a yellow plumeria lei around his neck. When several others offered him their hands in congratulations, he beamed with pride and suddenly something became very clear to Ashley. All this pageantry had little to do with Parker and herself. It was for her father.

Ashley raised her eyes back to his contented face and knew in her heart she was doing the right thing.

"Parker, about all these people…" she whispered before her father approached. "I know we didn't—"

"It's okay, Ash." Parker released her hand and put a silencing finger to her lips. His gaze drifted to her father. "He looks happy, doesn't he?"

Ashley drew in her lower lip, a surge of gratitude rendering her speechless for an instant. Then she laid her hand on Parker's arm. "Are you ready to do this?"

He swung his attention back to her and pierced her with a steady gaze. "I am." He recaptured her hand and they met her father midway. She accepted the flower and kiss her father gave her, then stayed close to Parker's side as they moved to stand before the minister.

Ashley felt rather than saw Parker looking at her. She tilted her head back and looked at him, bringing up a hand to shade her eyes. The lines of tension were entirely gone from his face as he moved to shield her from the sun. He took her hand away from her eyes and kissed it. "You look beautiful," he whispered as the preacher opened his Bible.

Ashley smiled, not because she believed him, but because he was playing the game so well. Yet a small part of her wanted him to think she was beautiful, and to her utter embarrassment tears welled up in her eyes.

She bowed her head and blinked them back while the ceremony progressed. She repeated the vows she was instructed to repeat, nodded when it was appropriate. And when the minister told Parker to kiss his bride, Ashley closed her eyes, lifted her chin and waited for him to brush her lips with his.

And waited.

"You may kiss the bride," the minister repeated deliberately.

Ashley slowly opened her eyes.

Parker grinned, slid his hands up her arms and pulled her to him.

She caught her breath and held it as Parker claimed her mouth. His kiss was long and hard and thorough. His hands caressed her back and he held her so close Ashley couldn't have breathed if she'd wanted to.

When the crowd erupted into cheers, she felt Parker's smile against her branded mouth, then he angled his head back and gave her a sleepy-eyed, lopsided grin.

Ashley felt the heat from her middle rise to her face. She exhaled a long, steadying breath and did her best to return his smile. Then she stepped back and clasped her palms together before one of them made sharp contact with his aristocratic face.

"Nice performance," she hissed and smiled at the same time.

"Thank you." The corner of Parker's mouth twitched. "But I think I need more practice."

Ashley stepped back and gave him a warning look before spinning away toward her father's waiting arms.

It wasn't hard to get away after that. The onlookers were satisfied, her father was on cloud nine and most of the patients were being herded back to their rooms.

After waving off Tom and Crystal, Ashley slipped into Parker's Porsche and rested her head back against the soft leather seat. "You can let me off at my apartment," she said once they were on the freeway.

"Is that where we're spending our wedding night?"

"Frankly, I don't care where you spend yours." In spite of herself, Ashley glanced at him. "But you can bet the resort it won't be with me."

Parker laughed. "Be careful. That resort will eventually pay for your community center."

Ashley casually shifted her attention out the window. She didn't need the reminder. What she needed was to get home and warn Crystal that Parker would be asking her about Magic Island.

Crystal was Ashley's best friend and loyal to the hilt. But she was also the worst liar Ashley knew. Forewarned, Crystal would be fine; but if cornered, there was no telling what would pop out of her mouth.

"Besides," Parker continued. "To get Mrs. Lee off my back, I had to promise her we'd go back to my...uh... excuse me, our place."

Ashley didn't answer at first, but she couldn't very well tell him to stuff it, since he'd been so civil about meeting the minister at the hospital. And besides, as long as she was with Parker she had time to get to Crystal.

"Fine. I'll go home after that." Parker's lips thinned and her conscience reminded her of how much that hospital visit had cost him. "Then if you like, we'll have dinner out later."

"Don't you have one romantic bone in your body?" Parker frowned as he shot her a sidelong glance before returning his attention to the road—the road, she noticed, that had long ago headed away from her apartment.

"This isn't supposed to be romantic," she reminded him slowly, almost swallowing the last word when he wickedly cocked one eyebrow up at her.

"Normal newlyweds wouldn't be dining out on their wedding night," Parker commented.

"We aren't normal."

"Speak for yourself." Parker chuckled. "Or I'll pull over and show you how normal I am."

His tone was pure suggestion and Ashley felt herself shrink toward the door, seeking oxygen from the open window.

"Never mind," she muttered, then changed the subject. "Where does Mrs. Lee think we're spending the night, anyway?"

"I don't know," Parker said. "She was driving me so crazy with rearranging the house, the subject never came up. Half the flowers on Oahu must have been delivered this morning. I think she had one of her bags packed, too. She probably thinks we'll be spending it at home."

She watched him sweep back the hair the wind had tumbled across his forehead. His hands were strong and tanned...and looked entirely too capable. And Ashley decided she didn't much care for the idea of spending the night with him. In fact, she'd had enough of him today. Period. Being with him was one thing, but being with him in front of an audience was quite another. It had been one heck of a strain. But she could indulge him and Mrs. Lee for at least the next half hour. Then as soon as Mrs. Lee left, so would Ashley.

They were about three blocks from his house by the time she'd formed a plan of action in her mind. She was about to propose it to him when the car swerved and Ashley looked up to see that they had just missed a parked car.

"What the hell is going on?" Parker sized up the long stretch of cars on either side of the street. "These people can't park on both sides like this."

"Someone must be having a party," Ashley offered and straightened to get a better look.

"Not someone," Parker said in a low, awestruck voice, while slowing down the car. "We are."

Chapter Seven

Parker was half tempted to step on the gas and get the hell out of Dodge. He was three seconds from doing just that when his sister and mother stepped out the front door and waved. Ashley's father was right behind them. Harvey Winton followed behind him.

Parker clenched his teeth as they coasted down the driveway and he noticed that two of the parked cars belonged to investors of his.

"I hope to God you don't know anything about this," he said through gritted teeth while trying to smile for their welcoming committee. He hadn't seen his father yet. Hell, he might not even have come. It would be just like him, Parker thought, to make it clear that once again he disapproved of his only son.

"You've been in the sun too long if you think I had anything to do with this." Ashley blew out a sharp breath, then her gaze riveted on her father. "What in the...he's not supposed to be out of the hospital."

"Yeah? Well, he looks fine to me." Parker shot her a suspicious look.

"I swear to you, I don't know what's going on." Ashley reached for the door handle with unsteady fingers.

"Look, Ash." He touched her arm and she swung her gaze back to him, her eyes wide and questioning. "I didn't mean to imply that you're involved with any of this." He waved his hand in a helpless gesture. "Whatever this is. We'll handle it, okay?"

"Okay," she whispered as he ducked in for a quick reassuring kiss. Their audience applauded and converged on the car.

They were hugged and jostled all the way to the front door, and as soon as Parker stepped inside, the events of yesterday and this morning came into sharp focus. Mrs. Lee's short temper, her furniture-rearranging frenzy, the delivery of roses, orchids and gardenias, which were now placed everywhere.

Parker shook his head, wondering who Mrs. Lee's accomplices might be. A large buffet table laden with an assortment of island delicacies extended the length of the glass window overlooking the pool, while waiters circulated with trays of canapés and champagne. His mother and sister were busy escorting in three musicians who had just arrived, but they immediately got them situated and headed for Parker.

"I haven't decided if I've forgiven you yet, but I figured you'd need this." Karen handed Parker a beer, then sipped from her own champagne glass.

"*I* definitely haven't forgiven you," his mother admonished. "I did all I could not to call you last night after Mrs. Lee phoned us. Parker, didn't you think we'd want to attend the ceremony?"

Parker fought with his conscience in silence for a moment. He hadn't wanted them to find out this way. They didn't deserve that. "Where's Father?" he asked and took a long pull of beer.

Karen looked at her mother, who was about to answer, and cut in. "We didn't have much notice, Parker. He already had an engagement. So did Don. But they both wanted to be here," she added hastily.

"Yeah." Probably playing golf together, Parker thought. Don was more than a son-in-law. He was everything Parker wasn't. But Parker had let go of that hurt years ago. "Well, this was last minute for us, too." He smiled an apology. "But I was going to tell you."

"Men," Karen muttered, shaking her head.

"Don't be sexist." Parker laughingly warned as several people approached. He handed her his near-empty bottle and added, "Make yourself useful, will you?"

"I'll get you later." Karen laughed at his favorite childhood taunt, then hugged him before she and her mother stepped aside for the next group of well-wishers.

Everyone was in high spirits, laughing, talking and drinking the free-flowing champagne. Several of his business associates approached to offer congratulations. Parker smiled, accepted the slaps on the back, did some slapping himself.

He couldn't wait to get the hell out of here.

Scanning the crowd, he spotted Ashley with her father in a corner.

"I can't believe they let you out of the hospital," she was saying when Parker installed himself next to her. "Those doctors should be shot for allowing this."

"Now, now, Leialoha." Keoki patted his daughter's hand. "I am fine. Look at me." Smiling, he spread his arms.

"Well…you do look good." Ashley worried her lower lip, then glanced at her new husband. "But it wasn't fair to Parker. He hates hospitals, yet he agreed to have the ceremony there for you." She took one of Parker's hands, her fingers a light caress, before her palm, soft and warm, pressed against his. Her eyes, golden and honeyed with gratitude, lingered on him.

Parker's heart swelled to his throat. Speechless, he gazed down at her. She had stuck up for him. Of her own free will, and not merely for the sake of their pretense, Ashley had chosen to stick up for him. Parker could see it in her eyes, feel it in her touch. And he had never felt so humbled as he did right then.

He wanted to tell her she was wrong, that he hadn't done

it for her father. He wanted to tell her that he'd done it for her. But he didn't trust himself to speak.

"Well, if it is any consolation," Keoki said, looking from his daughter to Parker, a satisfied gleam in his eye, "the white coats will be here for me in less than an hour."

"Pop," Ashley scolded. "I didn't mean that. Of course I'm glad you're here." She dropped Parker's hand to hug her father and Parker, in the midst of a hundred people, was struck with the sudden feeling of loneliness.

The feeling was odd, unfamiliar, and he didn't like it one bit. In fact, it frightened the hell out of him.

"Who's idea was this?" Parker asked as safer feelings of anger and irritation reasserted themselves. He ran a finger around the inside of his collar. "We didn't want all this...this..."

"Nonsense." Keoki guffawed. "You only get married once."

Parker and Ashley exchanged quick glances.

"You're right, Dad." Ashley patted his hand. "It's a wonderful surprise."

Several people interrupted to congratulate the newly-weds. And eventually Keoki was spirited away by a few of his old cronies, leaving Parker and Ashley by themselves for a few blessed moments.

"Have you figured out who's behind all this?" she asked behind a forced smile, as she continued to nod to people.

"No. And right now I don't care. I just want out of here," Parker answered in a hushed tone.

"We can't."

"Why not?"

Ashley turned wide eyes on him. "Because all these people are here for us."

"Precisely," Parker commented dryly.

"We can't just leave. It would be rude."

"Not if we were late for our honeymoon." Parker's brain scrambled for an idea.

Ashley's eyebrows drew together. "What honeymoon?"

"Trust me on this, okay?"

"Where have I heard that before?" Ashley sputtered before turning to wave to a friend. "Forget it."

"Look, Ash—"

Crystal popped out from around the corner, a glass of champagne in each hand. "Peace offering." Her grin was sheepish, her face red.

"So, you're the culprit." Ashley planted a hand on her hip. "Crystal—"

"Oh, Ashley...you know how your dad is. What else could I do?" Crystal extended the glasses to them.

Ashley took hers, but Parker only shook his head. "Now I may have two bones to pick with you. What do you know—"

Parker was interrupted by a loud cough from Ashley. He swung around in time to take the champagne glass she pushed on him, while she held her other hand flush to her chest. "Are you all right?" He passed the glass back to Crystal and drew Ashley into his arms.

She nodded, looking up at him, her eyes large and bright. "Too many bubbles," she whispered. Then, to his utter amazement, she stood on her toes, wrapped her arms around his neck and kissed him.

Parker had to catch himself from stumbling back. She'd taken him by surprise and was clinging to him as if her very life depended on it. And as much as he enjoyed her unexpected passion, they were creating quite a scene.

Parker glanced at a gaping Crystal, while gently prying Ashley's fingers apart. He pulled back and smiled at her. Her eyes were glassy, her mouth trembly. And in another minute he would take her straight to bed, wedding guests be damned.

"You were right," she whispered. "Let's get out of here." She flashed a come-hither smile that just about caused the rosebud on his lapel to bloom.

"Say good-night, Ashley," he ordered hoarsely, his gaze locked with hers.

"Good night." Her voice was barely audible, and she didn't even spare her friend a glance.

"Pass on our regrets, will you?" Parker said over his shoulder to a dumbfounded Crystal as he scooped Ashley up in his arms and strode out the front door.

"WHY MOLOKAI? I don't know why we couldn't have just stayed at my apartment." Ashley twisted the gold band around her finger over and over again.

"I thought maybe this might be a special night." Parker hadn't meant to sound so sarcastic, but the woman was making him crazy. They had gotten all of two blocks away from the party when she'd done a total about-face. What the hell ever happened to truth in advertising?

"Look, we didn't have time to argue about it," he continued. "If we'd waited any longer it would have been too dark for a commuter flight, then I'd have had to pull some strings."

"Do you always get what you want, Parker?"

He pulled the rental car out of the Molokai airport. "If I did, you'd have shut up an hour ago."

"That can be arranged." She crossed her arms over her chest, lifted her chin and angled it so she could look out the window at the jagged coastline. Waves foamed white and angry, spraying the aged lava rocks.

Parker had lost it. He raked a hand through his hair. Had totally lost it. He hadn't told anyone to shut up since he was eleven years old. He glimpsed Ashley out of the corner of his eye and his disposition immediately softened. Her crossed arms kept her fidgeting fingers restrained, but her tiny foot was tapping wildly. She was nervous.

That must be the reason for her sudden Mr. Hyde impersonation after that titillating scene back at the party. Armed with this new recognition, Parker relaxed and waited a few minutes for her to cool off.

"It was a stressful day, Ashley," he began after a short

time. "I'm sorry for anything negative I contributed. What do you say we make the most of this trip?"

Her foot slowed down, then she brought her face around to give him a slow contrite smile. "I'm sorry, too—"

"Enough said," he cut in before she tried to explain herself. "It's getting too dark for any sightseeing, but what would you like to do tomorrow?"

"I'm not sure." Ashley blinked and stared back thoughtfully. "I've never been to Molokai before."

"I'm surprised. There's more Hawaiian history here than on any other island besides Niihau."

"I know it sounds rather provincial, but I haven't been to all the islands. There's always so much to be done on Oahu." She squirmed a little, an attractive blush tinting her cheeks. "I guess this will be fun."

"There's a lot to see. We'll have to skip Kalaupapa, the old leper colony, and the wildlife preserve at the Molokai Ranch," he said, excited that he'd be the first to show her the island. "I have to be in the office on Monday, but I know exactly where I'm taking you tomorrow."

"Where's that?" she asked, smiling at his enthusiasm. He noticed she fingered the *maile* lei he'd given her. It pleased him that she continued to wear it. For Hawaiians, it was a symbol of luck. For Parker, the fact that she still wore it was a good sign.

"It's a surprise." He lightly touched the tip of her nose and winked. Ashley's tongue darted out to moisten her lips. She swiped at some loose tendrils. Parker settled back, willing his hands away from her. Even the most innocent touch made his senses reel.

He pulled into the hotel's circular drive and quickly surrendered his keys to the valet attendant. It hadn't really occurred to him until this moment that they had no luggage...no clothes. He smiled. That was more than okay with him, though he had a feeling Ashley might have a slight problem with that particular oversight.

They were promptly escorted to the suite that he had

arranged for them from the Honolulu airport, and Parker gladly tipped the bellman for *not* bringing the clothes they didn't have.

"This is quite a place," Ashley said once they were alone in the suite. Champagne chilled in a stemmed antique bucket near a cream-and-navy sofa. Heart-shaped petit fours were arranged on a paper lace doily, framed by a gleaming silver platter on the coffee table. The air was richly scented with dozens of roses in varying shades of pink, springing from tall crystal vases throughout the parlor.

"It's the honeymoon suite," Parker commented casually and opened the sheer drapes to let in the panoramic ocean view. Ashley darted him a nervous sidelong glance before peeking out the wide sliding-glass doors. A cascade of purple bougainvillea plunged from the balcony to the sea.

"Want to see the bedroom?" Parker asked, then had to suppress a smile when she swiped at her hair.

"This must have cost a bundle," she said, ignoring him.

"Oh, no. You're not going to give me another lecture on my errant ways, are you?"

"That depends."

"On what?"

"Where and when you're taking me to dinner. I'm starved." She grinned, and Parker was relieved to feel the earlier tension between them dissolve. "And where isn't half as important as *when*."

"I'll tell you what." Parker stepped forward and put his hands on her shoulders. She looked up at him with confusion in her eyes, and then her gaze lowered to rest on his mouth. She moistened her lips. His thoughts faltered.

"Did I ever tell you how ornery I get when I'm hungry?" she asked, swallowing hard.

"You mean, more than usual?" Parker forced a chuckle. He should get a medal for what he was about to do. Ignoring her unwitting invitation, he gripped her shoulders tighter and steered her toward the bathroom. "I'll give you first dibs on the shower, while I run down to the hotel boutique.''

''The hotel boutique?'' she questioned over her shoulder, then stopped at the bathroom door and faced him. Her eyes widened. ''Oh.'' She looked down at her wrinkled *holoku* and grimaced. ''You don't know my size.''

''This time,'' he said, hurrying to the door with a wicked grin. ''You really do have to trust me.''

SOMETHING VERY STRANGE was happening, Ashley decided, as she took her seat at the table set for two on the short pier. With the help of a nearly full moon, a crystal lantern and the illumination of the hotel looming behind them, she could clearly see Parker's face. Her heart had somehow moved to her throat and who knows where her appetite had gone.

Nothing had gone right yet today, and now conflicting emotions were threatening her very sanity.

Disappointment was the last thing she had any right to feel, Ashley chided herself...well, maybe second to the last thing. The green silk dress Parker had bought for her fit perfectly, was quietly elegant, undoubtedly expensive...and except for the thin straps, quite conservative. It was almost boring.

The trouble was, his demeanor had indicated something far more exciting, daring, tantalizing. And the longer she'd waited in her sinfully sensuous bubble bath, the more she'd wanted to excite him, dare him...tantalize the socks off him.

Except if she sent Parker one more mixed signal after the spectacle she'd made of herself back at the party, he'd surely have her committed. But when he had opened his mouth to ask Crystal about Magic Island, Ashley had acted on her first impulse.

And therein lay the larger problem. Why had that been her first impulse? She could reason that it had been the simplest thing to do, but she knew that would be a lie. For as much as she hated to admit it, Ashley had the sinking feeling she was falling for this…this… She sighed. Even her contrived thoughts allowed her no indignant respite.

"Obviously, making a menu selection from here would be impractical, so I've already ordered for us." Parker must have misinterpreted her sigh as he leaned forward, a questioning look on his face. His skin looked exceptionally tan against his starched white shirt collar. The breeze ruffled his hair, putting it into a state of sexy disarray.

"Fine." She blinked, then reached into the glass-bowl centerpiece and twirled the gardenias floating at the bottom.

"Don't worry. It'll be a lot."

"What?"

"Of food. I wouldn't want to be accused of starving you on our first day of marriage."

Ashley looked blank at first, then laughed after she got past the shocking *M* word. They really were married…if only in name…and land deed. "You know, I really hadn't planned on eating so much that you'd have been too embarrassed to be seen with me in a restaurant."

"I wouldn't take the chance." Parker shook his head.

Ashley flicked a light spray of water off her fingertips at him.

"If it's a water fight you want, I'd be happy to oblige." He grabbed her wrist, his eyes sparkling with challenge.

"Not in your fancy clothes, you wouldn't."

"Wanna bet?"

"No." Ashley laughed and pulled back her hand. "Why did you want to dress up, anyway?" She eyed his tuxedo, knowing it wasn't his preferred attire.

"I thought it an appropriate prelude," he said calmly, and Ashley nearly flipped off the unfamiliar gold band she'd been twisting around her finger.

His expression was serious at first, and Ashley felt a web of apprehension weave through her. Then his eyes began to crinkle at the corners, and he asked with pure innocence,

"Does prelude mean before or after an event? I always get that word mixed up."

Ashley thought of at least two answers she'd like to give him, but refrained from either.

Holding back a grin, he lifted his fluted glass. "To a smooth beginning."

"I think it's too late for that," Ashley replied and touched her glass to his, refusing him the satisfaction of any further reaction. "I don't suppose you bought me anything to sleep in."

The corners of Parker's mouth curved up, but his glass, in midair between them, distorted the true shape of his lips and made the smile seemed positively diabolical. "Of course. Otherwise that would be like..." He took a leisurely sip while watching her over the rim. "Forgetting dessert."

Ashley scrambled to think of something clever to say, but her heart competed with the distant pounding surf and her brain put all nerve endings on alert. She sipped the cool champagne instead and wondered if she could ever think of chocolate cake in the same way again.

With equal amounts of disappointment and relief, she noticed two waiters appear on the beach. She watched them approach with trays of silver-domed plates, grateful that she need not respond, ignoring the fact that she already had.

"You weren't kidding," she said when the food was placed before them. "It must've been embarrassing just ordering all this." She peered into papaya halves filled with crab and shrimp. Bowls of lobster bisque and plates of cold poached salmon were uncovered. Her mouth watered, her appetite firmly back intact.

"They'll bring my dinner next." He waved off the amused waiters, instructing them to bring the last course in an hour, then ducked the wadded cocktail napkin she threw at him. "Not enough for you?"

"Keep it up and I won't share." She forked a combination of shrimp and crab.

"Sure you will. Won't you?" The pleading he tried for fell a little short, but he leaned forward and waited.

"Well…" Ashley pursed her lips. "Just a little." Slowly she pushed the bounty toward him.

"Mmm. Superb! What else will you share?" He pierced her with a look that made her think he was talking about more than food.

Suddenly the meal held even more appeal. Ashley ate with relish, talking between mouthfuls, steering away from anything Parker implied. By the time the double chocolate mousse arrived, it didn't even seem tempting. But that didn't stop her.

"For a small thing, you sure can pack it away," Parker said after the dishes had been cleared and they were having their coffee.

"No short jokes or the truce is off."

"How about fat jokes?"

"You like fighting?"

"No. But I don't like considering this a mere truce, either," Parker said.

"How would you regard this?"

"Two people who can enjoy each other's company, while they each achieve their goal."

"We're too different, you know."

"To get along?"

She wasn't going to fall for this. There was no being led down the garden path for her. "We're getting along right now."

"Are we?"

"I enjoyed dinner, the conversation. And I didn't complain once about all this…this extravagance, did I?"

"You just did." Parker laughed. "In your own charming way, of course."

Ashley was glad he could make her blood pressure rise. It helped keep things in perspective.

"Care to walk off some of this dinner?" he asked before she could come up with a smart retort.

"Good idea." She pushed up from the table with a groan. "I don't think I could even get mad over a fat joke tonight."

"Good, because I was wondering how to broach this…" Shadows from the tide flickered across his face, giving him a pensive expression. "Are you one of those women who blimp out once they've snagged a husband?"

She stared at him for a moment, then punched his arm. "You turkey." He laughed, capturing her fist and bringing it to his lips.

"It would serve you right if I did." She lifted her chin and turned toward the ocean, letting the breeze cool her cheeks. He hadn't let go of her hand yet, and she didn't think she wanted him to. Gradually, she let her fingers relax from their balled position. His fingers slipped with ease between hers.

"Better take off your sandals," he suggested. "Unless you'd rather stick to the sidewalk around the hotel."

"Let's walk in the sand." She stooped down to do as he advised, and he removed his shoes as well. She laughed as he hopped on one foot and then the other to remove his socks.

"You could've helped me." The curve of his lips tempered his grumbling.

"I thought you were the floor show." She turned away with a smile and headed toward the shoreline, kicking playfully at the sand. "Besides, it was your profound idea to play dress-up."

In three strides he caught up, hooked her around the waist and hauled her up against him. He planted a swift kiss on her lips before she could do anything but breathe. "Today was special," he whispered. "Why not dress up?"

"Put me down or never complain about my weight again."

He pulled back in mock horror. "Me? Purposefully command your wrath? Surely you know I'm not that stupid."

"I know no such thing," she said and loosely put her

arms around his neck. He let her slide with agonizing slowness down the length of him, until her feet sank into the soft, moist sand.

"Know about what?" he asked, his breath a soft caress on her cheek, his arm still firmly around her waist.

"Why do you ask such absurd questions?" The ocean pounded in her ears, and stars twinkled their amusement against the cloudless tropical sky. She was tired of bluffing, tired of trying to remember what they'd been talking about.

His lips started at her temple, then trailed along her jaw, nibbling their way to her mouth. Ashley dropped her head back and felt the pressure of his hand in her hair, entwining it, pulling at it, until her throat and neck—and surely her heart—were fully exposed.

"What about our walk?" she asked, her voice at minimum service level.

"The goal is," he murmured, running his tongue down the column of her throat, "to get the heart rate up." He licked at her collarbone. "This works for me."

"A walk...hmm." She ducked slightly from his nibbling. "Would be more appropriate."

"Ah." He caught her earlobe between his teeth. "But not as much fun." She felt the vibration of his lips, felt the tiny bumps rise from her flesh.

"But safer." In spite of her words, she lingered in his arms, felt her toes curl down into the sand as she stretched up to him.

"For what? Your conscience?" He tried to snag her lower lip with his capable ones.

Ashley jerked her head back. Her feet sank back down hard. "My conscience is fine. Is yours?"

"Mmm. Everything is fine, honey." Parker tried to pull her back against him. His eyes were closed, a satisfied smile on his lips she'd love to erase.

"Try again." Her tone was as shaky as the hand she brought up to tuck her hair back.

"What?" He opened his eyes and gave her a puzzled look, one she did not find endearing.

He had no idea, she thought with amazement, then thought about it for another second and decided it wasn't worth getting into. "I'm tired. Don't bother walking me back." She pivoted in the direction of their abandoned shoes.

"What's the matter?" he called out.

"Nothing." He hadn't figured out that the truth hurt, that the only relationship they had was based on a strip of land and a piece of paper. But she was grateful for the reminder. Without it, no telling what kind of fool she'd have made of herself.

"I'm tired, that's all," she told him more gently and truthfully, realizing with great sadness that for them fighting was the best way to keep their distance.

Chapter Eight

"I'll go back with you." He scooped up their shoes and sandals, and they walked in silence up the torchlit path to the hotel.

It was later than Parker thought. There was no sign of life in the dimly lit hotel lobby set back from the beach. Most of the guest rooms were blacked out, and the restaurant overlooking the ocean appeared nearly empty.

He didn't know what had spooked Ashley on the beach, but it would be a shame to waste such a beautiful and private night. "Want to sit by the pool a while?" he asked, stopping at a plumeria tree and plucking one of the blossoms.

Ashley slanted him a wary look. "Don't you have a full day planned tomorrow?"

"We don't have a timetable." He positioned a lounger for her and gestured to it.

"I think I'll pass." She dusted the sand from her feet and took her sandals from him.

"What? Can't wait to get me up to the room alone, huh?" he teased, clapping the sand from his shoes. And then it occurred to him, that notion could be possible. His gaze jerked up to her indignant one. And then again, maybe not.

Wishful thinking, James. He bit back a resigned grin and

stroked a petal of the plumeria, then presented her with the fragrant flower. "I wish it were a gardenia."

"How did you know I like gardenias?" she asked with a slight frown.

"Simple." He shrugged. "Your perfume."

"I don't wear perfume."

He thought she was kidding at first, but he looked into her wide, questioning eyes and knew it was the truth. "I swear I can smell gardenias every time I'm with you." And when I'm not, he acknowledged wryly.

Ashley merely lifted a brow, a strange look on her face. Clearly she thought it was one heck of a line. And with her precarious mood, that wasn't a good sign.

"I mean it," Parker insisted. Good going. He rubbed his jaw. He'd surely get the line-of-the-year award.

"That's sweet, Parker." She put her hand to his cheek. Her lashes lowered for an instant and then her golden gaze bore into him. The angry green sparks were gone, but the warmth he craved wasn't quite there either.

"You don't believe me," he stated.

"Of course I do." She curved her hand to cup his face.

He relaxed, the tension he'd felt only a moment before dissolved. Mistakenly, he'd thought she'd been upset with him.

"Want to sit by the pool or go upstairs?" He captured her hand and pressed a long kiss to her palm.

She laughed, low and throaty, and gazing up at him, pushed her fingers through his hair. "It's so balmy. Let's stay," she said, her voice a sensual purr as she swayed against him, her long black hair flowing into the night.

He'd never been much for dancing, but Ashley's body pressed against his, oscillating with the flower-scented breeze, made his feet anxious to comply.

She let her head drop back, a bewitching smile on her lips, and she looked intensely at him. Exhilaration sparkled from her eyes, made all the more alluring by the shadows from the lighted water. Heat engulfed him. One shoe fell from his free hand, the other remained dangling from his fingers.

"Do you wear contacts?" she asked in a dreamy voice, her gaze unabashed adoration.

A sigh of relief almost escaped him. He was home free. Since he'd been a kid, women had fawned over his "bedroom blue" eyes. He cast silent thanks heavenward before answering in a modest voice. "Why, no."

"Good." She treated him to one more beatific smile, then put both hands on his chest and shoved.

He faltered in the middle of a sway. The one remaining shoe flew from his hand, an earthy curse from his lips. And with a large splash he landed in the kidney-shaped pool.

"That ought to cool you off…you…you arrogant, self-indulgent jerk." Ashley planted her hands on her hips. Parker kicked and sputtered, trying to stay above water.

"Me? Lady, you have one helluva nerve." He treaded water long enough to spit out his opinion before the weight of his anger—and his drenched tuxedo—dragged him down again.

"So have you," Ashley tossed over her shoulder as she headed for the path to the elevators.

Parker didn't know how he'd managed, in all his soggy leadenness, to make it to the edge and hop onto the decking. But he gained on her before she could make it to the building.

Ashley twisted in surprised horror as Parker pulled her against him. "Want to play rough?"

"You're getting me wet," she struggled in his arms. "Silk can't take water."

"And tuxedos can? You called the game, sweetheart."

"This is not a game. It was never a game," she hissed. "You tried to make it one." She gave him a futile push, then stumbled back against him. "Let go of me before someone comes to investigate the commotion."

"I'll tell them we're newlyweds." He shrugged, unconcerned, but she sensed a potent anger simmering below the surface. His lips were a breath away from her ear, his hands molded themselves to her wet, clinging dress. "That'll explain everything."

"What are you doing?" Ashley felt the first rise of panic. Her feet barely touched the ground as he propelled her back toward the pool. "Let's go to the room."

"Not yet. We have unfinished business here."

"Okay, I'm sorry." The tips of her toes skimmed the ground as she tried to put the brakes on. "Where are we going?" she asked, dreading the answer.

"To give you," he informed her in a hoarse whisper, his chest heaving beneath her hands, "a taste of your own medicine."

Ashley hit the water before his last word was out. She sank several feet and struggled against the urge to chop and slap at the water. She wouldn't give him the satisfaction. After several seconds she surfaced, swallowing a fair amount of water and indignation. She extended her arm and sliced through the water, reaching the side in several strokes.

"Nice job," Parker commented and reached a hand out to her, a smug smile on his egotistical face.

For a split second Ashley wondered if she had enough weight to pull him back in, but just as quickly she abandoned the whim. This particular war was over...for her, anyway. Maybe she had reacted too strongly. If only he weren't so...so...

"Staying in all night?" Parker left out his hand.

She looked up at him. Then again, maybe with the water's added weight, she could haul him in. "I'm tempted," she said, ignoring his offer, then placed both palms on the puddled deck and levered herself out.

"Tell me you didn't deserve that." He grinned and shrugged out of his dripping jacket.

"I didn't deserve that." With some remorse she watched him retrieve his ruined shoes, then looked down at her own irreparable clothes.

"I am sorry about the dress." He'd appeared beside her, his voice soft, the outside of his index finger rubbing against her upper arm.

"I'm sorry, too," she answered, hoping it didn't sound breathless. The air was mild, the water warm, his finger steamy. She shivered.

"Cold?" He slipped his arm around her. His face and seductive breath hovered above hers.

"No." She wouldn't look up. It'd be stupid. She pulled the fallen dress strap up her shoulder, then succumbed to temptation and raised her eyes to his. "I—I don't know why I did that. It was pr-probably childish." Her voice faltered under his intense gaze.

"Probably?" He laughed softly, hooking a finger under her dress strap, lightly scraping his knuckle back and forth across her skin. It caused an unbearable friction.

"Well, you irritate me." She made a halfhearted attempt to elude him, but his other arm encircled her.

"You *want* to be irritated," he corrected.

"Why would—?" His mocking expression stopped her. It would be pointless to deny it. She grabbed a handful of her hair, turned away and wrung it out. "It's better than doing anything foolish."

"Like this?" He stilled her hands and brought her head around.

She thought her chin actually tilted up before his fingers made contact with it. "Yes." Her voice was weak.

"Then let's be foolish." He brushed his lips against hers, then licked the moisture from the corner of her mouth.

"We really shouldn't," she murmured. They were both insane to be even thinking about getting involved. The arrangement could only work if they didn't. She had far too much to worry about as it was. This wasn't an option.

She closed her eyes and slid her arms around his neck.

A soft groan vibrated from Parker's throat as he tightened his hold. He lifted her up against his chest. He was tall and strong, and Ashley's feet no longer touched the ground.

She met each of his hard, hungry kisses, her neck arching back from their potency. His mouth left hers to forge a fiery trail down the column of her throat to the damp skin around her collarbone.

She heard his labored breathing, felt his chest heave against hers and understood the control he was fighting to maintain.

Pressing her hips against him, she began a slow rotation. She heard his breath suck in, missed its warm caress of her skin. His fingers bit into her buttocks, making the thin silk a useless barrier.

"No fair doing the hula now," he whispered, his protest a hoarse attempt. He shifted his own hips, then hiked her up higher in his arms. Her dress went up, too, leaving her thighs bare and vulnerable.

"I'm too heavy for you," Ashley murmured to the sky as she lifted her face to the perfumed air. Eyes closed, she could still see a thousand stars.

"Not even close." He nipped at her chin, then with his tongue traced sensuous patterns, dipping and darting to the top of her sagging dress. Her nipples pebbled and strained against the wet silk.

She clasped the sides of his head, fisting the wild half-wet tawny hair. One strap slid down her shoulder. Then the other. The weighty dampness dragged the flimsy material down low on her breasts. His tongue followed.

The ocean breeze glided over her skin, then sailed on through the night, stealing with it the rest of her willpower. His hot, moist mouth strained for her tender nipples. And Ashley offered them with each struggle for air.

A car backfired in the distance. Ashley opened her eyes and blinked. She stiffened. "Put me down, Parker." She took in a lungful of air, glancing from side to side.

"Hmm?" His eyes still closed, he nipped at the swell of her breast.

"We're right out in the open." She pulled up on her dress and adjusted the bodice.

"I can fix that." He lowered her, kissing her hard and wet when she was halfway down. "Come here." He pulled at one of her hands, pivoting toward the pool, while she rearranged a dress strap with her other hand.

"What are you doing?" Ashley planted both feet firmly together at the edge of the pool steps.

"Going where no one will see us." Parker had already placed one tuxedo-clad leg into the water.

"You really are crazy." Eyes wide and disbelieving, she shook her head. "I'm not going back in there. It's…it's wet."

"So are you." He gave her the final tug that brought her halfway down the steps. "I'm not giving you time to cool off, either."

She started to voice her irritation at his crass observation then repressed a giggle instead. The determined yet earnest look on his face was priceless. "Oooh." She backed up and shivered. "I think you're too late. The water seems colder this time."

"I'm not surprised." He tugged her forward again and grabbed both her hands. "We did heat things up pretty well." He found the sensitive area behind her ear and ran his tongue to her lobe.

"Someone could still see us," she whispered, hoping he didn't feel the goose bumps that surfaced on her skin.

"No one's around. Even the restaurant lights are out now. Relax, Ashley." He slid the straps back down her shoulders. "It's just you and me." He licked where each of the bands of material had been. "And we have all night."

Just one night, Ashley thought, closing her eyes. We'll steal this one small night. Reasons and regrets seemed far away as Parker reached behind her and pushed his hands up under her dress to her silk panties.

Her hands floated on top of the water until she could

stand it no longer. She plucked at one of his shirt buttons until it was free and then loosened the next. He pulled back when he discovered her mission, and although she couldn't quite meet his gaze his mouth was parted in anticipation. The third and fourth buttons were fast and easy.

Drops of water glistened from the dense thatch of hair on his chest. His nipples were distended and dark against the tawny hair. Ashley put her hands on him, shyly at first, but his groan of pleasure gave her confidence.

Stepping farther back, Parker slid the remaining inches of silk down over her breasts. She had no idea when he'd freed the zipper, for the top of her dress fell easily to float over the moonlit water. Only her long hair, tangled and clinging about her, shielded her nakedness from him. With aching tenderness, he peeled away the strands, kissing the sensitive areas they had guarded.

"You're beautiful," he whispered, cupping her breasts.

"Don't blow it now." Her laugh was short and nervous.

"You are. Like a Hawaiian goddess." He brushed the last of the hair away. His gaze rested on her face for a moment and then smoldered its way to her breasts. He circled the rosy tips with his thumbs, his head tilted in solemn fascination.

Ashley's voice stuck in her throat and she experienced an incredible sense of loss when his hands fell away.

"Come here." He reached under her arms and carried her up as if she were a child. "I want to feel you against me." As soon as he had her where he wanted, he locked his arms around her. Her nipples pressed to his hair-roughened chest. Slowly he swayed from side to side, while keeping her still. "You feel so good."

Anticipation bubbled and churned within her. Cool water, Parker's warm, hard body, air scented with a thousand flowers...surely she would drown in sensation.

To steady herself, she wrapped her unanchored legs around him. For a heartbeat, he stopped and looked down at her, his eyes masked by the shadows. She wanted to see them, wanted to be reassured. But when she gripped his shoulders, she felt the tension there and knew the next move would have to be hers. Before sanity could reclaim her, she undulated her hips, encouraging him to resume their sensual water dance.

It was all the inducement he needed. His mouth came down fast, his tongue like velvet against her skin. He changed the pace, made new rules, teased his way around her collarbone, then up to her lips. He lingered at her mouth, and with a sweet aching slowness tasted and probed.

Ashley began to breathe an even pattern when Parker deepened the kiss, his mouth demanding and rough with need. His fingers, woven through her hair, held her helpless. Not that she cared to go anywhere, do anything different. She kissed him back, matching his hunger.

"Oh, Ashley." He dragged his mouth away from hers, his words raspy and halting, his gaze roving her face. "We have to stop now if we're going to stop at all." He looked down at her breasts and watched the water ripple over them, first covering, then exposing them, the cycle repeating itself.

He cupped one breast, then put his mouth on her. She let out a small gasp, reveling in the feel of his warm tongue, the cool water. "No fair stacking the deck," she panted.

"I didn't say I'd be fair," he murmured against her sensitive skin and hesitated, holding her. Even the vibration of his words roused her tender need. But he was giving her a chance…a chance to preserve the relationship they could never again recapture.

Her body wanted to ignore the opportunity, but doubt niggled at her— even as she magnetized to his touch. Another moment, surely another moment wouldn't matter before she allowed reality to square off with emotion.

She tunneled her fingers through his hair and guided him to her other breast.

"Eh-hem. Excuse me, folks." The voice came from behind Ashley, her bare back up for the speaker's view. "I'm hotel security, and the pool is closed for the evening.'' If it were at all possible, the man's high-pitched voice sounded more embarrassed than Ashley was feeling.

She didn't turn to look at him, as mortification replaced desire. Heat climbed her face. She stared, wide-eyed, at Parker, who brought his arms around her, sheltering her from further discomfort.

"Sorry.'' Parker quietly cleared his throat. Looking over her head, he grinned at the man, and she was awed by his composure. "If you'll either turn your back or leave for a few minutes, I promise we'll be out of here.''

"No problem. I'll continue my rounds.'' The man's voice was already fading, but Ashley didn't budge.

"He's gone now,'' Parker said softly. He gave her a quick hug before releasing her and pulling up the front of her dress. "Ash, I'm sorry about this.''

She slipped each of her arms under the straps. The dress felt tighter, her breasts tender. She adjusted the fit, keeping her eyes lowered. "It wasn't your fault. I was just as much a participant.''

"I can still be sorry.'' He hooked a finger under her chin and nudged her face up. "I sure know how to romance a girl, huh?'' He chuckled. Her face burned. "Next time, I promise to do better.''

Ashley, tight-lipped, angled away from his grasp and reached around, trying to zip up the wet clinging silk. Parker buttoned his shirt halfway, then took the zipper from her hands and finished the job.

"Ashley?'' He waited patiently until with great reluctance she returned his gaze. The words "next time'' echoed in her head, and even as she vowed there wouldn't be one, she quivered with anticipation.

"He didn't see anything,'' Parker continued. "The man kept staring at his shoes. He was probably more embarrassed than you were.''

Quite impossible, but she didn't care to hang around and debate the point. She headed for the pool steps.

"Wait." Parker trudged up behind her just as she emerged from the water. His eyes lingered for a moment on the curves accentuated by the wet fabric. He looked as if he wanted to touch her, but he kept his hands fisted at his sides. "I need to know, Ash. What would have been your answer?"

Chapter Nine

Ashley had gotten very little sleep on her wedding night. Unfortunately, it wasn't for the traditional reason. She was confused. She'd spent part of the night thanking God for the security guard and the rest wondering how she was going to keep her hands off her husband.

She poked around at her breakfast of eggs Benedict and chanced several peeks at Parker. His unanswered question from the previous night hung between them.

After their romp in the pool the previous night, he'd left her an oversize T-shirt in the bathroom, then, without a single word, he had taken the couch. But with the birth of a new day, "tell me what you want" was the clear message in her eyes—his beautiful, compelling eyes. Had they always been that blue?

Ashley sighed out loud. Her gaze darted up to meet Parker's intense one. She looked away and coughed into her linen napkin. "What time did you want to get started?"

"As soon as you're through playing with your food."

She eyed the demolished egg concoction in front of her. His plate was clean. Obviously his appetite remained unaffected. She looked back at him in time to catch the twinkle in his eye.

She put down her fork. "I'm ready when you are."

"So agreeable. I like that in a woman." He grinned, then signed the check presented by the waiter.

He was trying to goad her. Ashley ignored him. "Can I assume this is suitable for what you have planned?" She waved at her new white shorts and lemon-colored halter top.

Parker stared at her a long time, taking in the V-neck top, the gold pendant with her scripted Hawaiian name dangling there against her tanned skin. His lips curved up.

Darn him for making her want to squirm. She was beginning to wonder what exactly he *did* have planned. "I thought we had a tight schedule." She pushed back in her chair and threw her napkin on the table.

"We could cancel and spend the day in the room."

"Forget it." She tossed her hair over her shoulder and headed for the door. "I didn't bring the checkers."

"Strip poker, then?" He strode up beside her, sounding almost comically hopeful.

Ashley bit her lower lip to keep from smiling. "Next you'll tell me you've never played the game in your life."

"Never. Scout's honor."

"You were never a Scout."

"No," he agreed. "Well, I was for a day. But I got caught sneaking into the Brownies' camp."

"Why am I not surprised?"

"Hey, I'm innocent. I thought they meant real brownies." He looked hurt at her skeptical look. "Scout's honor." They both laughed.

Ashley reached the elevator first and punched the button. "Since you ignored my question, I'll assume I'm dressed okay."

"Fine." Parker backed her up to the elevator doors, his hands bracketing her. "May I take the same liberty with my unanswered question?"

She staved him off with her palms against his chest just as the elevator dinged its arrival. He dropped his hands to allow for the opening doors but kept her gaze snagged with his. "I guess you've been saved again, Ashley James."

She took a deep breath and stumbled back into the waiting car. It was suddenly as clear as the brilliant midmorning sun. No matter what Ashley wanted, or what lies she told herself, she knew for certain it was only a matter of time. And deep in his very blue eyes, this undeniable truth was mirrored tenfold.

"PARKER, THIS IS incredible." She turned wide eyes on him, pushed her fingers through her hair, lifted it high, then let it cascade back down to her waist.

He watched the thick, glossy satin settle and wondered how it could be the color of midnight at high noon. Her face was alive with enthusiasm, fresh and glowing, free from unflattering makeup. Suddenly, he felt like the luckiest man on earth. The sparkle in Ashley's eyes had been put there by him. Well, he had a little help from Wailuku Village.

"You like it, huh?" Of course she did, but he wanted to bask in her gratitude a while longer.

"I love it." She grabbed his hand, hers so small and fragile, and pulled him toward one of the grass huts. "You're sure it's authentic?"

"From what I understand, this is an exact replica of a Hawaiian village years before any white men arrived. Our guide should be here any minute."

"This is exciting. Do they make the feather cloaks? How about food? Do they net fish and maintain taro patches?" She stopped for a few seconds, a small crease drawing her eyebrows together. "How about the *alii*? Is that established? That's Hawaiian royalty," she added for his benefit.

"I know what that means." He made a face, annoyed that she thought him so ignorant of the culture. However, his knowledge was limited and the last thing he wanted was a conversation that got him in over his head. He looked at his watch. Where was that guide?

"Hey, that looks like a ceremonial dance over there. My goodness." Ashley shook her head in awe. "Those canoes are hand carved. Look at the craftsmanship."

Parker watched her excitement grow, and contentment filled him. He hoped today would dissolve the new invisible barriers she'd raised after the pool incident.

"Look past the thatch hut near the carved figures," she said, and Parker bent his head to follow the direction of her extended arm.

Drawn to her unique scent, he lowered his face close to hers. She didn't appear to notice, so he ducked in for a quick kiss on her neck. She jumped and brought her face sharply around. Perfect. He kissed her swiftly on the lips.

"Parker," she scolded and shifted a small distance away from him, casting a quick glance in both directions.

"It's okay. We're supposed to be newlyweds. Remember?" She shot him a wry look as he slipped an arm around her waist. "Now, what were you showing me?" he asked before she could give him any grief.

"Over there. They're having some sort of ceremony. I wonder what they're passing around? I'll bet it's not coconut milk." She turned to him, bringing her face inches away. She hesitated and her gaze dropped to his mouth. Unconsciously, her tongue darted out to moisten her lips.

Parker was about to forget the entire plan and haul her back to the room. He glided his hand along her jaw and angled his face to hers.

"The tour starts now, so don't start anything else." They both turned to look at the grinning guide. He was short, brown and ample bellied, covered only by a loincloth. He held a spear in one hand and a clipboard in the other. "You folks must be the Jameses."

So now the idiot shows up, Parker thought. He glared at the man, while Ashley welcomed him with one of her beguiling smiles.

"Have you taken the tour before?" the guide asked. Ashley shook her head. Parker grunted something unintelligible.

"I'll give you some brief history before we start. When Captain Cook discovered the islands, he found that each one had its own monarch. The *alii*...'' The man droned on while Ashley nodded, totally engrossed in what he was saying. They strolled through the different areas of the village and it was obvious Ashley knew as much as their guide, if not more.

Parker, on the other hand, couldn't figure out half of what they were talking about, especially when they slipped into too much of the Hawaiian language. Holding his own, he laughed when Ashley did, nodded knowingly when he thought he should. He was curious about some things, but no way was he going to ask. That was out of the question. Why, that would be like...like asking for directions when he got lost.

By the time the two-hour tour was over, he was hot and thirsty and could think of nothing but a tall, cool drink and a steamy shower with Ashley.

"We have a couple of hours before our flight leaves," he told her as he steered the rental car back to the hotel. "Are you hungry?"

"Not at all. I'm too excited."

Great. Parker shifted his gaze to her without turning his head. All the more time for that shower.

Ashley laid her head back on the seat and let it loll in his direction. "That was wonderful." Her lips curved upward. "*You're* wonderful for taking me there."

He returned her smile and reached for her hand. Things were looking up. The tension between them was gone. She looked relaxed, even her hand rested easily in his. And all Parker could think about was how right it felt, being with her, trying to please her.

The realization hit him like a tidal wave. Somewhere along the line, Ashley had become important. Had it only been three weeks? At the moment, he couldn't remember how life had been before her. He gravitated toward the open window and gulped for a breath of ocean air.

This wasn't part of the plan. He clenched his jaw. It wouldn't work between them. She was too idealistic. He wasn't about to spend his life, or his money, building community centers. Especially now, when he was finally making a name for himself without his family's influence or money. He'd waited a long time and had worked hard for it. Ashley didn't understand that. They'd disagree for the rest of their lives. And their children were bound to suffer the consequences.

Oh, jeez. Now, he was thinking about kids. Sweat formed at the back of his neck. He withdrew his hand from hers and rubbed a clammy palm on his jeans before wrapping it around the steering wheel. He glanced over at Ashley. Her honey-colored eyes remained focused on him, a bit curious now but still soft and dreamy.

His breath sputtered in his chest. Was it possible? Could they make it work? If she kept looking at him like that, he'd begin to believe anything.

"You look happy," he said, his hand again finding hers.

"I am." She sighed. "I wish it weren't ending so soon."

He squeezed her hand. "Me, too."

She gave him a lazy, sensuous smile. "I'm impressed you knew so much about the village."

He shrugged and tried to look blasé.

"I'm embarrassed that I hadn't known of the village's existence before now. Maybe I need to widen my blinders," she said.

"Nah. Well, maybe a little." The village was the last thing he was thinking about when she lightly punched his arm and grinned. Somewhere deep down, Ashley had to know something was happening between them. And when she finally acknowledged it...

"We don't have time for much more than lunch, but since you're not hungry..." He briefly turned hopeful eyes her way before returning them to the road. "Ashley?"

"Hmm?" She twirled a long strand of silky hair, her head back, eyes half closed. Wind whipped through the open T-top of the rental car and teased the deep vee of her halter. It rippled against her golden skin and allowed him a glimpse of the piece of heaven he'd tasted the previous night.

"We have unfinished business," he said finally, immediately chastising himself for the use of the word "business." He gripped the wheel a little harder, determined that she not put him off. "Ashley?"

He steered the car around a curve in the road and into the hotel parking lot before glancing at her. She was asleep. Her lashes lay thick and dark against her cheeks, a slight part at the seam of her lips. If she'd gotten as little sleep as he had the night before, it was no wonder.

Her hands were curled together in her lap, her bare legs crossed at the ankle. It would be easy to scoop her up and carry her to their room. But he didn't think he'd make it to the lobby without her waking up and acting like a wildcat.

He turned off the car engine and sat there, watching the shadows of overhead coconut fronds sway across her face. The resort, her father, his father...everything seemed far away and unimportant. It had been a long time since the resort had had any competition for his attention. Harvey had assumed more and more of Parker's responsibilities. And Parker had been spending more and more time with Ashley and her tutoring project. He'd resented it at first, but lately he looked forward to it. He shook his head. Her idealism was contagious.

He watched her still form and the idea struck him. They needed another day off, plain and simple. She had to be exhausted with the grueling schedule she maintained, on top of worrying about her father. Construction on the resort would continue without him. He could rebook tomorrow's meetings. Who could begrudge him a short honeymoon?

More important, it was a good way for Ashley to get some long overdue rest. If they did manage to tangle a few sheets, he certainly wouldn't complain. It would be an added bonus. But at the moment, watching her sleep so peacefully, all he wanted to do was protect her from herself.

He got out and went around to open her door. After unfastening her seat belt, he hunkered down and took her face in his hands. "Ashley? We're here."

Her mouth stretched into a smile before she opened her eyes. From the innocence of sleep, she put a hand to his face and stroked his roughened jaw. He kissed her palm.

"I must have dozed off."

"That's an understatement. You were snoring like a drunken sailor."

"I was *not*." She dropped her hand to his shoulder and gave him a push worthy of a sailor.

"Tired, grumpy and can't take a joke." He grinned and offered to help her out of the car.

"Thank you," she said, taking his hand and levering herself. He grimaced. Those lovely nails of hers digging into his skin were no accident.

"I've got a great idea. Since we're having such a—"

"Oh, Parker." Her eyes were all honeyed with gratitude again. "I truly am." She slid her arms up his chest and hugged him. He knew it had been strictly on impulse, but he accepted it with relish all the same and locked his arms around her waist.

"Let's stay another day." He pressed a kiss to her forehead, then leaned back to look at her.

"How can we? That's not possible."

"Anything is possible."

"For you, maybe. I have classes to teach, a tutoring session." She threw up her hands. "I have to see my father. Then there's the lei-making contest I'm judging—"

"All small obstacles. Think about the cultural-enrichment aspect." Cultural enrichment, hell. She was going to spend tomorrow in bed...sleeping mostly. "All this exposure will make you a better teacher. How's that for justification?"

"Nice try. But I've got responsibilities."

"And I don't?" His hands slackened at her waist. His temper sparked, but he wasn't going to let her rile him, even though she'd conveniently forgotten he had a company to run.

"Oh, Parker, it's been a fantastic day." She cradled his face in her hands. "Let's not fight."

"Believe me, that's the last thing I want to do." He pulled her closer. "I merely thought another day would be nice."

"I'd love to say yes." She gave him a small, sad smile. "But it's simply not possible," Ashley said, then gave him an inquisitive look. "Exactly what did you have in mind?"

"Well..." He had to organize his offense. He cast his baby blues at her and tried to look a little wounded. After all, he was doing it for her own good. "Did you really like my surprise today?"

"Oh, Parker." She was in his arms again, all soft and grateful, smoothing his cheek. "It was one of the nicest things anyone has ever done for me."

Car doors slammed, murmurs echoed, but the fact that they were in the middle of an open parking lot didn't bother him. His hands rested on the curve of her buttocks as she looked up at him, her scent strong and intoxicating. He leaned back against the car, and cradling her between his thighs, brought her with him. Unresisting, she toyed with the buttons of his polo shirt.

"It doesn't have to end, you know." Over and over again, he combed his fingers through her hair. Ashley closed her eyes to the massaging motion.

"And you accuse me of having my head in the clouds." She laughed and tilted her face up to him. The sun caught a myriad of colors in her contented eyes. "You certainly do surprise me sometimes."

He lowered his head and she stretched up to meet him. Their lips touched in a light kiss. And then another. Her hands were still on his chest and he felt her tentative exploration through the shirt fabric.

The sun was hot, but no competition for Ashley's touch as she dipped in and out of his open collar. He caressed the bare skin between her halter and shorts, slipping his fingers up her top and along her delicate spine. She pressed into him and his control faltered.

"I think you do this on purpose," he whispered on a trail of kisses to her temple.

"Mmm, what?" She pushed at her hair, giving him better access.

"Start things in safe places. Or maybe you have a thing for cars and parking lots."

"Aren't you safe?"

"All depends." He nipped at her ear. "Wanna find out?"

"What did you have in mind?" She smiled. And somewhere in his foggy mind, Parker knew he had to have a portrait of her looking exactly as she did now.

"Stay another night and see for yourself."

"You're incorrigible."

"So I've been told a time or two."

"It is tempting, but I can't." Ashley brushed a fallen lock of hair off his forehead and sighed. "Tell me what you had planned, so I have something to look forward to."

Parker squinted at her. "Then it won't be a surprise. Wasn't that part of today's fun?"

"Partly," she agreed. "But you know what's best of all?" She leaned heavily against him and he felt her heart race. Her eyes were sparkling and her dimple flashed deep.

"What?" His own heartbeat picked up speed. It was only the two of them, no resort to worry about, no family problems. Ashley looked genuinely happy, and he knew he was largely responsible. He reveled a few more seconds in her intimate hazel gaze and waited expectantly.

"I can't wait to tell the kids about it."

"The kids?" He frowned.

"You know, the gang I tutor." She stepped away from him and he let her go. "They won't believe it. Maybe if they work real hard, we could take a one-day excursion here. We could have a car wash or something...." She chattered on and on, looking as animated as she had at Wailuku Village.

The hot afternoon sun replaced the warmth of Ashley's body as Parker watched the distance grow between them. She started in the direction of the hotel and had a hundred-and-one plans for the kids by the time they got to the room.

As a rule, it wasn't his style to sulk in silence. But Parker couldn't think of anything to say as they each filled their shared garment bag and small carryon.

He'd been arrogant enough to think her heart had skipped a few beats for him. But it simply wasn't so. It was those damn kids she thought about.

He picked up their bags from the bed and took them to the living room, where she was making a phone call. He plopped them down in no particular order.

Jealous. That's what he was. He raked a hand through windblown hair. He'd never been jealous a day in his life, and now…it was over a bunch of delinquents.

The worst part was, he had no right. He had bought and paid for Ashley's services…a fact that was becoming harder to accept.

He was waiting for Ashley to get off the phone when he noticed that the carryon's zipper was caught. He tried to free it, but it held fast to something inside the bag. He reached in and brought out a handful of Ashley's ruined silk dress. Images of her in the pool flashed in his mind and a smile of satisfaction tugged at his lips.

The previous night she'd been his. She could deny it, but he'd bet the resort she hadn't been thinking about those kids or anyone else.

But he wanted more. He wanted her trust. And from now on, the only thing he was going to buy was time.

ASHLEY HATED REDUCING herself to being a snoop, but she didn't think she could stand it a moment longer. From Parker's bedroom doorway, she glanced over at the garment bag they had yet to unpack since returning home the day before. She slowly meandered toward it.

Actually, it wouldn't be snooping, she told herself, since her clothes *were* packed along with Parker's. If she happened to run across the nightie she was certain he'd bought her, it would be purely accidental. Ashley didn't believe for one minute that the T-shirt he'd ultimately given her had been what he'd had in mind. Or maybe she didn't want to believe it.

Since returning to Honolulu, Parker had barely uttered three sentences to her. He hadn't even complained when she had elected to sleep at her apartment the night before. And since Mrs. Lee was on another island visiting family until tomorrow, Ashley had the same choice to make tonight.

It would be a whole lot simpler if she didn't feel so guilty, she acknowledged, or if she actually *had* classes to teach, students to tutor, a contest to judge. But the fact was, all those reasons had nothing to do with her having refused to stay on Molokai another night. An important meeting concerning Magic Island this morning had everything to do with it.

Ashley swung the garment bag from the luggage rack onto Parker's bed and unzipped the side pouch. She figured she had at least another hour before Parker got home from work. Plenty of time to retreat to her apartment…after she satisfied her curiosity. Although she wasn't sure what that would prove, except…

She wasn't going crazy. Ashley smiled and pulled at the familiar cream-colored boutique sack. It caught on a tangle of clothes, but she could see a sliver of something pink… lacy…she couldn't quite…

"You beat me home." Parker's voice came from behind her. Ashley dropped the sack and clutched her chest.

"You scared the devil out of me." She jammed the package back in and turned to the door, her heart pounding like a war drum.

"Sorry." He grinned. He looked tired.

"I was just unpacking." Ashley realized she was still stuffing things back in and stopped.

"I see." Parker jerked his tie loose. He started to fling his jacket onto the bed, but settled it on the valet instead.

It suddenly occurred to Ashley that she was sitting on Parker's bed, in his bedroom. And he was undressing. She stood. "I can do this later."

"Everything's probably ruined." Parker paused. His eyes seemed to darken and memories of their pool escapade rattled Ashley's last strand of composure. "But we probably ought to at least give the dry cleaners a go at it."

"Good idea." Ashley snatched up the entire garment bag and staggered under its weight. Parker came from behind to circle her with his arms, absorbing the bag's weight and steadying her.

Ashley straightened. She felt shakier now than without his help. "I'll drop it off on the way home," she said, trying to subtly free herself.

"Home?" Parker turned her toward him and took the bag from her arms. "What do you think this is?"

Ashley forced herself to look up. She was prepared for sarcasm, maybe even anger. But the trace of uncertainty he blinked away surprised her.

"I'm not sure, Parker," she replied honestly. Then she left both him and the garment bag and hurried out the room.

"ARE YOU STILL TALKING to me?" Crystal asked as she pulled out a chair opposite the table from Ashley.

"Barely." Ashley looked up and frowned at her friend. "I thought about ignoring your message and standing you up for lunch."

Crystal grinned. "And forgo the chance to tell me about your wild and crazy honeymoon?"

"It wasn't a honeymoon." Ashley felt the heat start at her neck. She quickly picked up her menu, burying her face in it.

"Really?" Crystal laughed. "You were so hot to trot at the reception, I about dropped my nose ring."

Ashley abruptly lowered the menu and peered closely at her friend. "You don't have a nose ring."

"Gotcha." Crystal leaned forward. "Tell me everything."

Ashley sighed. Her father had already admitted guilt regarding his role in initiating the wedding reception. It hadn't stopped Parker from chewing out Mrs. Lee for her complicity, but Ashley knew admonishing Crystal would be useless. Besides, there was a far more important matter to address. "Don't talk to Parker."

"Why? Will he have a better version?" Crystal's dark eyes sparkled with curious delight.

"I'm serious. He thinks you're linked to Magic Island."

"Well, I am, in a way."

"Yeah, well, he wants to know what you know."

"Oh." Crystal settled back in her chair. "If he asks, what should I tell him?"

"Nothing." Ashley shook her head. "Right now he's busy with the resort." Or so Ashley supposed. He certainly hadn't been busy with her in the past three days, since they'd come back to Oahu. "But if he brings it up, tell him that you offered some legal services but no one has contacted you about it."

"Does he know about you?"

"Heavens, no." Ashley's eyes widened, her voice lowered. "And he's not going to find out. The committee met yesterday morning and will meet two more times this week. We're gaining a lot of support, especially now that we have some concrete proposals for the state. And I don't need Parker throwing a wrench into the works."

Crystal said nothing at first. She pressed her lips together and studied Ashley until the waiter came, took their orders and left. Finally Crystal said, "You're still going through with it."

"Going through with it?" she echoed cautiously.

"Your service center for Magic Island." Crystal narrowed her eyes on Ashley. "After the way you left the party, I thought—"

"I had to do that, Crystal." Ashley flipped her hair back. "It was the only way I could keep him from surprising you with a question about Magic Island."

Crystal's eyes widened. "I really thought..."

Ashley shook her head and lowered her gaze. "It was an act. That's all." She looked back up at her friend, who returned her stare with a suspicious frown.

"Okay," Crystal said after a thoughtful silence. "I won't say anything to Parker."

PARKER OPENED THE entry door and sniffed the air. Roast pork and fried rice. He wasn't surprised that Mrs. Lee had cooked his favorite dish. She'd been totally unrepentant this morning when he'd picked her up at the airport, but when it came down to it she knew that the party had not been a great idea. Especially since Parker Senior had elected not to show up. And being the peacemaker that she was, Mrs. Lee was making it up to Parker in her own way.

"What died in here?" Parker called teasingly out to the kitchen.

Mrs. Lee came through the swinging door, snapping her dish towel in the air. "If it weren't for your new bride, I'd take this towel to you like I did when you were a *keiki*." She stopped and looked around. "Where is she?"

"Ashley?" Parker laid down his briefcase and picked up the newspaper, casually glancing at his watch. "Isn't she home yet?" For the past three days, he'd been patient with Ashley's decision to remain at her apartment, but his equanimity was definitely waning. And if his lovely wife didn't get her sweet fanny home soon, he was going to wring her lovely neck.

"I thought she'd be with you." Mrs. Lee's finger came up wagging. "What kind of lovebirds are you?"

"Cuckoos are more like it," someone mumbled from

down the hall—or so it sounded to Parker, and he glanced that way.

Ashley breezed in. "I was right behind you, Parker. But I came in through your…uh…our suite entrance. I had something to drop off." She darted Mrs. Lee a nervous look, then gave them both a bright smile. "What smells so good?"

She started to brush past Parker, but he caught his housekeeper's inquisitive look, hooked an arm around Ashley's waist and hauled her up against him. When she opened her mouth, Parker took full advantage of her beginning protest by slipping his tongue between her lips. He felt her relax against him for a moment, then she jerked her head back and looked directly at Mrs. Lee. Her chin quivered as if she wanted to say something, but she kept her mouth clamped shut and sent Parker a murderous look.

"It's about time." Mrs. Lee chuckled and made an about-face for the kitchen. "Dinner is in half an hour."

Ashley edged a safe distance away from him and as soon as Mrs. Lee was out of earshot, she hissed, "Try that again and I'll bite your tongue."

"Mmm. Sounds kinky." Parker smiled while pulling his tie through his collar. He tossed it onto the back of an overstuffed chair and took a step closer to Ashley.

"Sounds painful to me." She took two steps backward.

"Maybe." He shucked off his jacket and advanced three steps.

"What is this? A striptease?" Ashley laughed nervously and tried for a nonchalant pivot toward the kitchen.

"If you like." Parker shot out a hand and grabbed her wrist.

"I don't like," she said through clenched teeth as he brought her up hard against him. Her gaze sparked angry green as she lifted a defiant chin and looked him right in the eyes. "Do *not* take advantage of the fact that Mrs. Lee is here. Or I warn you—"

"Don't make idle threats…" Parker advised. Ashley narrowed her I-dare-you gaze on him before he could remind her of what she had to lose, and he quickly amended what he was about to say. "Because it turns me on."

Her eyes widened. So did Parker's smile.

"A warthog would turn you on," she whispered fiercely and twisted away from him.

Parker laughed out loud. "Give yourself a little more credit than that."

Ashley gave him a dirty look. "I think I'll help Mrs. Lee," she said pointedly and made it to the kitchen door.

"Wait a minute." Parker crooked his finger, beckoning her to him.

Ashley stared at him with a disbelieving shake of her head. "You're crazy. I ought to just have you committed and be done with it."

Parker lowered his voice even further, his face serious. "I merely want to remind you that this is for real." He paused when the spunk disappeared from her expression, and he mentally cursed himself. But Ashley had made herself so scarce since their return, they hadn't discussed much about Mrs. Lee. And Parker had to admit he had hated to even bring up the nasty business that so crassly described their relationship. "We have to be convincing, Ash," he said gently.

"Don't worry, Parker." Ashley hesitated with her hand flat against the kitchen door, her proud face focused on him. "You'll get your money's worth."

"PASS THE SYRUP, please." Parker watched his new wife fumble with the small pitcher of freshly made pineapple syrup while he restacked his pancakes.

"Thank you," he said once she had placed it in front of him.

Ashley gave him a small nod. "Butter, please."

Parker obliged her with a bland smile and the white ceramic crockery.

The sun was at the horizon, spouting off its usual

fireworks of orange and pink and promising the start of a fresh new day, but Napua Lee's heart was heavy. She was dreadfully worried about her two wards.

It just wasn't natural, she lamented to herself, as she watched Parker and Ashley eat their breakfast in silence. Newlyweds should be laughing, touching, smooching, as they had in her day. She strained her memory back to when her Leonard was alive. She smiled. It was so long ago, but she could still remember the carefree days of shared whispers, secret touches.

Her smile faded. But not these two. Normally, they stayed clear of each other, and when they were together and thought she wasn't listening, they fought like cats and dogs. But Napua prided herself on keeping on top of things and little escaped her. Parker liked to call it nosy. She sniffed. But the way he managed things, what did he know?

"Mrs. Lee, do you have a cold?"

Napua met Parker's concerned gaze. "No. Do you two want to go out to dinner alone tonight?"

Parker arched a brow and darted a quick look at Ashley. "I don't think so," he answered slowly.

Ordinarily, Napua would have laughed at the confused look on his face. He obviously thought he'd forgotten some occasion. But she didn't laugh. She was peeved.

"Everything you make is so wonderful, Mrs. Lee," Ashley added politely. "I'd just as soon eat here."

Humph. Napua did not return Ashley's smile. She drummed her plump fingers on the table and covertly regarded Ashley's stiff posture and her shadowed eyes. She was just as bad. Stayed away for hours at a time, that one did. And was as quiet as a church mouse whenever Parker was around. Worst of all, Napua had a keen suspicion that Ashley didn't always sleep in Parker's bed.

"Well." Parker placed his napkin on the table and stood. "Got to get to work."

"Are you going to be late tonight *again?*" Napua asked.

"I don't know." Parker picked up his keys and started

for the door. He stopped, as if remembering something he'd forgotten, and brushed his wife's cheek with a hurried kiss. "I'll call."

Ashley gave him a tight smile of acknowledgment and he left.

Napua fidgeted. She counted silently to ten and waited for Ashley to do as she had done every day this week—wait for Parker to pull out of the garage and then leave for the day herself. Generally, Napua would consider their obvious rift none of her business, but she saw the longing looks Ashley gave Parker, saw the melancholy helplessness in Parker's eyes. And it all but broke her maternal heart.

Ashley predictably thanked Napua for breakfast and had headed out the door just as the phone rang.

"Hi, Mrs. Lee." Napua recognized Crystal's voice immediately. For a day and a half before the wedding they'd been thick as thieves, planning the surprise party. And despite Crystal's odd appearance, Napua liked the young woman.

"Is Ashley still home?"

"You just missed her." Napua wondered what Ashley's friend made of all this.

"Do you know if she went to her apartment?"

"Her apartment?" Napua was horrified. "Why would she still have that?"

Silence greeted Napua's ear. "Hello?"

"I'm here, Mrs. Lee. But I've got to run."

"Just a minute, Crystal. I'm worried about the kids."

Crystal chuckled. "I'm sure there's nothing to worry about. The kids are fine."

"I don't like it that Ashley still has an apartment. They don't spend enough time together, as it is."

"Well...I'm sure she'll have it cleaned out and be outta there in no time." Crystal hesitated. "The party may have been a mistake, Mrs. Lee. I think they need to be left alone."

Alone. Apartment. "How big is it?"

"What?"

"The apartment. One or two bedrooms?"

"One, but—"

"That's it. Crystal, you are a very smart girl. My *aloha* to your family." Napua could hear Crystal still calling out to her as she replaced the receiver. But Napua had no time to dally on the phone. Smiling, she patted her bun and pulled out the Yellow Pages.

Chapter Ten

Ashley knew something was wrong as soon as she pulled into the circular drive. The front door was open and she could see Parker gesturing frantically to Mrs. Lee. Reluctantly, Ashley left her faithful Toyota and trudged up the sidewalk.

"*When* did we discuss this?" Parker was asking his housekeeper. His hands had landed on his lean hips and Mrs. Lee's spread fingers were firmly planted at her plump ones. If the woman had been seven inches taller, they'd be nose to nose. "We *never* discussed this."

"You are as stubborn as your father. Do you think I would make this up?"

Whatever had riled Parker to begin with was nothing compared to the look on Parker's face at the mention of his father. "*When,* Mrs. Lee?" he ground out once more.

"A year ago. Maybe two." Mrs. Lee shrugged, looked away, then caught sight of Ashley.

"*Two* years ago?" Parker bellowed.

Mrs. Lee sent him a disgusted frown. "Maybe one." Then she turned back and smiled at Ashley. "Good," she said, stepping forward to pull Ashley into the circle. "Your wife will settle this."

Ashley looked from Parker's angry face to his house-keeper's determined one. Actually, in Ashley's opinion, she didn't think his wife would be settling anything. She tried to step back and then she smelled it.

"Whew! What is that?" Ashley wrinkled her nose, her gaze bouncing back and forth between Parker and Mrs. Lee.

Parker threw up his hands.

"Paint," Mrs. Lee answered, unconcerned.

"Paint?"

"We're remodeling," Mrs. Lee went on patiently. "*Your* husband…" She glanced at Parker and lifted both sets of chins several degrees. "Your husband and I discussed it some time ago. But I never got around to it."

"If we *had* discussed it, which I seriously doubt…" Parker stopped pacing long enough to send her a threatening look down his nose. "You picked one hell of a time to start."

"Oh, Parker. It can't be that bad." Ashley laid a hand on his arm.

"My bed…our bedroom is all torn up."

"Well…" Ashley's mind spun as she tried to calculate exactly how that would affect her.

"The guest rooms are *also* torn up," Parker added meaningfully. "The only damn room that isn't is Mrs. Lee's." He skewered the older woman with another accusing look.

"O-okay…" Ashley offered and lightly squeezed Parker's arm in an effort to calm him.

"What's the big deal? I already made your hotel reservations." Mrs. Lee sniffed.

"Ouch!" Parker pulled back his arm. He lowered his gaze to the red mark Ashley's nail had left.

"Sorry," Ashley mumbled. She pushed the offending hand through her hair to ease its weight off her back. The temperature had suddenly climbed ten degrees. She didn't want to stay in a hotel. Not with Parker, anyway. Staying together in one room was far too close, too intimate. No way. They didn't do at all well in hotels. "How long are we out of commission here?"

"A week." Parker and Mrs. Lee said together.

Ashley scrambled in silence for a suggestion to make, a plan to offer...a way to get the hell out of this.

"I've put out your suitcases." Mrs. Lee headed for the hallway, then stopped and slid them a sly glance. "It's too bad you don't still have your apartment, Ashley. But the honeymoon suite should be nice." The housekeeper patted her bun and continued down the hall.

"Honeymoon suite?" Ashley lifted a brow at Parker.

He jammed his hands into his trouser pockets.

"Apartment," they both said at once.

Ashley quickly picked up Mrs. Lee's trail. Parker followed right behind her. The strong odor of fresh paint assaulted them immediately.

"I'm not happy about this," Ashley whispered over her shoulder.

"Oh, and I am?" Parker was close. She could feel his breath stirring her hair. If she turned now, she could be in his arms, feel the strong wall of his chest, feel the soothing rhythm of his heartbeat. And she could get herself in a whole lot of trouble. How could he so effectively irritate and arouse her at the same time?

"After all," he groused, "I'll be the one stuck in enemy camp."

Enemy camp? Ashley stopped cold.

Parker didn't. His arms came reflexively around her as he tried to ease the collision.

But it wasn't arousal that she felt. It wasn't even irritation.

Enemy camp? Magic Island? A wave of dread stormed her. Ashley had just made a horrible mistake.

"You didn't tell me you had cats." Parker toed the litter box, an expression of contempt on his face.

"You hadn't told me you had a dog," she shot back.

"I didn't know I had to clear it with you."

"You didn't. Just like I didn't feel I had to clear Kiwi and Cinnamon with you."

"Kiwi and Cinnamon? What kind of names are those?" His good humor had gone the same way of his unattended libido. He'd never known a woman who could confound him so thoroughly.

"Perfect ones." She picked up the fat calico and nuzzled its neck. Lucky bastard, came Parker's unbidden thought. "Because you're both so sweet," she cooed in a nonsensical lilt. The cat squirmed when Ashley stopped to send a skeptical frown at Parker, and she set the bundle of fur down. "What about your dog…Prince? Isn't *that* original? Or maybe it's symbolic?"

"Look," he began through clenched teeth. Ashley was upset about something and was doing her best to annoy him. In fact, she'd been trying to annoy him since they'd gotten back from Molokai. Unfortunately, her success rate was phenomenal. He was about to tell her that they would not be opening a zoo back at the beach house, when a loud squawk from another room halted him. "What was that?"

"A bird." Ashley turned to straighten some books.

"As in, *your* bird?"

"No," she answered sweetly. "*Our* bird."

"This is getting ridiculous." Parker felt his hands making their newly automatic route through his hair.

He looked into Ashley's sparkling eyes and knew she was enjoying his irritation. He summoned a long-deserted patience and said, "I can't wait to hear what you call it."

"It's a him."

"What's *his* name?"

"Pilikea." Ashley quickly busied herself with some paperwork she'd left on the table, careful to avoid his eyes.

She was flipping at her hair again—a sure sign of trouble. "What does that mean?" Parker asked with a modicum of dread.

"Trouble," she muttered on her way to the kitchen.

Parker snickered out loud at the irony. "Any symbolism there?"

"You want some coffee?"

"I want to know about your feathered friend out there. I *really* don't like birds." Parker had followed her and now paced the narrow kitchen that was much too small for such an activity. "They're noisy, stubborn and a general pain in the ass." He stopped and leveled her an I-mean-it-this-time look.

"Well..." She angled her head a bit, drawing her eyebrows together, a sly smile tempting her lips. "So are you, but it looks like I'll have to put up with it."

He stared back, his annoyance dissolving. She had the most expressive eyes. Right now they were animated with humor and mischief. She was silently laughing at him, and he wanted to hear that laughter out loud. He loved her laugh. He loved her ability to make him want to laugh—when he didn't want to strangle her, that is.

"I suppose you're right. But it doesn't seem fair that I'll have two of you to contend with," he said, grinning.

"Touché."

Parker affected a pensive look. "Does that mean 'touch' in French?"

Ashley eyed him for a long moment, then produced a can of coffee from the cupboard. "We need to set some ground rules while we're here."

"Oh, let me guess." He briefly closed his eyes and held a hand to his temple. "No touching, right?"

She snapped her fingers in the air. "Give the man a prize."

"Of my choosing?" Parker did all but rub his hands together.

"It's a figure of speech, James." She slanted him a wry look, then popped the lid off the new coffee can. She leaned over to inhale the potent aroma.

Parker angled his head back for a better view of her enticing bottom and gorgeous legs, which this new position afforded him. It was going to be a long week, he decided.

It had already *been* a long week. His self-imposed hands-off policy since returning from Molokai was killing him.

"Is there something I can do for you?" Ashley asked in a clipped tone.

He leisurely raised his gaze to her face and grinned.

She rolled her eyes and automatically tugged at the hem of her shorts. "Which brings us to rule number two."

"Nice try, sweetheart, but my thoughts are off-limits."

"Don't call me sweetheart."

"Now you're confusing me. Is that rule two or three?"

Ashley puffed out her cheeks and loudly exhaled. She fussed with the coffeemaker, plugging and unplugging it, then plugging it in again. She whacked the top of it and it gurgled to life.

"Think we can afford a new one?" Parker crossed his arms over his chest and lounged back against the counter.

"That's exactly what I mean." She slammed one cabinet shut, then bumped a drawer closed with her hip. "This is *my* apartment. No changes, no negotiation." She turned to face him and shoved her hair back. "And no answering the phone."

"What?" He straightened. "You're joking, right?"

Ashley shook her head. "I'm serious about this, Parker."

"You know how many calls I can possibly receive a night...calls from the construction site. I can't operate without a phone."

"Use your mobile."

Parker just stared at her.

"I'm not saying you can't call out." She turned to wipe off the counter. There wasn't a crumb on it. "And if I'm home and it's for you, of course I'll answer it and turn it over to you. But when I'm not...well, I'd prefer...I insist you don't answer it."

Parker watched her straighten the small appliances that didn't need straightening, watched her jiggle the coffee carafe. The coffee didn't perk any faster. He studied his shoes for a moment, then looked back up at her. "Why, Ash?"

"Why?" she echoed faintly.

"Why?"

"Because I receive a lot of important calls."

So did Parker, but he elected not to point that out. He didn't think he could do so without heating up the discussion. "I *am* capable of taking a message."

Ashley gave him a look of dismissal that was his undoing. The hell with trying not to show he was angry, because damn it, he was. "Besides, none of this should be a problem. You're always *here*. You certainly haven't been at our house."

Ashley stopped her aimless straightening and plastered him with a haughty look. "I'm surprised you've noticed."

"Yeah, well, I'm surprised you're surprised. Because you haven't been around enough to notice if I've noticed." He'd promised himself he wouldn't raise his voice.

She opened her mouth to speak, then closed it again. A frown puckered her brow. "I think I take exception to that."

Parker stared back angrily at first, then a slow half grin spread across his face. "Which part?"

"I'm not sure." She laughed unevenly. "I think you lost me."

Parker watched her dimple flash, the honey color touch her eyes. No question about it. *He* was lost.

"Parker?" Her voice was soft and imploring.

"Yeah." He took her hand.

"About the phone." Her fingers moved restlessly against his.

"Yeah?"

"I need your promise." She squeezed his hand when he didn't answer right away. "I really would like to keep my affairs private."

Parker stepped back suddenly as if he'd been slapped. *Affair.* The single word had the impact of a full-blown tidal-wave alert. He dropped her hand. It fell to her side and a guarded look darkened her eyes.

Trapped oxygen threatened to explode from his chest. He let out a large breath.

His wife had a friggin' boyfriend!

Parker watched Ashley moisten her lips, watched her graceful hand flutter to her throat and wished to God he didn't still want her.

Shell-shocked, he continued to stare and waited for the numbness to ebb.

"You do understand, don't you?" Ashley asked. "After all, I'm sure I don't know everything about your life. And I don't expect to. I don't even want—"

"You're wrong." His voice was low, almost too low.

Ashley shut up and inclined her head to him.

"What you see is what you get," he said, slowly shaking his head. She simply didn't want what she saw, and that saddened him far more than he would have thought possible. "Who is he, Ash?"

"Who's who?"

The fact that she had the gall to look puzzled irritated the hell out of him. It was a welcome respite. "Oh, please. Let's be adult about this." Parker threw up an exasperated hand. Good advice, he warned himself, and brought his hand back to lean on the counter. "I asked you before if you had a boyfriend. You should have—"

"A boyfriend!" Ashley's expression went blank. Then she actually started laughing just as the telephone rang.

Parker looked from her to the noisy wall instrument, but she just kept laughing and made no attempt to answer it.

After the third ring, Ashley gulped back her last giggle. The phone stopped. A noisy click came from the other room, then Ashley's recorded voice sailed through loud and clear.

All amusement disappeared from her face. Her eyes widened in horror.

The caller's message began.

Ashley dove for the phone.

And to his utter amazement, so did Parker.

"OH, NO. EVERYTHING is fine. But I'll have to call you back." Ashley watched Parker out of the corner of her eye. He'd allowed her not a speck of privacy by stationing himself at the door. His hands were locked at the top of the frame as he leaned in toward her, glaring the entire time.

"Yes, I'll be there." She hid a smile when Parker let out a deliberate and impatient sigh. "And…" She roughed up her voice, going for a breathless quality. "I'm looking forward to it."

She kept her head down while she hung up the phone, furiously willing away any sign of a smirk. Manuel Gomes of the Make Magic Island a Reality committee must be thinking she was a few bricks short of a load, but it was worth it to see Parker's disgusted expression. Ashley wondered how long she ought to let him think she had a boyfriend.

She schooled her expression to pure innocence and looked up at him. "Now, where were we?"

"You were about to tell me who he is."

"Who? Him?" Ashley sent a pointed look at the phone. Parker's expression was thunderous at best and she had to swallow another chuckle. If she didn't know any better, she'd think he was jealous. "He's a student."

"You're seeing one of your students?" Parker dropped his arms to his sides. "I don't believe it." He shook his head in bewilderment.

"Not in the way you obviously think, Buster." Ashley pushed herself away from the counter and gave the stalled coffeemaker a jolt, then faced him. "I hate to pull the role of victim out from under you, but read my lips. I don't have a boyfriend."

And Parker looked as if he was doing just that. His gaze locked on her mouth for a long moment, then he ran it up to her eyes. Ashley held her breath at the strange look he gave her.

"Then why the cloak-and-dagger?" he asked slowly.

She laughed. "A little overstated, wouldn't you say?"

"Not from where I stand. You've looked as though you're about to jump out of your skin ever since we got here. And then this idiotic phone thing."

If he only knew, Ashley thought, he'd probably prefer that she *did* have a boyfriend. "Look, it's just that this apartment is so small." So was a hotel room. "Maybe we should stay with your family."

Parker let out a choice word. "You know better than that."

"Do I? Actually, I don't know a damn thing. All I know is that you have some kind of problem with them—I think that's pretty obvious to everyone—but other than that, you haven't told me diddly-squat."

He issued a long-suffering sigh.

"I believe it's fair to know what I've gotten into." She leaned a hip against the counter and stared at him.

"You married me, not them." Parker added another jostle to the coffeemaker. "All you have to worry about is acting like it once in a while."

Ashley knew by his tone she should let the subject drop. "How often do you see them?"

"How often do you see the Kings?" he shot back.

She felt herself jerk as if she'd been dealt a physical blow. She didn't want to think about her father's estranged family, about the mother she had never known. Unconsciously, she crossed her arms and hugged them to her, watching Parker's blue eyes turn the color of regret.

"Look, Ash, about the bird." He rubbed the back of his neck and glanced away for a moment. "It won't be a problem."

"I've decided to keep him here, along with Kiwi and Cinnamon."

"What about when the house is finished?" Parker asked slowly.

"I'm keeping the apartment, Parker."

"We hadn't agreed to that."

"It wasn't up for discussion." Ashley uncrossed her arms and searched a cabinet for two mugs.

"It is now."

Ashley looked at the childish drawings taped to her refrigerator, the collection of logo magnets Crystal had started. Though the apartment had never truly felt like home, it was familiar. No strings attached, it was hers. She set down one mug and faced him. "I need to keep it, Parker."

He didn't answer right away. He just stood there looking at her, and she could tell he was trying to understand. A small part of her wanted him to.

"Did you and your father live here together?" he finally asked.

"No. We had to sell the house. I moved here after he entered the hospital." She lifted a shoulder and glanced away. "It was a matter of economics."

"And what about all your belongings?"

"You're looking at them." She sent a pointed look at her refrigerator art and started to laugh. Until she caught the hint of condolence in his eyes. An ugly knot coiled in her stomach. She slammed down the other mug. "Don't you dare pity me. I didn't ask for it. And I sure as hell don't need it."

Parker issued a short, humorless laugh. "Furthest thing from my mind." He shook his head and drilled her with such an intense gaze it took the wind out of her temper.

She helplessly returned his stare until another thought crossed her mind. "And I'm not a martyr," she warned, watching him effectively mask any clue to his thoughts. "Make no mistake about that."

Ashley felt the stubborn lift of her chin and cursed her reflexive reaction. She felt open and vulnerable while he stood there silently, looking as if he knew all her secrets. She wanted to blurt out about Magic Island, wanted to see his smug, knowing look turn to shock.

She didn't want his understanding, didn't want his support. All she wanted was the security and financial independence his name and connections could afford her.

Ashley braced herself against the counter and looked into his heart-melting blue eyes. And most of all, she didn't want to feel the way she was feeling right now.

"Keep the apartment, Ash," Parker said finally.

"And the phone situation?"

"It's your phone."

"No further questions asked?"

"None."

"Don't think you're doing me a favor." Ashley took a deep breath. "Because you're right, it's my apartment, my phone."

Parker nodded, his gaze still fastened to her wary one, and Ashley was left without a doubt that he fully understood her need for independence. The bond that stretched between them was as real as the oxygen deserting her lungs.

"You give me far too much credit, Ash," Parker said, unplugging the coffeemaker. "I have a far more basic motive."

"What are you doing? The coffee isn't finished."

"I have a better idea." He moved closer.

"Parker?" She backed up.

His lips curved into a slow, sensual smile. "Let's neck."

Chapter Eleven

"Are you crazy?" she asked with a nervous laugh.

"Just trying to set the mood." He snaked an arm around her waist and pulled her flush against him. "We already have fighting down pat, I figure we need to practice the other part." He'd pressed his lips to her neck and his words came out garbled. She felt his grin punctuate his outrageous excuse.

"You *are* crazy." Her pronouncement came out weak on the tail of a giggle. His chin was stubble-rough and it tickled.

"Maybe," he agreed, and took full advantage of her exposed neck as she arched away from him.

"Stop that." She pushed at his shoulder, but again a small, traitorous giggle weakened her position.

"Isn't this more fun than fighting?" His tongue trailed behind her ear, flicking at her lobe until he pulled it into his mouth and nipped boldly at it.

"No."

"Sure it is." His lips traveled her jaw until he made contact with her mouth. He pressed a long, soft kiss there until she attempted another protest. Then he slipped his tongue between her unsuspecting lips before she could utter a word.

She meant to stop him. Had every intention of getting away. But he held her firmly against him and his hands felt strong and good, his desire blatant. And for a moment Ashley forgot that this was the very last thing she should be doing.

Her tongue danced with his, her breasts pressed to his chest. Her head spun with denial. It wasn't supposed to be like this. She pushed back a little, self-conscious that he could feel how wildly her heart pounded.

Parker broke the kiss and pulled back, too, gazing at her with such intensity she wanted to look away. "Isn't this better?" Using his thumb, he brushed a soft caress across her lips before tracing her jaw. "Say it, Ashley."

"No." Her voice was damnably weak.

"It's not so hard to admit." His whisper was hoarse and close, his breath mingling with hers.

"No." Ashley shook her head, refusing to give up that last shred of protection, that remaining bridge to sanity.

"Okay." He chuckled. "But would you mind sounding this breathless for company. That ought to fool everyone."

"Damn you, Parker James." Ashley spun away from him and seriously considered dumping the half pot of coffee over his arrogant head. Without intending to, she glanced down at his pants. He needed a cold shower, not hot coffee.

"Life's not fair," he said, grinning when he noticed where her attention was directed. "Guys always get caught."

"Go home." She marched out of the kitchen.

"Aren't you forgetting something?"

He followed her, and when she realized she actually had forgotten, she turned and faced him with a groan. "Rule number—"

"I thought I already showed you what I think of your rules." Parker nudged her chin up. "Shall we go over it again?"

Ashley stared into his amused gaze and willed herself not to react. Slowly, calmly, she slid her hands up his chest and around his neck. She got up on her toes and touched her nose briefly to his. She tipped her head back and parted her lips in invitation. Parker's expression of utter surprise was her reward.

He let his hand slip from her chin to curve around her, his lips forming a satisfied smile. Before the chuckle that threatened to erupt could escape her, she slanted her mouth over his, leaving only a breath between them and whispered, "Enjoy the couch."

PARKER RESIGNED HIMSELF to the fact that he was never going to be able to understand women. One in particular was on his mind as he sat on Ashley's uncomfortable couch and flipped on the television with the remote control.

It had been five days since he and Ashley had moved into her apartment. Five even longer nights. And Parker didn't remember ever having watched so much television in his life. But even with all the work he had to do at the office, it was virtually useless to stay late or bring paperwork home. All he could think about was Ashley...and her damn clandestine phone calls.

For the most part, he'd at least convinced himself that there was no boyfriend involved. Ashley was stubborn, argumentative and altogether too maddeningly enticing, but she wasn't a liar. She had said there was no boyfriend, and Parker believed her. He had to.

He'd scanned several channels when he heard the key in the lock.

"Hi. You're home early," Ashley said brightly as she came through the door, a large grocery sack in one arm.

Parker ignored his automatic inclination to get up and help her. If he'd learned one thing in the past five days, it was that Ashley wanted and needed zilch from him. That fact did more than irritate him, it downright ticked him off. He sprawled deeper into the couch and grunted.

Ashley paused for a few seconds, commented on the heat and the blissfulness of married life, then breezed on into the kitchen. Parker skipped through four more channels.

"Want a beer?" Ashley asked when she reappeared. She flicked on a ceiling fan and held out one of two moisture-beaded cans to him. He accepted his with a mumbled thanks.

She pressed hers to her bare neck for a moment and briefly closed her eyes before taking a long sip. Parker watched a drop of moisture slide down her smooth tanned skin and disappear into the scoop of her pink T-shirt. He took a long pull of his beer and jabbed another number on the remote control.

"You really ought to get more exercise than channel surfing," Ashley said and hitched one hip up on the opposite end of the couch back. She wiggled into a more comfortable position and ended up with one bare thigh a scant foot away, eye level with Parker.

He gave her a murderous sidelong glance that didn't quite reach her face. She tugged at her shorts. He tipped the can to his lips.

The phone rang.

"I'll get it," Ashley said, hopping off the couch, while Parker made a face and silently mimicked her exact words along with her.

"No sh—" Parker shook his head and finished his beer. He heard Ashley's delighted laughter float above the television voices and he quickly lowered the volume.

He'd just about had it with being a nice guy. When he'd agreed to play her phone game the previous week, he hadn't anticipated that it was going to be like a veritable switchboard operation around here. The phone rang constantly, and Ashley either spent her time on calls or running out to meetings. And Parker was damn tired of feeling like the only person left out on a joke.

The only thing he did know was that she was working on something…something big…something she'd elected to keep from him.

He picked up his empty can, strolled soundlessly toward the kitchen and stopped within hearing range. From the glimpse he could get of her, Ashley's back was to him, so he waited with his fingers wrapped around the can, on the verge of crushing it, and listened for all he was worth.

"How about lunch tomorrow?" Ashley asked the caller. "We can go to the meeting from there."

She paused for her answer, then lowered her voice. "I haven't heard yet, but I only submitted the bid ten days ago...yes, but..."

Her dark head started to swivel in his direction. Damn. He squashed the can with a loud crunch and smiled at her when she laid her gaze on him, lifting his foot as if he'd never broken stride.

"I really can't talk right now." Ashley's tone was hurried as she gave him her back once more. "Tomorrow, then."

Parker tossed the can in the recycling bin under the sink. Ashley replaced the receiver and immediately opened the refrigerator.

"Any ideas for dinner?" she asked. Her voice was calm, but she made the mistake of swiping at her hair as she made an inordinately thorough inspection of the fridge.

"Maybe we should go out." Parker reached around her for another beer. As always, the scent of gardenias assailed him. He gripped the top of the door and lingered a moment, his face inches above her shiny black hair, his very aware body a tempting proximity to her hula-enhanced hips. He swallowed. A dry, painful swallow.

"Why?" Ashley backed up. "Oh..." Her curvy little bottom met Parker's growing interest.

He reluctantly backed up, too. Ashley flashed him an oh-my look that was almost comical as she ducked under his arm and scooted past him.

"You're right," she said, grabbing her abandoned beer from the counter. "Maybe we should go out for dinner."

Parker chuckled. "That wasn't my reason, but you're probably right." He snatched the beer he had originally been after, closed the refrigerator door and imitated her earlier actions by bringing the cold can to his neck. That wasn't exactly what needed cooling off, but it would have to do.

"Why did you want to go out?" she asked, easing her way toward the door.

"I didn't want us to have to mess with cooking and cleaning up." He followed her. "I've got to go out in a couple of hours…"

Ashley plopped on the couch, tucking one tanned slender leg under her, and looked up expectantly at him.

Why hadn't he thought of it before? If he included Ashley in more of his dealings, maybe she'd be more open with him. Maybe she'd tell him what she was up to.

"Actually, I've got to attend a meeting with some resort reps, investors, city council members…" Parker laughed. "Don't roll your eyes. It's something you might be interested in. It's a real hot topic tonight," he drawled enticingly and sat next to her.

Ashley arched a brow and the corners of her mouth started to lift. "Really?"

"Maybe we could go to that little restaurant in Chinatown you're so fond of…." He shrugged. "Then you can go along with me."

"That might work." Ashley drew up her other leg as well and settled back into the cushions. She gave him a brilliant smile. "What exactly is this hot topic?"

Parker knew he had her now. Her eyes were turning that golden-honey color he'd come to know and crave. She looked relaxed, sinking into the floral pillows, her hair fanned out like a veil of black silk. The former edginess he'd felt began to slip away. It appeared the evening might have possibilities after all.

He put down his beer can and angled his body toward her. "Magic Island," he said. "Know anything about it?"

ASHLEY PACED HER SMALL kitchen and darted several looks out the window. For the second time, she picked up the phone receiver and listened for the dial tone. It was still working. So why didn't it ring? She returned the instrument with a little too much force and quickly picked it up again, listened, then replaced it with as much care as her sorely tried patience would allow.

Manuel simply had to call before Parker returned. It would kill Ashley to have to wait until tomorrow to find out what had gone on at Parker's meeting.

She'd called the Magic Island committee chairman as soon as she'd gotten rid of Parker. No easy task in itself. She couldn't actually remember all of what happened after Parker had dropped the bomb. She'd been too stressed out. But she had managed to send him off to dinner by himself, which had given her enough time to notify Manuel Gomes so that they could send a spy out to the meeting. She did, however, remember enough to know that Parker had left angry.

Ashley glanced at the clock and out of the corner of her eye, caught the sweep of headlights across the grassy area outside the apartment. Damn. She grabbed a diet cola out of the fridge, dove for the couch and struck a nonchalant pose.

The unnecessary jabs at the lock were a dead giveaway as to Parker's mood before he came through the door. She heard his mumbled curses and looked up as he flung his keys onto the rattan side table. She offered a tentative smile.

"Headache any better?" he asked, rubbing the back of his neck.

The blank look she gave him didn't help the skeptical gaze he fastened on her. "Headache. Yes. I mean, no. It's gone." She nodded her head. "Back to normal."

"Great." He couldn't have made the single word sound more sarcastic if he'd practiced an hour.

"How was your meeting?" She sipped her cola.

"A damn three-ring circus."

A flood of the carbonated drink swooshed down Ashley's

throat. She grimaced against the burning sensation. "What happened?" she asked warily.

"What didn't?" Parker asked over his shoulder on his way to the kitchen. He came back with a can of guava juice. "Halfway through the meeting, some idiot starts spouting off about how we're ruining the islands by allowing the tourists to 'trample our culture.'"

Ashley cringed. Why would Manuel have sent John Aoki?

"And then the other one starts in on—"

"There were two?" Ashley realized her slip immediately. Her gaze darted to his. He frowned. She lifted a shoulder. "I mean, I didn't realize this was a pro-and-con type meeting," she offered lamely.

"It wasn't." Parker kept his attention focused on her a long time. "And there were four."

She swallowed back her surprise. Obviously nothing had gone as planned. And now Ashley *had* to know what happened, if not from Manuel…she took a quick breath and gave Parker what she hoped was an indifferent shrug. "Was anything resolved?"

"Hell, no." Parker pinched the bridge of his nose. "Those people are insane. The whole lot of them. There isn't a logical bone in their fanatical bodies. They won't listen to a single word anyone who disagrees with them has to say."

"That's quite a generalization," Ashley said with a tight smile.

"Believe me, I know." Parker gave her such a strange look, it made her squirm. He doesn't know a thing, she assured herself, it was her conscience knocking things out of whack.

"Do you know what they want to do?" He gestured to the air, obviously not wanting an answer. "They want to turn Kahoolawe into some sort of Disney-type island with an amusement park, casinos and resorts."

Ashley shifted her weight from one hip to the other and widened her eyes. "So?"

"Don't tell me you think that would be a good idea?"

She put her palms up and gave him a half shrug and a noncommitted smile. She wanted to give him a strategic jab in the solar plexus. It was, in fact, a damn good idea.

"Do you know how long that would take? That island is totally barren. We don't even know if it's safe. The military bombed the hell out of it, using it for target practice for a number of years. The whole thing is probably as stable as a piece of Swiss cheese."

"That's not true." Ashley bit her lip.

He gave her an odd look. "The point is, we don't know. The thought of planning an amusement park, of all things, gives me the creeps. Would you want our kids going there?"

Our kids? A lump blocked Ashley's air passage.

Parker blinked several times. He shifted positions. "I know that's overreacting," he said, "but I think it's foolish to take a chance on that island, when the floating casino idea makes so much more sense."

He was wrong about the risk and definitely wrong about the floating casino being a better idea. She wanted to tell him so, but instead she offered matter-of-factly, "Some civic groups have already begun replanting on Kahoolawe."

Parker narrowed his gaze on her. "What do you know about any of this?"

"Nothing, really." She got up. "Want more juice?"

"Has Crystal been filling your head with this...this Magic Island nonsense?"

Ashley silently counted to ten and headed for the kitchen, trying to put some distance between them. When she turned to answer, she came face-to-face with him. "No," she said slowly and truthfully.

"I knew I should have spoken to her before this." Parker

unbuttoned the top of his shirt and pulled the collar away from his neck.

"Crystal does not influence what I think." She sent the empty cola can rattling across the counter. "I even have a mind all my own. Imagine that?"

"I didn't mean it that way." Parker put his hand out and the can came to a halt. He moved in, slipped his hand under her hair and cupped the back of her neck.

"I know I'm touchy on the subject. But the implication that the rest of us don't care about these islands really gets me. That's just not..." He shook his head in such sad earnestness, Ashley had to press her lips together to keep from spilling her guts. "Look, Ash, no matter how I feel personally, this is business and people know how cause oriented you are. I just don't want you to get hurt."

With firm but gentle fingers, he kneaded the tense muscles at her nape. He held her with a steady gaze and a lopsided smile. Ashley quickly lowered her lashes. It was a little hard to be loyal to the cause while he was regarding her with those beautiful blue eyes.

He crooked his finger under her chin and nudged her face back up to his. "Tell me you won't get involved and I'll drop the subject."

"Parker, I appreciate your intentions." She tried to draw back. He wouldn't let her. "But what I am or am not involved in is none of your concern."

"Sorry, sweetheart, but this time it would be. I've got too much on the line, and I don't need my name tied to the likes of Sam Chun or any of those other crackpot zealots."

"Sam Chun?" Ashley echoed faintly.

"Not that I'm accusing you of keeping company with them."

"Was *he* at the meeting?"

"Sam? Yeah, *was.* We took care of that."

Ashley felt her body go boneless and Parker brought his other arm around her. Had Manuel Gomes gone out of his mind? First John Aoki and now Sam Chun, two of the most irrational, hotheaded supporters of Magic Island. Ashley shivered. She didn't even want to know who the other two attendees were.

"Are you feeling okay?" Parker pulled her close. "You aren't cold, are you?"

She shook her head but snuggled against him. She didn't trust the expression on her face.

He smoothed her hair and rested his chin on top of her head. Gingerly, she pushed her hands up his chest. She felt his heartbeat gaining momentum, felt her own racing toward him.

"Whose foolish idea was it to talk business?" Parker angled back a bit and smiled down at her.

Ashley exhaled. "Not mine." Her return smile came easy in the wake of the most truthful thing she'd said all night.

"Well, since I was the one who initiated such an unacceptable discussion," Parker lowered his face several fractions, "I think I'll remedy it."

Ashley arched her head back in time for his lips to brush once, then twice across hers. Her eyes drifted closed, and her mind tumbled beyond rhyme or reason. With quickened pulse, she waited for the next touch of his lips.

His warm breath transfused her skin as he dipped his head to nuzzle the side of her neck. Her shirt slipped off her shoulder and he ran his tongue along the unguarded path. A sensitive shudder rocketed through her, and Parker stopped long enough to give her a long, blazing look.

Ashley's lips parted. Something had to be said, someone had to stop this.

He circled her waist and hoisted her onto the counter. Her sandal slipped from her foot, and with it the last vestige of denial.

She tunneled her hands through his hair and met his mouth with equal hunger. His tongue plunged after hers and she gladly gave up her last breath to dance the dance with him. He propelled one hand up the gaping cuff of her shorts, stroking her bare thigh, leaning her back, taking what she offered.

Out of the sensual fog, a bell sounded. Parker kissed and kneaded, but it rang again. He slipped a finger under the elastic of her bikini panties and the bell shrilled. What was happening?

He took a ragged breath and reached around her with his other hand.

As if mired in an out-of-body experience, Ashley watched the phone receiver make contact with his ear. She heard his voice but his words didn't register.

Moments of endless silence penetrated the fog.

She looked into Parker's stunned eyes only inches from her own. The sensual blue turned a somber navy.

Parker handed her the phone. "It's the Honolulu county jail," he said quietly, and turned to walk away. "Sam Chun needs bail money."

"MRS. LEE, PLEASE have Ashley pass the syrup." Parker sat rigid in his chair. His hair was in need of a cut, his eyes lacked their normal sparkle.

Ashley pushed the pitcher of coconut syrup a tad short of his reach.

"Thanks." Neither woman missed his sarcasm.

"Mrs. Lee, may I have the butter, please?" Ashley gave Napua a smile, but its usual warmth was as toasty as a Hawaiian snow cone.

Parker handed Mrs. Lee the butter, which was well out of her reach. Napua sighed heavily and nudged it across to Ashley. Things were bad...very, very bad.

She watched Ashley nibble on a piece of waffle that wouldn't keep a mynah bird alive. Napua eyed Parker. He was assaulting his waffle as if it were the devil himself.

Napua shook her head. *Disastrous.*

It had been four days since the house had been completed and Parker and Ashley had returned home. Napua had had the rooms filled with fresh flowers, had excitedly cooked a dinner fit for King Kamehameha himself. She'd even arranged to spend the weekend with a friend in order to give the lovebirds their privacy. It had all been in vain. Napua had known it the minute they'd stepped from the car, and if she hadn't, the deliberate slam of each door would have convinced her.

And then things got worse. Ashley stayed at home less and less, and when she was here she and Parker quibbled over everything from how many chocolate chips should go into Napua's cookies to what time the sun would set.

Napua plopped her elbow on the table and rested one plump cheek in her hand. What had gone wrong? And what was she going to do about it? She'd only heard bits and pieces of their various arguments, but it had been enough to know that Parker was unhappy with one of Ashley's charity involvements. And Ashley was unhappy in general.

And although she still thought the apartment idea had been a good one, Napua felt terribly responsible. But now she was at a complete loss about what to do.

Parker pushed back from the table and stood. Napua watched him through narrowed slits. Surely this morning he would at least kiss his wife goodbye.

Ashley continued mashing her waffle without looking up. Parker picked up his briefcase. "Ashley, could I see you a moment?" he asked, darting Napua a quick glance.

The younger woman took an inordinate amount of time dabbing her mouth with her napkin, and Napua could see Parker's patience slipping.

"I'll be in the kitchen," Napua said and rose quickly, taking along her barely touched plate.

Immediately she discarded her breakfast and stationed herself at eavesdropping distance.

"We have to talk at some point," Parker said in a low, controlled voice.

"I think you've done enough of that," Ashley replied sweetly.

"I wish *you* had." Parker's tone was curt.

"I've already told you everything you need to know."

"The hell you—" Parker sighed heavily and lowered his voice. "Nothing, Ashley. You've told me absolutely nothing."

Napua heard Ashley's chair scrape the floor and immediately thought of her poor wood parquet which had been freshly polished. She put a hand to her mouth to keep from being discovered.

"That's because I don't have anything more to say, Parker. I'll see you tonight."

"Don't walk away from me," he warned.

"Then don't push me."

Silence stung Napua's ears. She bit down on her finger, listening to the fading footsteps, waiting to hear a door slam.

None did. Instead, Parker's faint voice questioned Ashley as to what she had expected.

Napua straightened. Expected? Or had he said expecting? She strained her ears, clutching her chest.

The door slammed. Twice.

Napua rounded the corner and stared dumbstruck at it. And then a slow, knowing smile settled on her round, relieved face. If there was going to be a *keiki* around the house, she'd have to act fast. And she knew just the person to help her. She hurried to the telephone and punched out a set of numbers.

"Karen?" She waited for Parker's sister to finish her yawn. "How would you like to be an aunt?"

Chapter Twelve

"You should have checked with me first," Ashley grumbled as she threw some Dramamine into her purse.

"Sorry, Your Highness." Parker stomped past her with some clothes he'd grabbed from the closet. "But you weren't home long enough."

"She's *your* sister," Ashley warned. "If you want to start something before we meet her and Don for the afternoon, that's up to you."

Parker sighed. "No, I don't want to start anything. And you're right. I should have checked with you first."

Ashley kept fiddling with the contents of her purse, but slid him a furtive sidelong glance. That was the most civil he'd sounded in over a week.

Parker pulled off his shirt and stood fumbling with the buttons of another. Curly, dark, tawny hair swirled over his tanned chest and around his flat nipples. His jeans were tight and low, and not yet snapped at the top.

Ashley swallowed. Damn him. She peered back into her purse, trying to remember what she'd been looking for.

"Ash, can you give me a hand with this?" He frowned in concentration at the button tab.

Reluctantly, she dropped her pocketbook onto the bed. And then she heard the tear.

"Oh, great." Parker exhaled. "I think it's beyond help now." He gave her a sheepish smile and held out the shirt.

The once too small buttonhole was now large enough to drive a truck through.

"It can be fixed." She took the shirt from him and raised her gaze to his face. His hair was framed by the sunlight that streamed through the open door from the hall skylight. If she didn't know any better, he'd look like an angel. But she did know better. And Parker James was no angel. "But not in time for today."

"I'm sure Mrs. Lee will do it." He reclaimed the torn article, wadded it up and tossed it on the bed.

"You'll pay dearly for that." Ashley arched a brow in the direction of the crumpled-up heap and laughed.

Parker gave her a strange look. "I'll pick it up before she does." He stopped, but kept his eyes narrowed on her. "It's good to hear you laugh again, Ash."

She ran a palm up her bare arm and struggled against the pull of his gaze. She allowed it for an instant, then broke contact.

Mentally, Ashley shook her head. It was either laugh or cry, she thought wryly. This past week had been the week from hell. First, the third degree from Parker, lurking from Mrs. Lee, then silent treatment from Parker, crazy demands from the Magic Island committee, and to top it all off, her father was having delusions about being able to leave the hospital.

And worst of all, Parker believed she was being manipulated into helping with the Magic Island "cause," as he called it. He thought of her as so darn altruistic that the real reason hadn't occurred to him. Money...basic greed, plain and simple. Well, the desire for security wasn't exactly in the same category as greed, Ashley reasoned, but that didn't make her feel any better. Parker might be a shark, but he'd been an honest shark, and right now she merely felt like the rear end of one.

Ashley took a deep breath and chanced another peek at him. His hair was longer than she'd ever seen it and curled in an aimless arrangement at his neck. His lips were pursed in uncertainty, his chin dimpling slightly with the action. Once again, a familiar ache settled in a grudging spot in her southern hemisphere.

She wanted to spill her guts to Parker. She wanted to tell him he was wrong about Magic Island. She wanted to prove to him that the concept could work. She wanted total honesty between them. She wanted to stop their unspoken war.

Instead, what she did was reach in the closet for another shirt. "Are you going to be ready on time?" she asked and tossed it to him.

He rubbed his jaw. "If I don't shave."

Ashley bit back a smile. She wondered what his sister would think of his new beach-bum look.

"But I guess that won't matter," Parker grumbled. "No chance of running into anyone twelve-thousand feet in the air. Have you ever taken one of these aerial tours before?"

"No. And don't use that tone with me. I'm not the one who agreed to this."

"I know. I know." He pulled the shirt over his head. Ashley breathed a sigh of relief and returned to organizing her purse. "But Karen wouldn't take no for an answer. She went on and on about how she and Don haven't gotten to know you. Plus, she did the guilt-trip thing about me not informing her of the wedding in advance...."

"And you fell for it like a two-ton sack of rice." Grinning, Ashley turned back to him. His hair was in disarray from pulling on the shirt, and Ashley automatically leaned forward to smooth it out.

One tawny curl had caressed her little finger before she realized what she was doing. She grazed his neck and felt the heat of his skin as she tried to pull back her imprudent hand.

He wrapped his long fingers around hers and held her hand in midair. He gave her a long, searching look, then slowly buried his lips in her palm while holding her gaze.

She froze for an instant, then closed her eyes, tentatively flexing her fingers against his cheek in a stroking motion.

"I've missed you," he whispered.

"I've been here," she answered in a soft voice.

"Not here." He banded his arms around her and pulled her up against him. His mouth descended upon hers with an urgency that should have been frightening. But it wasn't. Parker's taste, his scent, his touch...they were all becoming familiar to her. More than familiar, they felt unbearably necessary.

She opened her mouth to him and he pushed his tongue to hers. It was like velvet on satin, satin on velvet. He explored her mouth, while his hands rubbed a path down her back and over her buttocks. The spandex of her biking shorts felt skimpier and skimpier with each pass of his hand as he stroked her over and over.

"I want you, Ashley." His breathing was heavy, and she could feel evidence of his arousal.

"I know," she whispered. Why couldn't she admit it? She wanted him, too. *Chemistry,* her brain chanted, it's only chemistry.

"You feel so good." Parker kissed and licked and suckled until Ashley didn't think there would be enough oxygen left in the room. His fingers hesitated at the top of her shorts. He played with the elastic for a few seconds. When she didn't make a move to stop him, he dipped inside. His warm and sure fingers glided over her hipbones, past her bikini panties and down her thighs.

She buried her face in his neck and glanced down to see the shape of his knuckles moving under the clingy material. He'll stretch the fabric, she thought with irrational hysteria, as he neared the place he'd never been.

The elastic of her panties gave way, and his thumb grazed the nest of curls guarding her desire. She was hot and wet, and she wanted to rip the shirt right off his body. But uncertainty slackened her grip on his shoulders. Reflexively, her thighs moved together.

Parker immediately stilled his hand on her thighs. "It

isn't right yet, is it?'' he asked, stroking her cheekbone with the thumb of his other hand.

''I don't know,'' she whispered and averted her gaze, knowing she was a liar. She didn't want him to ask. She wanted him to take what she didn't have the guts to give.

''What will it take, Ash?''

She moistened her lips and forced her gaze back to him. ''Something more than chemistry.''

The twitch was there at his jaw again. She saw the convulsive movement in his throat. ''Is that what you really think?''

Ashley slowly nodded. His embrace slackened.

The doorbell chimed.

Parker briefly closed his eyes. ''What timing,'' he said and gave her a weak grin. Slowly, he slid his hand from her shorts and unabashedly adjusted the tightness of his own pants.

''I'm sorry,'' Ashley said, not even sure what she was sorry about. She turned her cheek to his heart and rubbed it against the exposed vee at his chest.

''Me, too.'' He sighed and rested his chin atop her head for a moment. Then he pulled back and tilted her gaze his way. ''Because, sweetheart, you're dead wrong.''

''I THOUGHT THIS TOUR was of Oahu only,'' Parker said, frowning as the small plane made a wide turn and headed out over the Pacific.

''Oh, didn't I tell you?'' Karen waved an unconcerned hand. ''We're doing Maui, too.''

''What!'' Parker's voice thundered above the roar of the laboring engine.

Ashley had been about to protest, too, but from the look on Parker's face, he was about to do enough of that for both of them. So she settled back in her seat and looked from brother to sister.

It felt good not to be in the hot seat for a change, although she didn't believe Karen ever truly had to worry about that. Parker obviously adored his sister. He'd been his most charming self ever since she and Don had arrived at the house to pick them up. No one would ever know that he and Ashley had been fighting all week…or jumping each other's bones just moments before.

Ashley loosened her seat belt a notch and let out a breath. She wasn't sure what Parker had meant about her being wrong, wasn't sure if she wanted to know. Hopefully, this extended plane ride would provide the necessary distance from their crazy lapse of sanity.

Parker waited a minute until the plane began to level off and the engine quieted a bit. "Look, Karen——"

"You're missing Hanauma Bay." Karen excitedly pointed out the window to the reef-crowded inlet. Hundreds of snorkelers assumed the appearance of ants as the plane continued to ascend into the cloudless sky.

"I'm going to be missing a hell of a lot more than that if you don't have this plane turn around." Parker cupped his hand over his watch, blocking out the sun's glare.

"Don't tell me you have to work today." Karen wagged a finger at him. "For goodness sakes, Ashley, don't let him get away with that. You two should still be on your honeymoon." She gave her husband a sly wink that was not missed by Ashley. Don returned a leave-me-out-of-this look, before feigning a copious interest in the fading Hanauma Bay.

Ashley swiped back her hair and shifted against the seat belt. Karen looked far too pleased with herself. It made Ashley uneasy.

"I have a meeting at three o'clock, Karen," Parker warned. "And I had better be back for it."

His sister waved him off. "You're just like Dad," she said, and Ashley's eyes darted to Parker. His mouth tightened. "You worry too much," Karen continued, grinning. "Haven't I always taken good care of you?"

"Yeah, right." Parker let out a disgusted sound. His gaze

drifted to the horizon as he drummed his fingers on the armrest of his seat.

Actually, Ashley had a meeting, too, and she hoped Parker wasn't going to give in to his sister. Ashley had purposely scheduled it for this afternoon because she knew Parker was going to be tied up. And this was one meeting she had to attend.

She had to warn the committee to back off. Too many hotheads were getting involved, and although they all wanted the same thing, Ashley disagreed with the way they were going about it. They, of course, were free to choose their own way, but she didn't appreciate them using her access to the land as a pawn. If they couldn't come to a compromise, she'd have to rethink her involvement.

"And what do you think?" Karen turned her bright smile on Ashley. "Parker shouldn't be going to the office on Saturdays, should he? Surely you don't work on weekends."

"Actually…" Ashley glanced over at Parker. He turned and lifted a brow at her. "I did have something planned for this afternoon," she said, hearing the involuntary defiance in her tone.

"Yes, well, Mrs. Lee thinks—" Karen stopped short as two pairs of eyes snapped to hers. She sent a wide-eyed plea to Don, who did nothing but crane his neck farther toward the window. "She thinks that…that I should have brought our kids. Parker loves children, you know." Her smile was all bright innocence again. "Expecting any soon?"

"What?" Parker choked out the word, then issued a short, humorless laugh. "You practically went from honeymoon to kids in one breath." He shook his head. "Amazing."

Ashley said nothing. A nervous laugh was the best she could produce.

"Stranger things have happened during honeymoons."

Karen nodded sagely. "You do realize Lindsey was conceived during ours." She put her hand in her husband's.

Don patted it and cleared his throat. "Been playing any tennis, Parker?" he asked, making only his second attempt to enter the conversation since they'd first taken off nearly two hours ago.

"Not lately. How about you? Playing any golf?" Parker asked, and for the next twenty minutes the conversation took a blessedly neutral turn.

Ashley let the small talk float around her. She chimed in occasionally, but mostly enjoyed lounging back and listening to the friendly banter between Parker and Karen.

Though not once did she feel excluded. All three made her feel comfortable, like part of the family. And the whole trip would have been quite a nice experience, she decided, had she not felt so terribly guilty. Deceiving people was difficult enough, Ashley was quickly finding, but deceiving people you liked was a killer.

After a while, Karen leaned forward to talk with the pilot and Don resumed his post at the window. Ashley snuggled into her seat and watched the occasional cloud sail by, while Parker fidgeted with something in his hand.

Several minutes passed before curiosity got the better of her and Ashley sidled over in her seat to see what had so captured Parker's attention.

Around and around, Parker twisted the simple gold wedding band he wore. He pushed it a fraction up his finger and studied the ring of paler skin it left behind.

As if compelled by her gaze, he lifted his face to hers. "I'm a marked man," he said, grinning at the untanned skin. "After only three weeks and two days."

His gaze returned to hers and his grin softened into a smile.

Ashley felt a flutter catapult from her chest to her belly. Quickly, she did a mental calculation. He was right. Exactly three weeks and two days.

She looked back down at his long lean fingers, tenderly

stroking the textured gold, and she swallowed around the lump in her throat.

Parker touched her arm. "Almost an anniversary already. Can you believe it?"

She looked up into his eyes—eyes so earnest and blue they made hers sting. He gazed back for a moment, then lightly dragged the tip of his finger down her arm.

Ashley shivered. Excited bumps surfaced on every inch of her bare skin as he wrapped his strong hand around hers and brought it to his lips. She felt his contented smile rub the top of her hand, felt her heart surge with warmth, and in total awe she wondered when pretense had merged with reality. Dazed, she sank back into her seat.

He leaned forward and touched her lips briefly with his. "Don't start feeling too safe," he whispered. "I might just blow off my meeting."

Ashley sighed.

A soft groan left Parker and he swooped in for a harder kiss. Ashley gasped for breath. "Unless you want to join the mile-high club," he whispered so loudly that Karen and Don straightened in their seats.

Ashley widened her eyes at first, then narrowed them on him—giving him a slow, saucy grin—and said in her best Mae West imitation, "Don't start anything you can't finish."

The plane dipped suddenly.

"What the devil—" Parker swung his gaze to the window. "We're landing." Ashley shot a look to Karen and Don. Don slumped in his seat. Karen reached into the cockpit and pulled out two very familiar-looking overnight bags.

"Surprise!" she yelled. "Happy honeymoon."

Parker looked at Ashley. Ashley looked at Parker. "Honeymoon?" they echoed.

"Don't worry about a thing. Harvey is covering for you, Parker. And Crystal has you taken care of, Ashley," Karen gushed on, her face brimming with excitement as the plane touched ground. "And we'll be back for you in a week."

"A week?" Parker and Ashley repeated together.

Ashley coughed.

Parker laughed and slipped an arm around her sagging shoulders. "Well, sweetheart, what was it you said about finishing what I start?"

PARKER KNEW HE SHOULD be angry, furious even. He was far too busy with the resort to be railroaded like this. But as he watched Ashley unceremoniously jerk clothes out of the bags that had been packed by Mrs. Lee and smuggled to Maui by Karen, he just couldn't seem to find an angry bone in his body. Besides, Ashley was doing well enough in that department for both of them.

"Which side of the bed do you want?" he asked, nodding to the king-size bed and hiding a smile. He knew damn well which side she wanted—both, with him on the parlor couch.

Ashley favored him with an icy green stare and ignored his question. "Why didn't you simply refuse to get off the plane?"

"Why didn't you?"

She ejected a frustrated sigh and tossed a cosmetic bag into the bathroom. "I didn't think of it." She plopped one of the bags on the luggage rack and pinned him with a suspicious glance. "You don't seem too ticked about this."

He shrugged. "What good would it do? Karen assured me that Harvey has already cleared my calendar and is stepping in where necessary. Besides, you don't know my sister. Once she sets her mind on something…" He shook his head. "Look how elaborate this scheme was. I figure we can kick back for the weekend…go our separate ways if you like." He gave her a covert glance. "Then make arrangements to get ourselves back on Monday."

Before Ashley could verbalize her air of eager agreement, he added, "Unless we find something more… interesting to, uh, engage in."

She sent him a look. Parker pressed his lips together and

busied himself with unpacking. One more suggestive tone out of him and she'd probably swim back.

"Oh, great." Ashley planted her hands on her hips and inclined her head to the phone's blinking message light. "I don't think your sister's through with us yet." She paused and lifted a suspicious brow. "Unless someone else knows we're here."

Parker ignored her ridiculous implication and reached for the phone. At the same time, a knock sounded at the door. Ashley threw up her hands and headed for it. Parker frowned and jabbed zero.

Moments later, a room-service waiter pushed a cart holding chilled champagne and an enormous basket of tropical fruit just ahead of Ashley. Parker gave the man a tip and finished listening to his voice-mail message. Ashley plucked an elaborately scripted envelope from the basket and opened it.

She scrunched up her nose. "Who's Herman Voss?"

"Son of a—" Parker slowly replaced the receiver. He gave her a blank look. "What?"

She eyed the offending phone and met his narrowed gaze with a concerned one of her own. "Herman Voss. He sent this." She dropped the announcement to the table. "What's going on?"

"Beats the hell out of me." Parker worked at the kink in his neck. "Herman Voss is one of my investors." He motioned toward the phone with a toss of his head. "That message was from Walter Ito. He's another one." He paced to the sliding-glass doors and stared pensively out over the ocean.

Ashley made a soft sound of exasperation. He looked over his shoulder at her. "And he's kindly arranged to entertain us for the week."

"Entertain...for the week?" Ashley threw back a thick swatch of hair. "Parker? How do these people know we're here?"

"I don't know," he said, shaking his head. "I'd blame

Karen, but I'm not sure she even knows either of them. Mrs. Lee, Harvey and Crystal are the only other possibilities. And Mrs. Lee is out.''

"So is Crystal. Of course, you'd think she and Harvey would have both known better to begin with.''

"Well, my money wouldn't be on Harvey either. But I don't suppose we're going to find out any time soon. Walter Ito has quite a week planned for us.''

"We don't really have to stay…'' Ashley gaped. "You said we could get back on Monday.''

"Not now, I'm afraid. I'm not stirring up any speculation.''

She sighed heavily. "A whole week,'' she muttered, as she trudged up beside him and pushed the drapes further aside. "Look at this place.'' A long stretch of beach curved into a bay, where it met jagged lava cliffs. A green cloud-capped mountain hovered to the left. Not a person was in sight. "It's…it's deserted. What could there possibly be to do?''

Out of the corner of his eye, Parker watched Ashley blow out a puff of air and he bit back a chuckle. He didn't think she'd appreciate his answer to that question, so he kept his mouth shut and enjoyed the view of her delicate profile against the setting sun.

Ashley's forehead puckered in thought for a few seconds, then she flashed him a crooked grin. "Is this the resort they joke about being for newlyweds or nearly deads?''

Parker's attention snagged on the tiny dimple that flexed at the corner of her mouth. He knew he'd stared a moment too long when her tongue darted out to moisten her lips. She started to back up, but he snaked an arm out to capture her waist. "That's us, Ash. Newlyweds.''

Her tongue made another swipe at her lips, then her chin lifted a notch. "Take too much Dramamine, Parker?'' she asked sweetly, as she stomped on his foot and pulled out of his reach.

Parker glanced down at the scuffs on his deck shoes and

chuckled. She was so light, he'd barely felt it. He looked back up into her smug expression, then reached out his hand to draw the drapes. "No," he replied, ambling toward her. "Too much testosterone."

Ashley's amusement fell away. "You're joking." She sidestepped the bed. "Right?"

"Right." He allowed a slow smile to cross his face.

Her eyebrows drew together in a threatening manner and she slanted a glance toward the vanity night-light that had illuminated with the closing of the drapes. She seemed about to make her move for the bathroom door, when Parker lunged forward and gripped both her wrists.

"One scream and security will be here in two seconds." She flexed her hands back but his fingers locked around her.

"Wanna bet?"

"What do you want, Parker?"

He bunched her wrists together and held them tightly with one hand. With his free one he lifted her chin. "You."

Ashley met him with an unblinking gaze. "You already have that." She raised her chin yet another degree. "Bought and paid for."

Parker felt the blow somewhere in the vicinity of his gut, but he wasn't going to let her get away with it. She always started trouble when he got too close to her—and used it to distance herself. But not this time. He swallowed back the dose of useless pride she had so adeptly summoned.

"You have a very sassy mouth," he whispered. "But we already know that, don't we?" He kept hold of her chin and used his thumb to outline the corner of her mouth. "Hard to imagine such tart words come from these soft lips."

"I'll give you something even harder to imagine," Ashley warned.

"Hey." Chuckling, Parker touched her dimple. "That's my line."

Ashley smiled, displaying a disarming flash of white

teeth before they clamped down on his unsuspecting thumb. He jerked back and she pushed away from him.

Biting back a curse, he caught her around the waist and toppled them both to the bed. "Very childish, sweetheart," he scolded, grinning, and successfully pinned her beneath him.

Chapter Thirteen

The light from the bathroom streamed across Parker's face. Ashley watched in fascination as his cheeks and jaw worked to suck away the throbbing from his thumb. Desire, raw and primal, spiraled through her.

"You're too heavy for me. Get off." Her voice wasn't quite normal. He chuckled and she knew he recognized that fact, too.

"You wanna be on top?" His shoe made a soft thud when it hit the carpet. His toe trailed a promise up her calf. "Teacher's choice."

"There's a couple of things I'd like to teach you right now." Ashley twisted to the side, but Parker imprisoned her shoulders with his elbows and captured her face between his hands.

She felt his tongue first, teasing her tightly closed lips. His fingers stretched back into her disheveled hair, massaging her scalp, sending little shivers down her spine. She debated a token struggle, but her thoughts tangled with a more primal need and she reached for him instead.

His shirttail was already loose, so it was easy to travel the length of his warm, naked back with her palms. Muscles flexed and relaxed to her touch. Large, ragged breaths expanded his width beneath her fingers. The thrill of power surged through her and she opened her mouth to him.

Parker's tongue dove smoothly between her eager lips.

His hands molded her shoulders, her waist, her hips before he rounded her bottom and pressed her to him. Ashley whimpered softly and he broke the kiss for a moment.

"It's time, Ash."

"I know." Her voice was low, almost inaudible. To erase any mistaken uncertainty, she initiated another kiss, sweet at first and then, fueled by love and desire too long denied, her tongue matched his fire, delving between heaven and hell.

"Ashley?" After a moment, Parker was the one to pull slightly away. "No turning back, okay?"

"No." She reached for him again.

"No distractions," he said, maintaining a slight distance, a satisfied smile tugging at the corners of his mouth as she looked at him through glazed eyes. "No excuses. No interruptions."

"No." Her impatient tone brought a full grin to his lips. Any other time she would've liked to smack him, but right now all she wanted was for him to kiss her.

"And, honey?" His face was somber now. A cold shiver tempered Ashley's heat, until he gently framed her face with his hands. "Most important." He stroked her cheek. "No regrets."

"None." A feeling of serenity, of rightness settled over her. She loved him. And that made it right. Even the other "no" he'd neglected to mention could not extinguish her longing at this moment. Expectation and commitment had not been part of their bargain. Ashley had no illusions now. "No regrets," she stated, strong and certain, and pushed up toward him.

"Ah, sweetheart. I've been waiting—" Parker murmured against her lips.

Ashley kissed him into silence, then allowed a couple of breaths between them. "One more no, Parker," she half whispered, half panted, bringing a finger to his lips. She smiled at his quizzical look. "*No talking.*"

The words were barely out when he banded her with his

arms and rolled her over on top of him. He smoothed his palms over her shorts until fabric met skin, and then slid his hands up under her bikini panties. He toyed with the elastic, tracing patterns with his fingers over the swell of her buttocks.

His kisses were gentle and teasing, nipping at her lower lip, moistening it with his tongue. His hair carried the scent of sunshine and promise, and with it the memory of his unfailing support. He'd been patient with her unruly students, kind to her father and so unlike the picture she'd painted of him just a few short weeks earlier. Ashley's breasts strained against him, her body anxious for his exploration. She reached between them and undid the last button of his shirt.

Parker slid his hands from her, kissed the exposed shoulder where her T-shirt had slipped, then lay back against the pillows. His arms rested on either side of him, away from her, his eyes dark with challenge and desire.

This was her test, Ashley knew. It was also her final chance to back down. Her hesitation was brief as she was left to straddle him while he watched. She pushed his shirt aside and ran her palms against the taut skin, wondering at the softness of the thick, dark blond chest hair. She felt a small quiver beneath her hands and smiled to herself.

She made the return trip down, grazing his flat nipples, tracing the dip between them, delighting in the small bumps that appeared on his skin. But her control was short-lived.

"Damn," Parker swore through clenched teeth. "You like making me crazy, huh?" He sat up and pulled her legs more tightly around him. Reaching around, he pulled up the hem of her top and with it the brief camisole. He tossed them aside and shrugged out of his own shirt.

Ashley's hair fell forward but he brushed it away and fisted a handful behind her. "I want to see you." He released it and she felt it glide down her back, reminding her of her nakedness.

"I'm going to turn on the light," he whispered, and with deliberate slowness Parker stretched for the bedside lamp.

Any other time, Ashley would have cringed from the exposure. But when light flooded their half-naked bodies, assurance cocooned her heart. She was exactly where she wanted to be.

She met Parker's smoldering gaze with one of her own, then let it drift to the tempting expanse of flesh and hair that tapered to the waistband of his unbuttoned jeans and below, to his straining fly.

She shifted unnecessarily on his lap. A smile quickly appeared on his lips.

"You little devil." He grasped her about the waist and set her farther back from harm's way. "Careful, or this will be over before you know it."

"C'mon, Parker, don't chicken out on me now," Ashley chided and wiggled forward, grinning.

"If the teacher wants an apple, she'd better behave." He raised himself up to a sitting position and brought her up against him, seeking the tart sweetness of her lips. Her sensitive breasts tingled with the friction of his hair-carpeted chest. They pebbled and pouted awaiting his velvety tongue, which was making its way from her mouth down her neck.

He didn't disappoint. Suckling one breast and then the other, he gently laid Ashley backward until she was fully reclined, her hair spread out about the satin sheets. He slid his hands to the back of her thighs and massaged and kneaded until he'd worked his way up under the leg of her shorts. She reached for his zipper but he ducked away.

She felt his ever-hardening manhood graze her fingers through the rough denim fabric and knew she could easily have it her way. A smug cloud was beginning to shroud her senses when she felt his deft fingers slip inside her panties, finding the wetness there. A surprise jolt brought her shoulders off the bed.

"Relax," Parker whispered, soothing her back down, his fingers stroking a gentle inquiry. "I won't hurt you."

Yes, you will, was Ashley's last feeble thought before his magical fingers erased the reality of the future.

Rainbows. Fireworks. Forked lightning. They all collided under her tightly closed eyelids. It was hot, then cold, just before the tidal wave swept her into a pulsing native dance. She could hear the drums in the distance. Her heart echoed their beat. Her senses begged their encore. And then the waves became swells, dwindling to ripples, nature's prudent restoration of order.

"Shh, baby."

She opened her eyes and Parker was smiling, stroking her cheek. "Everyone will think I'm beating you."

Oh, my. The fog began to lift. She'd been crying out his name. Embarrassed, she tried to turn her face into his shoulder.

But he wouldn't have it.

"Don't do that," he said softly. "You're beautiful." He stretched out beside her, still holding her, caressing her. "And a wonder for my ego," he added, chuckling.

"You don't have to say those things," Ashley said, ignoring his teasing. She wanted things kept straight between them. It was bad enough she'd climaxed so quickly.

"You're right. I don't. I call it like I see it." He rested his hand under her breast, cupping its light fullness, rubbing his thumb over her responsive nipple. "Now, in your own words. No talking." His hand left her breast. She tackled his zipper, and this time he did nothing to discourage her.

A remnant of her pride was restored when she discovered how hard and heavy he was. But it was no match for the renewed desire that commandeered her wits.

They both shook free of their remaining clothes and lay face-to-face, their bodies inches apart. Parker twirled a long strand of her hair around his finger until he came upon her breast. He traced a light finger around her nipple as if memorizing the texture. Ashley felt the heat beginning to pool again, and partly out of shock, partly in self-defense, she fastened her hand around the length of him. She had the satisfaction of hearing him take a quick and unsteady breath.

With tentative strokes, she worked her own brand of magic. He whispered her name, mixed with endearments. His kisses faltered, his chest heaved. He grabbed her hand to stop her.

"I wanted to take it slow." His voice was hoarse and gravelly. "But you'll have it your way." He rolled toward her, pinned her hand under his until she was flat on her back.

Startled by his sudden move, Ashley's immediate response was to bring her thighs together. Gently, Parker parted them. He knelt before her, fully aroused, his tawny hair sexily disarrayed, a slight tremble in the hand that touched her cheek. "Heaven help me, Ash, but something's happening that shouldn't be."

He bowed down and kissed her with renewed tenderness, then filled her with his explosive desire.

Ashley gripped the sheets. His breathing was hard and heavy, hers nonexistent. She moved her hands to his sweat-slickened shoulders and rode the wave that threatened to wash away every principle in her body.

He murmured her name into her hair, kissed the damp tendrils at her neck. And when she thought she could stand no more, the impossible happened and fireworks once again graced her night.

IT WAS DRIZZLING AGAIN. Or maybe it had rained all night and Ashley simply hadn't noticed. She gazed out through slitted eyes at the ill-fated attempt of dawn's hues slanting in through the partially opened drapes.

She knew where she was, but something felt different. She propped herself up on one elbow, glanced down and quickly pulled the sheet up over her bare breasts. With a furtive glance over her shoulder, she eyed the bare spot next to her. Parker was gone.

A loud sigh left her lips as she sank back into the pillows and stared at the ceiling. She didn't know if she should be happy or disappointed. Then she remembered how gentle he'd been while the pulse had raced wildly at his neck and his fingers shook with restraint. He had been a far better lover than she could have imagined...or maybe it was because she was in love with him.

Ashley sighed again. It didn't matter. There were no promises, no guarantees. There'd only be the memory...and one big mess called Magic Island.

Ashley had had every intention of calling Manuel Gomes the night before to explain her absence, and to find out what had transpired at the meeting. Other priorities, however, had prevented the call.

But now, alone, with reality cooling the sheets beside her, Ashley knew she had to make some decisions about her stand with the committee. And it was time to explain her role to Parker.

The thought sent a shiver clear down to her toes.

And then she pictured his understanding blue eyes, replayed the sweet endearments he'd whispered in the dark, and she stretched like a contented cat. The warm feeling of being sheltered in his arms lingered in every unfamiliar ache in her body.

Ashley swung her feet to the thick carpeting and headed for a much-needed warm bath. The previous night had been her choice and she was certainly prepared to live with that. It bothered her, though, remembering his words. Something was happening that shouldn't be. Was he already having regrets? She turned on the water to full power and prayed it would wash away any trace of doubt.

PARKER HEARD THE WATER draining from the tub as he entered the room and set the tray of food on the bed. He plucked the red rose from the vase he'd set on the night-stand, closed his eyes and inhaled its scent.

Funny, he'd never thought roses were especially fragrant before, but this one…well, it was perfect. He replaced it in the vase, careful to face it toward Ashley's pillow, where he hoped to have her lying before long.

What was keeping her? It would be a shame if she were spending any time fixing her hair. He expected it would be for nothing. He smiled at the thought and rubbed his stubbly chin. This would have to go. He'd shave while she ate. He hadn't wanted to wake her, so he'd showered in the parlor bathroom earlier, but he hadn't had the foresight to take a razor. This morning had to be perfect. Ashley deserved it.

"Parker?" Ashley peeked out from a crack in the door. Her face was freshly scrubbed…and glowing. He hoped he had something to do with that.

"There better not be any other strange men in the room," he growled playfully and shot a hand through the door opening, grabbed her wrist and pulled her to him.

She wore a short red silk kimono which she automatically tugged at. Her hazel eyes wary, she settled against his chest, head tilted back. He tightened his arms around her.

He kissed the tip of her nose and then paid a swift tribute to her lips. "Good morning."

"Good morning back." Her smile was shy and endearing. Then she sniffed the air. "Do I smell food?"

"Thrown over for scrambled eggs." Parker cast a woebegone look to the ceiling. Grinning, he cinched the belt to his robe, then gently pushed her toward the bed.

"Where did that come from?" Ashley's eyes widened. Bacon, buttered toast, fluffy yellow eggs, steaming coffee all awaited her.

"The love fairy. He wants to keep your strength up."

"Parker." She laughed. Lashes fluttering, she looked away.

It was amazing that she could still blush after all they'd

shared the previous night. His gaze traveled the black silk-iness of her long hair to the smooth, tanned skin of her thighs. All that and a heart as big as the moon. He felt a stirring of desire that could very well cancel their breakfast.

"Eat," he ordered, and urged her to the bed, setting the tray across her lap. He sat beside her and helped himself to a strip of bacon. Munching on it, he watched her dip into the eggs. "Do you like your bacon crisp?"

"What?" Ashley laughed.

"Maybe I shouldn't have ordered your toast buttered." He pursed his lips. "It's strange. Sometimes I feel I've known you forever. But I have a lot to learn about you, don't I?"

Ashley picked up her coffee cup and swiped at her hair. He didn't like the caution he saw in her eyes as they tried to avoid his. He reached out and grabbed the small bare foot she'd tucked under her leg. "Like are you ticklish?"

"Knock it off, Parker." Ashley gulped down her coffee and let out a half giggle. "I'm warning you..."

"Or what?" He kept a firm grasp of her ankle and ran a light finger across her instep. Giggling, she discarded her cup and clutched at his arm, but only managed to lose the kimono halfway down her shoulder.

"Ah, good idea." Grinning, he removed the tray and set it on the nightstand.

"What?" Ashley inched to the other side, tugging up her sleeve, anticipation curving her lips.

Parker was quick. He yanked the sash of her kimono. It fell open. His own robe slid to the floor. He stood before her, naked and fully aroused.

Ashley did only a fair job of hiding a large gulp that made his heart smile. There wasn't any wariness or doubt on her face now, and he certainly aimed to keep it that way. He allowed himself a few more seconds of feasting on her beautiful face, then crawled along the bed until he reached her bare thighs.

"Honey, I had every intention of shaving first." He

kissed her calf, then dragged his lower lip up past the inside of her knees. His tongue took over the search.

"I truly did," he murmured, and heard her gasp as he reached his satiny destination.

"THAT WAS FANTASTIC." Ashley's chest heaved with exhilaration and she gasped for the breath that had been knocked out of her.

"It's also illegal." Parker pointed to the No-Trespassing sign nailed to a huge mango tree and grinned. "Want to go again?"

Ashley frowned at the sign. "Should we?"

"Sure. They need to cover their butts so we won't sue them. Besides, it's the high school kids they probably worry about most." Parker took her hand and led her back up the jungly mountain path.

"High school kids?"

Parker stopped and looked at her. "Didn't you ever cut class to go fluming?"

"Cut class?" Smiling, she lifted her chin and a brow.

"Oh, I forgot. You were probably too busy saving the world," Parker teased, but when her expression tightened, he grabbed her hand. "Hey, Ash. I wasn't being critical." He slipped his arms around her and hugged her to him. "I admire what you do, your dedication, your plans for the community center. I admire *you*."

Ashley managed to accept the swift kiss he gave her without cringing. Why did he have to bring up the community center? The secret phone calls to various Magic Island lobbyists she'd had to make over the past five days had been bad enough. She pushed up on tiptoe and returned his kiss. "Tell me about your rebellious fluming days."

"Rainy days were the best. With the surge of water, we really did some flying. Although at times, it could be dangerous."

"I'm surprised you didn't get your fannies thrown in jail."

Parker threw his head back and laughed. "We did. Well, we got arrested a few times anyway. But the plantation owners never pressed charges. And we always managed to sneak back." He shrugged, a broad smile firmly in place. "We figured that since the flumes weren't needed for irrigation anymore, they needed to be put to good use."

"How thoughtful of you." Ashley plucked a nearby wild ginger blossom and tickled his nose with the soft petals.

"Wasn't it?" He made a grab for her, but she managed to dodge him.

"I'll race you to the top."

"Hey, no fair." He swatted at some overgrown ferns and scrambled after her. "The path isn't wide enough."

"Don't be a quitter, Parker." Ashley laughed over her shoulder, then leapt over some fallen bamboo.

She made it up the steep path another six yards before she realized that the only response she'd gotten was the rush of a nearby waterfall. She clutched the fronds of a coconut tree for balance and turned to him.

He hadn't followed her, but stood motionless, a peculiar expression on his face.

Ashley's smile faltered. "Parker? What is it?" She released the frond and stumbled more quickly than she'd intended, back down toward him.

Narrowly escaping bodily injury, Parker caught her in his arms as she came barreling down, the momentum of her speedy descent nearly knocking them both off their feet.

"Hey, lady, I've already fallen for you," Parker joked as he righted them on the path.

She turned in his embrace to face him. The smile he gave her didn't quite reach his eyes. "What's wrong?"

"What's wrong?" He glanced down at her knee. "You just about wiped out the need for birth control."

"You know what I mean." She waited, watching him, knowing that he wanted nothing more than to ignore her probing.

"Nothing, really." He paused, but Ashley remained

stubbornly silent. "It was a seventies kind of flashback, you know," he added in his best surfer accent and grinned.

Ashley didn't buy his sudden nonchalance for a minute. Her brain replayed the past few minutes of their conversation, but she'd only teased him about being a...

"Parker? Did this flashback have anything to do with quitting law school?"

Parker's hands fell away from her. One made it to the back of his neck, the other sliced through the air in a helpless gesture. "What do you know about my going to law school?"

"Not much." She shrugged. "Just that you went but didn't like it."

"Didn't like it," he repeated in somewhat amazement. "Who told you that?"

"Mrs. Lee. Was she wrong?"

"No. She wasn't wrong." Parker laughed. It held no humor. "I didn't like it."

"So?"

"My father liked that fact even less."

Ashley moved closer, circled her arms around him and took over the task of massaging the back of his neck. She slipped her fingers under his and found the knots of tension there. "That doesn't make you a quitter, Parker."

He looked down at her and brushed the pad of his thumb across her cheek. His eyes crinkled at the corners. "I know," he whispered.

And Ashley wished she could believe him.

"I WISH THIS WEEK HAD never ended." Ashley zipped up her toiletry bag and stuffed it into her carryon.

"It hasn't yet." Parker snuck up behind her, grabbed her around the waist and tumbled them both to the bed.

"If we don't want to miss the plane, it has." Ashley laughed and pushed his long hair away from his eyes. His face was more tanned than usual from all the outside activities they'd been treated to, which made his eyes seem even bluer.

"What plane?"

"Parker..." Ashley tried to sound admonishing, but the giggle blew it. "You know we have to go back."

He sighed. Ashley did, too. She didn't want to go back any more than he did, but if she didn't she wouldn't be surprised to find the whole Magic Island committee on her hotel-suite doorstep. Talk about the natives getting restless. Only after she'd threatened to pull out altogether had they finally quit phoning her at the hotel. She'd had a couple of near misses as a result. And although that had been handled on her second day here, when the phone rang it still made her jump.

It also made her acutely aware that the time had come to be totally honest with Parker. The mere thought sent the usual shiver down her spine.

"Do you want the air conditioner turned off?" Parker asked.

Ashley blinked. "No. I'm fine." She rolled away from him, rubbing her bare arms. She had to tell him. Today. When they returned to Oahu. The longer she took, the harder it was going to be. Oh, God, it was already hard.

She lined up her bags and reached for her hat.

"If I didn't know any better, I'd think you were anxious to get away from me," Parker commented with a puzzled look on his face.

"I need rest," Ashley joked.

"And you think you'll get it once we get home?"

"I have a feeling I might," she mumbled, and hurried to the phone as it sounded its first ring. It's not that she thought anyone from the committee would be stupid enough to still try her here, but...

As soon as the front-desk clerk identified himself, Ashley's breathing eased. "Your limo will be here in fifteen minutes, Mrs. James. I'll send someone up for your luggage. Is there anything else we can do for you?"

"Nothing. We've had a marvelous time." She looked up at Parker, who was about to answer a knock at the door, and returned his knowing smile. "And I believe the bellman's already here."

"Oh, yeah," the young man rushed on. "Someone left a message for you. They wouldn't leave it over the phone, said you wouldn't want that, but they left an envelope instead."

Ashley bit back the indelicate word that came to mind and immediately focused on Parker. His back was to her as he carried on his muted conversation with their visitor. "I'll be right down for it."

"That's not necessary," the clerk assured her. "I've already sent someone up with it. He should be there—"

Ashley replaced the receiver, unsure as to whether she'd thanked the young man or not. She paced a couple of steps toward Parker and watched his back stiffen as he closed the door.

He pivoted toward her, an envelope in one hand, an unfolded sheet of paper in the other.

He looked up, his jaw twitching.

"Congratulations," he said, blandly. "The state accepted your bid."

Chapter Fourteen

Parker shoved the last of the luggage into their closet and slammed the door in the middle of Ashley's protest that they needed to be unpacked.

"Not this time, Ashley Leialoha." He took several menacing steps in her direction. "We are not skirting the issue. Now tell me what the hell you have to do with those Magic Island idiots."

Ashley took a casual turn around the bed and dropped her watch on the nightstand.

"And Judas Priest, *don't* tell me your approved bid for the airstrip has anything to do with our homestead land."

She swiped at her hair and Parker knew for certain. He knew whatever she had to say, he didn't want to hear.

"Tell me, Ashley. Tell me everything."

She took a huge breath. "Make up your mind," she muttered and tried to sidestep him.

He blocked her exit. "What do you have to do with all this, Ash?"

She looked up at him, her eyes bright with green specks. "Do I know everything there is to know about your resort project?"

"Anything pertinent to you. And, hell, anything you choose to know. I don't keep secrets from you."

Ashley flinched. "Is your implication that I've been lying to you?"

Parker studied her silently for a moment. "I don't even know what to imply. I just want to know what's going on." He let out a chest full of pent-up air and reached for her. "Look, sweetheart, if Crystal has involved you—"

"No. Please." Ashley shook her head and put out a restraining palm. "You're right. I need to tell you everything. And, no, Crystal has nothing to do with this. In fact, she tried to talk me out of it."

She sat at the edge of the bed, twisting her wedding ring. Parker sat beside her and put his hand over hers. "Talk to me. It can't be that bad."

"Wanna bet?" She raised her reluctant gaze to his. "Parker, at this point, I practically *am* Magic Island."

He felt his mouth go dry. "I don't get it."

"If you'll only listen to all the advantages of diverting tourists to a single island—"

"What do you mean you *are* Magic Island?" he demanded in a low, even tone as his gut twisted in anticipation.

"When I came up with the service center and airstrip idea…" She lifted a sagging shoulder. "Everyone got excited about it all over again."

Recognition dawned and Parker slowly nodded his head. "That's why there was a sudden resurgence of the committee." He had wondered why the recently renewed interest. One mystery solved. He narrowed his gaze. "Service center?"

"Yes. To accommodate the airstrip."

"This is like pulling teeth, Ash."

She sighed. "I've proposed to both the committee and the state that I could provide a tourist center for translation services, information, money exchange, you name it. And, of course, the airstrip would be used for shuttling the people over. That strip of homestead land is the perfect location." Her gaze roamed his face as her mouth tensed, waiting for his rebuttal, waiting to deliver her protest.

Parker sat quietly, his expression carefully bland, trying

to organize his thoughts, regain his composure. He met her expectant gaze and something in her guileless eyes pierced his cynicism.

Maybe she had no protest, maybe she'd finally realized that it wasn't going to work, maybe she was sorry for having gotten involved in the first place.

He patted her hand and half smiled. "You realize, don't you, that there isn't enough land for a service center, an airstrip and a community center."

Ashley nodded sadly and took a deep breath. She lowered her lashes for a moment before looking him straight in the eyes. "There is no community center."

Parker blinked. "No community center. But you…" He dropped her hand. "You lied to me?"

"I never did that."

"The hell you—"

"Technically, the service center could be considered a community center, because it will be manned—"

"That's a bunch of crap and you know it."

"You didn't let me finish," Ashley pointed out, her eyes gathering storm clouds in its depths.

Parker slowly, painfully rose from the bed and put some distance between them. "Trust me, Ashley," he said through clenched teeth. "You are finished."

CHEERFULLY HUMMING Rock-a-bye Baby, Napua Lee meandered down the hall with a tray of freshly cut pineapple and two mineral waters. Life was good, she decided, on this fine Sunday afternoon. Her two wards had returned and by now, well… She smiled and continued humming.

Napua reached Parker and Ashley's room, balanced the tray on one hand and raised her fist to the door. Before her knuckles made contact with the wood, she froze. The smile fell from her lips. Her eyes grew saucerlike.

Voices rose and fell from the room beyond. They weren't distinct voices, but Napua knew they were angry ones. Her heart heavy, she yanked a linen napkin off the wobbly tray and pressed it to her flushed cheek. "Dear Lord," she whispered. "What are we going to do now?"

"WHAT DO YOU THINK you're doing?" Harvey Winton stood at the entrance of Keoki King's hospital room with a wary look on his face.

"Unpacking." Keoki gave him a disgusted look, then grimaced at the clothes he had only an hour ago deposited in his bag.

"You're supposed to be going home today." Harvey adjusted his shirt cuffs. A nervous habit Keoki knew well. "I'm supposed to be picking you up. Remember?"

"Things have changed." He glanced back up. "Lose the poker face, my friend, we have new plans to make."

"Keoki…" Harvey drawled in warning.

"I know Karen has called you. Do not pretend she has not." Keoki pulled two wadded-up aloha shirts out of the duffel bag. "Crystal has called me. Mrs. Lee has called *everybody.*" He shook his graying head and sank down next to the bag. "What do you think they are fighting about *now?*"

"I don't know. And I don't care. *You* shouldn't care. We did what we set out to do. We got them together. Now, old man, we back off."

Keoki slanted him a menacing look. "Who are you calling old? At least I remember what love is about. I say we up the ante."

"And I say you're out of your mind." Harvey strode over, picked up the discarded shirts and stuffed them back into the duffel. "If you aren't planning on going home like you're supposed to, I'll be happy to drop you off at the psychiatric ward instead."

Keoki absently watched his friend repack his bag. "We'll have to come up with something else. Something that will make them see how far they've come."

"No, Keoki." Harvey snatched the shaving kit from the bathroom sink and threw it in with the shirts.

Pensively, Keoki pulled out a cigar and bit off the end. "Do you think it could be true about the baby?"

"Baby?" Harvey dropped the bag altogether. Obviously this was the first he'd heard of the rumor.

Keoki chuckled. "Karen didn't tell you." Enormously pleased with the dumbstruck look on his friend's face, Keoki lit his cigar.

"They're not having a baby?"

"Maybe this is a good thing. We could revise the contract, make provisions for an heir. That would give them all the more reason to stay together." Keoki lazily blew a smoke ring toward the ceiling, contemplating their best avenue in securing the newlyweds' relationship. He doubted the validity of the baby—Mrs. Lee had been near incoherent when she had called both him and Crystal. Still, it was something to consider.

"I have it." Keoki stubbed out his cigar, his black eyes wildly excited. "We will tell them a mistake has been made, that the land is not homestead land."

"How do you know there's going to be a baby?" Harvey ignored Keoki's blossoming plan and calmly took the nearest chair, staring at him the entire time.

"We will tell them that the land is actually privately owned. And…" Keoki paced to the window, his fingers to his temple. "And that the owner will agree to lease them the land, if they can provide an heir of Hawaiian ancestry. That's it." A slow grin blossomed on Keoki's face as he ignored the other man's gaping disbelief. "Of course the owner will remain anonymous."

"You *aren't* serious." The very proper Harvey pushed his hand through his hair with such force that the gray strands poked comically out of place. "That's the most absurd thing you've come up with yet."

"You have a better idea," Keoki snapped, then put a soothing hand to his belly.

"Yes. Let things be." His friend enunciated each word with purpose, then ran a skeptical gaze over Keoki's pitiful expression and down to his fraudulent middle. "And save your antics for your daughter. It doesn't work with me."

Keoki shrugged and removed his hand. "Crystal still does not need to know anything—"

"You really don't get it, do you?" Harvey shook his head. "We knew they'd eventually find out about our…our plan, but if you think for one minute Parker will believe…"

Keoki had patiently resumed emptying his duffel bag, waiting, as the inevitable dawned on Harvey. When the look of grudging relief softened his friend's features, Keoki smiled.

It was almost over. Harvey understood that now. Parker and Ashley would never fall for this newest scheme. How they reacted to it, however, would be the biggest gamble of all.

Keoki knew that, too. But he also knew his daughter. And he knew for a fact that she would get to the bottom of this. Even if it meant conspiring with the enemy.

Whistling, Keoki dumped out the last of the bag's contents. "It is a glorious day after all, is it not, my friend?"

ASHLEY DROPPED HER PURSE on a chair in the corner of Harvey's office and motioned through the glass window to Crystal who had just stepped off the elevator. "Do you know what this is all about?" she asked her friend before Crystal could get through the door.

Crystal shook her newly tinted auburn head. "Harvey mentioned something about unexpected revisions to the contract. Doesn't Parker know anything?"

Ashley felt the starch creep up her spine. Her lips thinned. "That insufferable, self-absorbed jerk wouldn't know his butt from a—"

"So, things really are that bad." Crystal pulled a long face, then quickly lowered her head to flip open her briefcase when Ashley gave her a quizzical frown.

"He knows about Magic Island and my role in it," she said, wondering at the rather odd observation Crystal had made. The previous time they'd spoken, she and Parker had been getting along well...very well...too well. Ashley sighed.

"How?" Crystal peered at her over the top of the open briefcase.

"I told him." Ashley passed a hand over her cheek and felt the heat there. "I didn't have much of a choice."

"And he gave you a rough time." Crystal nodded sympathetically. "Is that why you don't look so good?"

"I stayed at my apartment last night. I didn't get much sleep, though," Ashley admitted and let her hand drift down to rest against the butterflies in her stomach. First the horrible scene with Parker and now this secret emergency meeting. "So I haven't been totally with it this morning."

Crystal's wary gaze followed the descent of Ashley's hand. Gradually, her eyes widened as Ashley applied pressure to the havoc being wreaked by her morning coffee. Crystal opened her mouth to speak, but nothing came out.

"They're here," Ashley warned. "I'll fill you in later." She took the seat on the other side of Crystal, as far away from Parker as she could get.

He'd told her he was going to fight her every step of the way on Magic Island. And she believed him. She was prepared to do the same. Unfortunately, it didn't mean her disloyal body would be a willing ally. She clasped her hands together, kept her focus straight ahead and waited for the two men to take their seats.

She was surprised to see that Parker wasn't wearing a suit today. From what she could tell out of the corner of her eye, he had on a rather rumpled sport coat and...jeans?

Casually, she turned her head a few degrees his way. His eyes immediately found hers. They were just as blue, just as compelling as she'd always found them to be. But tired lines fanned out more deeply than usual at their sides. He gave her a sad crooked smile.

"Good morning, Ashley, Crystal." Harvey nodded to

them, unlocked his desk and pulled out a folder. "I know you're anxious to find out what this is all about."

"Yes, we are," Parker stated in an impatient tone.

Ashley and Crystal exchanged quick glances. Not even Parker knew what this was about? Ashley scooted back in her chair and leaned forward a bit, listening intently for what Harvey was about to say.

"There seems to have been a misunderstanding." Harvey adjusted first one cuff, then the other. Parker slid Ashley a brief sideways glance. "About the homestead land, we have a slight problem." Harvey cleared his throat twice. "It appears it isn't governed by the homestead act after all."

"Appears?" Parker shouted. "Appears? What exactly *is* the status, Harvey?"

"It's privately owned. Your current contract is void."

Ashley felt the first arrow of realization reach its target and her heart sank like a lead canoe. The land wasn't theirs. She looked over at Parker, who sat in stunned denial, a faint red surging up his neck.

"This isn't like you, Harvey. What the hell went wrong?" Parker finally asked in a controlled voice, and Ashley had to admire his regained composure. If it weren't for the tick at his jaw or the low rumbling of his voice, no one would know how upset he was. And if that same low, rumbling voice didn't remind her of intimate whispers on a moonlit night, maybe she would be more concerned about the future of Magic Island. Instead, the fact that there might no longer be a reason to stay together weighed heavy on her heart.

"I don't want to get into that now," Harvey replied. "I think we need to spend the time reviewing our options. You see, there's still a chance of keeping the land."

Ashley held her breath and darted a look at Parker. He sent her an expressionless one back. Crystal, speechless for one of the few times in her life, threw up her hands.

Harvey took a large gulp from a mug of cold coffee,

then stated, "If you will earnestly promise to provide an heir."

Parker let out an irreverent word, and Crystal added a far more colorful one. But for the next two hours Ashley watched, listened and said very little as Harvey outlined the new conditions and fielded questions. Parker also became increasingly quiet, and by the time they all agreed to call it quits for the day, the contract remained unsigned.

Crystal said she had a client to meet and was gone in a flash. Harvey suddenly had to leave for a luncheon meeting. Another meeting was scheduled for the next day.

Ashley folded up the scant notes she'd taken and deposited them in her purse. Parker had risen and stood near the door, watching the lunch crowd head for the elevators, his hands stuffed deep in his pockets. The fit of his jeans was snug enough, and the action caused the worn denim to enticingly caress his taut rear end.

Ashley felt the first surge of residual anger. How dare he have criticized her for such a lamebrained scheme only yesterday and still look so damn good today. She jammed her pen and notebook into her purse.

"I don't buy this," Parker said quietly, continuing to look out the door. "But I can't figure it out either."

Ashley hitched the strap of her pocketbook up on her shoulder and drew her brows together. "Did Harvey seem strange to you?"

"Strange?" He turned and gestured to the air. "That man hasn't been so disconcerted since he had to be potty trained."

Ashley chuckled and Parker gave her a small, tired grin. "What kind of lunatic would come up with a crazy plan like this anyway? No wonder the owner wants to remain anonymous." He shook his head. "Something's amiss, all right. But I'll be damned if I know what."

"You know, Crystal's been acting sort of strange, too." Her purse slid back down her arm. She dropped it to the chair and paced to the window.

"How so?"

"Nothing I can really pinpoint...." She sighed, a long, tired sigh. "And then again, it may be my imagination."

Parker picked up his copy of the contract off Harvey's desk. "Maybe not." He scanned the pages for a moment and asked, "Does Kinwin Corporation sound familiar to you?"

"No. I don't think so." Ashley tapped her finger on the windowsill.

"It does to me." He frowned in concentration. "But it doesn't make sense. The guy wants to remain anonymous, yet allows this company name to appear on the contract...."

Ashley bit her lip. "What do you want to do, Parker?"

He looked up. "Get to the bottom of this."

"And in the meantime?" she asked slowly.

"You're not suggesting we sign the contract?" He dropped his hand to his side. The sheet of paper fell to the floor.

Ashley crossed her arms over her chest. "We both need the land."

Parker ran an insolent gaze over her. "And you're ready to make a baby for it."

"Why, you..." She felt the heat erupt to her face. "No, Parker, that's not what I meant. But you don't want to believe that, do you?"

"Ashley, I'm sorry." He moved forward and put a hand out to her. "I really didn't—"

She stepped back. He hadn't forgiven her for her deception regarding the community center. And he never would. She knew that now. "I'm not apologizing for wanting or needing the security that service center would provide me and my father. I know you can't understand that...."

"You're wrong—"

"Am I, Parker?" Her laugh was humorless. "Your father should be damn proud of you. Karen's right, you're just like him." His expression pinched in aggrieved confusion and she knew she'd be sorry for her hasty words. But he'd hurt her, and Ashley's need to strike back overwhelmed her.

"You pigeonholed me, Parker. You put me up on some damn pedestal." She gestured high in the air. "*Your* pedestal. And when I stepped down, you couldn't take it." She raised her chin, holding back a sniffle. "Sorry I didn't meet your expectations."

Parker took a deep breath. "Ashley, you're—"

She stopped him with a raised hand and reclaimed her purse, along with her copy of the contract. "We need some space, Parker." Sudden tears burned the back of her eyes when she realized the stark truth of that statement, and she hurried to the door. "We'll talk later, try to figure out what this new deal is all about."

Parker watched her go. She didn't bother waiting for the elevator, but took the stairs instead. It was ten flights down. He picked up the legal papers he'd dropped earlier, rolled them up and smacked the inside of his hand with them.

So, they were back to business...back to square one. She'd be willing to talk to him all right, to talk about securing the land.

Well, hell, he didn't care about the land anymore. Had quit caring about it almost a month ago. About the time he had fallen in love with Ashley. About the time that what she'd just accused him of would have been accurate.

But now, today, Ashley had been wrong. That burden was no longer Parker's to carry. For the first time in his life, he knew that he'd truly let it go. Parker no longer needed his father's approval.

Just as Ashley didn't need his.

Parker smiled at the mere thought of Ashley needing anyone's approval. He'd learned a lot from her. He'd even learned that he was worthy of her love.

What she *did* need, however, was a wake-up call.

She didn't need the damn contract, didn't need Magic Island or the land for security. Didn't she realize that? She already had all the money and security she needed, for as long as she wanted it.

Parker leaned his arm up along the window frame and rested his forehead against the back of his hand. Or maybe she did realize it. Maybe she simply didn't want what he had to offer. Or maybe…maybe she didn't want him.

He drew in a large, shaky breath. That wasn't true, he admonished himself, this was his insecurity talking. She was stalwart, proud. She didn't want anything handed to her. He understood that. Like himself, she worked for what she got. He still didn't agree with her manipulation of the community-center situation, but he respected her determination and independence—two of her many qualities he'd grown to love.

He smiled to himself again. Her stubbornness he could probably do without, but it was a small obstacle. Because deep down, he knew she loved him, and he was about to prove it.

Chapter Fifteen

"This better be good, Parker," Ashley said as she opened the door to her apartment. She hadn't seen or spoken to him since that awful day in Harvey's office, and she hoped she didn't look as nervous and wretched as she felt.

"Define the word good." He pushed a large legal folder into her hands and went straight to the kitchen. He had the most unusual smirk on his face when he returned with two beers.

"Help yourself," Ashley murmured, eyeing the cans. She couldn't help that touch of sarcasm even though she was immensely relieved at his easygoing manner—as if nothing had happened, as if she hadn't said those ugly words.

He handed one to her on his way to the living room. "You might want this."

She accepted it and their unspoken truce, and joined him on the couch. She'd barely read halfway down the page when she let it slip from her hand and looked up into Parker's I-told-you-so expression. He gave her a wry smile and took a large gulp of beer.

She took one of her own. "I don't believe it."

"Believe it. I checked and rechecked because I had trouble with it myself."

Ashley picked the paper back up. "Kinwin stands for King/Winton, doesn't it?"

"You got it. Now, what are we going to do about it? That's the question." Parker sprawled back on the couch and Ashley had the irrational urge to smack him. He might not be the guilty party, but he looked so relaxed over it and here she was ready to scream. Of course, she admitted, he'd had time to digest this information. Plenty of time, in fact—it had taken a whole week to hear from him.

She counted silently to ten, then asked, "How did you find this out?"

"That's the damn thing about it. It wasn't that difficult."

"Then why has it been a week?" she blurted out and felt the heat reach clear to her hairline.

Parker grinned and straightened. "Did you miss me?"

"Hardly." She left the couch to prowl the room. "Wait until I get my hands on that conniving old son of a gun...." Ashley suddenly spun on Parker. "And if you make one crack about it running in the family, so help me—"

He held up his hands. "Didn't even cross my mind." He gave her a large grin. "Especially since we're going to be allies again."

She lifted her chin and spent a few seconds relishing the sensation of looking down on him before her curiosity got the better of her. "How so?"

"Well, I'm pretty ticked at Harvey, myself," he said, an odd tilt at the corners of his mouth. "And I figure you may have a score to settle with your father, as well."

"No doubt about that."

"And the way I see it, two heads are better than one."

Ashley brought a finger to her lips. "Maybe," she admitted, mulling over the possibilities.

When the phone rang, she automatically jumped for it. She glanced at Parker. His old guarded expression went into place for an instant, and then they both laughed. It felt good.

Her conversation with Crystal was brief, and when she returned to the living room she was surprised to find Parker with the television on, indifferently flipping through channels. Once again she was struck with the feeling that he wasn't nearly as upset as he might be, as she surely was.

He muted the volume and looked up as she approached. His eyes were clear and blue and filled with something so soft and tender it made her insides go all mushy.

"Well, are you in?" he asked.

"Hmm?" She sank down near him, brought both legs up and rested her chin on her knees. "Do you think anyone else was in on this scheme?"

Parker frowned and glanced heavenward. "I hadn't thought about it." He started to shake his head slowly. "Mrs. Lee may seem culpable, but I know her well enough to know she couldn't keep her mouth shut that long." He blinked. "But she did act rather strangely... Nah, she's just nosy...I think."

"And Karen?"

Parker lifted an uncertain shoulder, a suspicious glint in his eye. "What about Crystal?"

Ashley wrinkled her nose. "She, of all people, should have known better, but she's said some odd things lately—"

"It's a damn conspiracy." Parker slammed his can down and beer sloshed over his hand.

"We don't know that." Ashley watched him lick the liquid from his fingers and unconsciously ran her own tongue over her lips. Parker's gaze snagged on the action.

"Well," he slowly raised his reluctant gaze to her eyes.

"Well," she echoed and put her feet to the floor. "What are we going to do about it?"

"Get even."

"I like your thinking." A lazy smile stretched across her face and she stuck her hand out. "Partner?"

"No kiss?"

She moistened her lips once again and rubbed her palm up her thigh. "Parker...we...I..." She left the couch and put a chair between them. After this was over, there would be no more us, no more we...and she didn't want things to be any more difficult than they already were between them. "Why do you think they did it?"

Parker gave her a long, measuring look. "Maybe," he said, his eyes suddenly looking very tired, "they saw something we didn't."

"I SIMPLY CAN'T FIGURE out what's wrong." Ashley laid a hand on her stomach, put on her best woe-is-me face and peeked out from lowered lashes at her friend. "This is the third day this week I've felt queasy. Have you heard if the flu is going around?"

Crystal visibly swallowed. "Not that I'm aware of." Her glance flittered from Ashley's face to her stomach and back again. "Maybe you should go to the doctor."

"I'm sure it's nothing. Now, where were we?" Ashley leaned over Crystal's desk and did all she could to keep from laughing.

"Are you sure you want to sign this contract?" Crystal asked, her fluorescent orange-tipped finger tapping the sheet between them. "It sounds so…so permanent."

Ashley laughed. A light, tinkling laugh. No easy feat, since she was actually ready to bust something. She couldn't wait to tell Parker. "That's silly. It only requires that we promise to try for an heir. Besides, Parker and I are getting along fabulously."

"Then why aren't you living in the same house?" Crystal squinted at her friend.

Even though it was an obvious and expected question, it stopped Ashley for a moment. "Because I'm trying to sort out my stuff. After the party on Magic Island this weekend, everything will be settled. You'll see."

"Magic Island? A little premature, don't you think? The last I heard, they still call it Kahoolawe."

Ashley shrugged daintily and tried to look glowing.

"And that's another thing. Why are you two having it there, anyway? I know Parker couldn't have given in on that issue yet."

"No," Ashley answered more truthfully than her friend would ever know. "Let's just call it symbolic, but I can't tell you any more or it will spoil the surprise."

Crystal picked up a pencil and drummed it on the desk. "There isn't something you should be telling me, is there?"

Ashley flashed all hazel innocence. "Why, no. Is there something you need to tell me?"

Crystal's response was an impatient sigh, then she busied herself with the contract, making notes in the margins, mumbling to herself.

Ashley leaned back and smiled. This was their second such meeting since Ashley and Parker had devised their plan. Her father had been her target the day before, just as Karen had been Parker's.

"Well," Ashley said a half hour later. "I really feel like a nap." She stretched out her arms and yawned for good measure. "Let's meet one last time before the party on Saturday, shall we?"

Ashley hurried out of the office, leaving Crystal with a puzzled frown and reaching for the phone as soon as Ashley had cleared the corner.

When Ashley pulled up to her apartment complex, she was delighted to see Parker's car already there.

"How'd it go today?" she asked as soon as she came through the door.

Parker had been coming from the hall and stopped dead in his tracks. "You wore that to see Crystal?"

She looked down at the long oversize muumuu and grinned.

He burst out laughing. "I wish I could have seen her face."

Ashley puffed out her flat stomach as far as she could and patted it. "Is that anyway to treat your brainchild?"

Parker continued laughing, hooked his arm around her waist and swung her around.

Laughing along with him, Ashley laid her hands on his

chest and fought to catch her breath. She looked up into his smiling blue eyes and nearly lost the battle for oxygen. She pushed at him and slowly he let her slide to the floor.

"How did it go with Mrs. Lee?" She straightened the ridiculously large floral tent around her small frame.

"It was priceless. When I told her that I wanted one of the guest rooms redone in blue and another in pink, I thought she was going to pop her girdle."

"Parker," Ashley admonished but couldn't keep a straight face as she made her way to the kitchen. "What does she think the party is about?"

"She hasn't a clue. I told her the same thing we've told everyone else. Only that we have an announcement to make." He followed her, rubbing his palms together. "The only thing that could possibly go better is if I invite the new decorator to the party." He stroked his chin. "In fact, maybe I will."

"What new decorator?" Ashley ducked her head in the refrigerator and pulled out the makings for a salad. Ironically, during the past week, she and Parker had settled into a comfortable routine of meeting at the end of the day, reviewing the day's strategy and then sharing dinner.

Ashley bumped the refrigerator door closed with her hip. She was going to miss these evenings, she acknowledged, more than she cared to admit. But all that would come to an end after the party Saturday night…the party to announce their pending divorce. Her gaze found Parker's intense one and she swallowed. "The decorator?" she reminded him.

"Oh, yeah. Raquel."

She laughed. "Raquel?"

"Yup. Straight out of the Yellow Pages. Who would have thought she'd be made to order." Parker reached around her and snitched a baby carrot. "Met her for lunch yesterday and today. I'm sure tongues are wagging as we speak."

"Why?" Ashley swept a deceptively casual hand through her hair.

"Tall redhead, legs that won't quit." Parker made a clicking sound with his tongue Ashley had never heard him make before. Then he had the absolute nerve to wink. "Nice touch, don't you think?"

She shot a furtive glance down to her own short legs, wildly camouflaged by the monstrosity of a muumuu. No, as a matter of fact, she didn't think so at all.

"Right," she said and rammed the bag of carrots into his hands. "Glad you had such a great lunch. Dinner is canceled."

ASHLEY WAITED AT THE pier, arms crossed, foot tapping. Her father puffed on his cigar while he talked to Mrs. Lee, Harvey, Karen, Don and Crystal a few yards away. He had been miraculously discharged from the hospital two days earlier. Ashley couldn't wait to hear how that particular feat had come to pass.

But right now she was more interested in why the yacht she and Parker had hired stood waiting, along with everyone else, while her soon to be ex-husband was five minutes late. Picking up Legs, no doubt.

Ashley changed feet and resumed tapping furiously. She was far angrier with herself than Parker, for having reacted as she had the previous night. Her only saving grace had been that it seemed he'd been too preoccupied—or stupid—to realize that she'd been jealous.

Jealous. She had actually been jealous. Renewed mortification sent her foot into a frenzy.

Five minutes later, Parker's cherry red Porsche pulled up. And, sure enough, Legs, the decorator, got out...with Parker's eager help.

The woman had at least seven crummy inches on Ashley. And a gorgeous red mane. Probably out of a bottle, Ashley figured and straightened her spine. She tossed her freshly brushed hair back and tried stoutly for a wide smile. She settled for a smirk.

When several pairs of eyes seemed to settle on her as the couple approached, the corners of her mouth forced themselves up.

"Ashley?" Parker guided Legs forward by the small of her back. "This is Raquel Moore."

Just Ashley? Not "this is my wife, Ashley."

"Nice to meet you." Ashley pushed her hair back and looked up into the woman's flawless face. "I'm glad you could make it."

"I wouldn't have missed it." Raquel gave Parker a ongcy wink.

"Everyone ready to get on board?" Parker clasped his hands together, a large grin on his face.

"Have been for the last ten minutes," Ashley called over her shoulder and headed for the yacht.

Their guests were mumbling among themselves as they headed toward the ship's plank, and Ashley could only imagine what they were saying about Parker's companion. Sighing, she slowed her pace. Her actions surely weren't helping matters either.

When Parker caught up to her, she carefully positioned herself on his side opposite Legs. She smiled when the woman eyed her curiously, then whispered in a hushed voice, "We've come this far, don't you dare blow this now."

He surveyed her with faint amusement. "How and why would I do that?"

Ashley darted a meaningful sidelong glance at Legs, then glared at him.

Parker laughed. "You mean Raquel?" he asked with surprised innocence—loud surprised innocence.

Ashley intensified her glare, then marched ahead of them. As soon as her initial irritation wore off, an undertow of sadness swirled tears to the back of her eyes.

This was it, she acknowledged, as she boarded the yacht.

This was really it. No more pretending, no more wishing. And no more hoping. Because foolishly, for the past week, Ashley had hoped.

"Are you all right?" Mrs. Lee took her arm, glancing down belly level.

"I'm fine." Ashley's fingers flew to the single drop of moisture that seeped from the corner of her eye. If she weren't so miserable, she'd laugh at the housekeeper's dubious preoccupation with her stomach.

And then the sickening thought wormed its way into her overtaxed brain. Oh God, maybe she really was pregnant! Wouldn't that be the crowning touch? She fought back the hysteria rolling around in her stomach.

"She will be fine." Keoki took Mrs. Lee's free arm and blew a stream of cigar smoke up toward the clear blue sky. "You will see."

"Only if you quit smoking." Ashley plucked the smelly stub out of his fingers and flicked it into the water.

Keoki puffed out his chest, his expression combative at first. Then he grinned. "Parker?" he called out over his daughter's shoulder. "I am glad she is all yours now."

Parker had been watching the exchange. He laughed. "Yup," he said, winking at Ashley. "All mine."

Ashley closed her eyes. She wasn't going to make it. She wasn't going to get through the evening. Scheming and plotting this payback all week had been fun, just being with Parker again had been fun. But now, as he continued to joke, as if he had not a care in the world…and her replacement in the wings…her heart began to crumble piece by piece.

She felt the yacht glide away from its slip and she took her father's arm to steady herself. She opened her eyes and found it was her husband's arm she was clutching for dear life.

"Are you okay?" Parker asked, his beautiful eyes shadowed with concern as he ducked his face close to hers.

"Of course," she whispered back. "It's part of my

cover, remember?'' She made an attempt to stick out her tummy and laugh. Only her tummy cooperated.

''Okay.'' Parker breezily accepted her explanation and strode away.

Ashley watched him go. She fumbled with her purse, pulling out a pair of sunglasses and quickly pushing them on. For the rest of the trip, she did her best to mingle with everyone. Either she looked really nauseous or she was doing an exceptional job of playing her part, because she was ready to scream from everyone asking her if she was feeling all right.

As they homed in on their destination, her father found her leaning over the rail, watching the orange sun dip into the horizon.

''Leialoha, I believe we are approaching the wrong side of the island.'' Keoki squinted at the stretch of forsaken brown landscape. Waves slapped its deserted shores, and even the disappointed birds swooped down for only moments before returning to the more bountiful sea.

A gleeful smile sprang to Ashley's lips, but before she could respond Crystal sidled up to her other side.

''I know you're not into decadence….'' Crystal pointedly looked out over the flat, soulless island. ''But what gives?''

Mrs. Lee, Harvey and Don gathered around, also interested in the answer.

Parker strolled up along with Karen and Raquel. ''I get it.'' Karen slipped her arm through Parker's, looking rather relieved. ''The party is actually on the yacht.''

Parker patted her hand. ''Wrong.'' He pulled away and motioned to one of the ship hands to prepare for their arrival. Then he slid Ashley a secret glance and grinned.

Her own lips gladly followed suit. It was easy. Too damned easy. Smiling at Parker, laughing with Parker, sharing his secrets…his bed.

Ashley heard the nervous murmurings and turned to see their guests shooting confused glances at each other. The deckhand had tied a rope to the short pier. Unstable looking as it was, it was the only sign of human existence. She felt the giddy return of delicious revenge and looked back over at Parker.

His head was tilted toward Raquel's, his lips inches from her ear, uttering whispers that only a week earlier had been for Ashley.

She pressed her lips together to keep her weak, traitorous chin from quivering. The end of the story had already been written. That was for certain. The only control Ashley now had was focused on how much dignity she could maintain. She took a deep breath and tried to tell herself that it would be worth it to see the smug smile wiped off her father's face.

The whole affair had begun on a lie and now Ashley was even lying to herself. It wasn't going to be okay at all. She indulged in one last private sniffle, then forced the corners of her mouth up and led the group off the yacht.

"What is going on, Leialoha?" Keoki's thick black brows drew together as he patted his pockets in search of a cigar.

"This place is creepy." Crystal ran her hands up her arms, her gaze surveying the craterlike surface of the burned-out island.

Several others nodded and Ashley moistened her lips to hide the smile that was forming. Her attention was drawn to Parker, as if he'd magically compelled it.

His eyes, darkly intense, registered her every movement. He stuffed his hands deep into his pockets and his shoulders hunched forward slightly as if he were cold. It was at least eighty-five degrees.

Ashley swallowed hard and slowly made her way to his side.

"Well..." She gave him a small shrug. "I guess there's no use waiting."

"No," he agreed and pulled his hands from his pockets. She made an automatic sweep of faces and found Raquel nearby, watching them. Ashley swallowed once more. "I'll, uh…" She let her hand wave through the air. It looked helpless and pathetic, so she straightened and in a stronger voice continued. "I'll get their attention."

"Wait, Ash." Parker put a hand on her arm.

Her gaze flew to his.

"Do you want to announce the divorce, or shall I?"

"I…no. You do it." Ashley swept back her hair, then faced their curious guests with her chin lifted.

And waited. But nothing came from Parker. She looked over at him.

His eyes were dark and stormy as his hand shot out to grasp her arm. He pulled her back far out of earshot, and she would have stumbled if he hadn't anchored both his hands firmly around her upper arms.

"God, Ash. How can you stand there and look so cool about this?" He let go of her and pushed one hand through his hair. She opened her mouth to say something, but he put a finger to her lips.

"I wanted to say something clever, do something earth-shattering. Hell, I don't know." He shook his head. "This isn't going anything like I planned."

He had the strangest look on his face and she put a comforting hand on his forearm.

"Look, Ash, I want you to marry me. Again. Now."

Ashley's eyes widened.

"Don't you dare say it." Parker ran a hand over his face. "You know I love you. And you love me."

She wanted to say something, tried to speak, but only a small, guttural sound came from her throat.

Parker sighed. A large, shaky sigh. "Don't you?"

"What about…" Ashley sent a quick glance at the other woman.

"Raquel? She'll do it."

Either he was going crazy, or Ashley already had. She squeezed the arm she had in her grasp. "Parker?"

"She's a judge, Ash. Raquel's a judge. I brought her

here to marry us. But I want this time to be different. I want to hear you say you love me.''

Ashley had never seen such sweet vulnerability as she saw on her husband's face at that moment. She touched her hand to his, but his shook so badly that she had trouble entwining their fingers.

''I do, Parker. I do love you.'' She raised her other hand to his face and stroked his cheek. ''And I don't need to repeat the vows, but I will.''

Parker let a slow smile spread across his face, then lowered his lips to hers while he picked her up and pressed her close to his heart.

After a long, tender kiss, Ashley pushed to the ground and glanced over at their smiling friends and family. She'd almost forgotten. ''What about them?''

Parker smiled again. ''I say the rest of the plan stays in effect.''

Ashley centered her attention on her father's smug face. He clapped Harvey on the back, stretched his arms to the heavens and then clasped his hands behind his neck. His chest puffed out like a proud peacock. ''Me, too,'' she said, grinning.

Parker followed her gaze and surveyed their audience. ''Karen's going to kill me,'' he whispered, his blue eyes alight with amusement. ''Harvey, too.'' The attorney stood ramrod straight, his eyes ever watchful.

''Mrs. Lee won't make us dessert for a month,'' she pointed out cheerfully. The housekeeper had wound a white linen handkerchief around one pudgy hand, the other she used to grip Harvey's arm. Happy tears glistened from her eyes.

''She probably won't feed us at all,'' Parker added.

She would if I were pregnant. The stubborn thought reinsinuated itself and Ashley drew in her lower lip. She couldn't be, could she? Her hand made a reflexive journey to her nervous belly. ''Parker?''

He looked down at her, touching her with his beautiful

eyes and loving smile. She stared up at him, the question dying on her lips as she found the answer she needed.

But Parker's gaze drifted to her hand, then his eyes searched hers. He covered her hand with his, his long fingers stroking her stomach. "Ashley?" There was a sweet urgency in his voice.

She shook her head and turned her hand over, their palms meeting. "I don't think so." She smiled. "But would you mind if I was?" She felt only slightly guilty for already knowing the answer, yet wanting to hear the words.

"I love you," he whispered, his eyes the soft color of promise. He swallowed, then lowered their clasped hands to their sides. "I say we get out of here."

"I agree."

He angled back in mock surprise. "That may be a first."

Ashley lightly socked his arm and laughed. He brought her fist to his curved lips for a quick kiss, then steered them toward the yacht. They motioned for Raquel to follow.

"Hey. Where are you going?" Crystal was the first to holler. She'd taken a step forward, her ludicrously made-up eyes wide with suspicion. The others stood paralyzed with confusion.

"Giving you time to think," Ashley called out once they were safely aboard. "Don't worry. We'll be back tomorrow." She grinned as she watched the stunned group move toward the departing ship in comical slow motion, disbelief echoing in each leaden step.

Then a small frown settled between her eyebrows, as she brought a thoughtful finger to her lips. "You know, this island is going to work out even better than I thought. I bet there's room for at least five casinos."

"Oh, no. Look, Ash." Parker took a deep breath, his beautiful blue eyes widening with wariness. "About Magic Island..."

Ashley laughed, then kissed him into silence.

American HEROES
AGAINST ALL ODDS

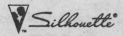

HARLEQUIN®   Silhouette®

Please address questions and book requests to: Harlequin Reader Service U.S.: 3010 Walden Ave.,
P.O. Box 1325, Buffalo, NY 14269 CAN.: P.O. Box 609, Fort Erie, Ont. L2A 5X3   PAHGEN

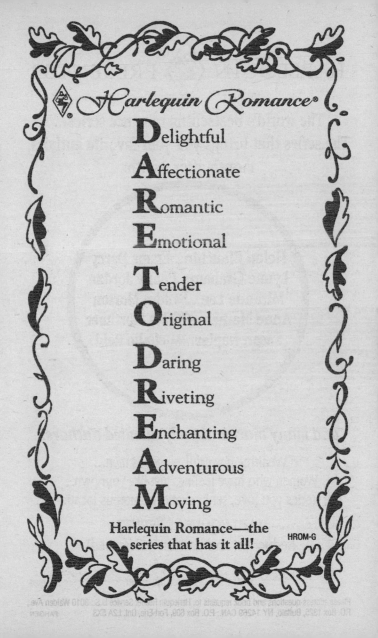

Harlequin Romance®

Delightful

Affectionate

Romantic

Emotional

Tender

Original

Daring

Riveting

Enchanting

Adventurous

Moving

Harlequin Romance—the
series that has it all!

HROM-G

Please address questions and book requests to: Harlequin Reader Service, U.S. 3010 Walden Ave.,
P.O. Box 1325, Buffalo, NY 14269 CAN.: P.O. Box 609, Fort Erie, Ont. L2A 5X3   PAHSERV

Harlequin® Historical

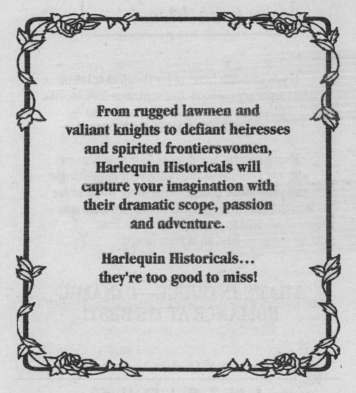

From rugged lawmen and
valiant knights to defiant heiresses
and spirited frontierswomen,
Harlequin Historicals will
capture your imagination with
their dramatic scope, passion
and adventure.

Harlequin Historicals...
they're too good to miss!